As soon as he stepped in front of the Army Remington, butt-forward on his left side.

Toby saw it happen, and dove to the floor to get out of the line of fire.

The Winchester and Remington roared at the same time, but both men were diving to the side as they fired, and both missed.

Toby scrambled on through the batwings as Kev dove behind the cover of the bar and Starkey backed away, knocking over a table and chair as he did so.

The Winchester was too long for the tight space, so Kev pulled the Colt. Two shots in rapid succession splintered the corner of the bar, then Kev heard rapid steps and the slamming of a door. He stood quickly, ready to snap off a shot, but Starkey was nowhere in sight. There was a door at the rear of the small saloon. Starkey was at a dead run, heading for the barn, firing blindly as he ran, trying to make sure Kev kept his head down so he could make the barn in safety.

But realizing Starkey was heading for where Caitlin and Sean were holed up, Kev jumped to his feet. Starkey was a good seventy-five feet away, at a dead run, when Kev snapped off a shot. Starkey spun a complete circle and went down, but almost as quickly was back on one knee, leveling the Remington at Kev. His shot cut through Kev's coat, and Kev again dove to the side as Starkey, holding his bloody side, scrambled to and through the barn door.

Kev heard the report of the shotgun as Starkey charged inside the barn.

BOOK YOUR PLACE ON OUR WEBSITE AND MAKE THE READING CONNECTION!

We've created a customized website just for our very special readers, where you can get the inside scoop on everything that's going on with Zebra, Pinnacle and Kensington books.

When you come online, you'll have the exciting opportunity to:

- View covers of upcoming books
- Read sample chapters
- Learn about our future publishing schedule (listed by publication month *and author*)
- Find out when your favorite authors will be visiting a city near you
- Search for and order backlist books from our online catalog
- Check out author bios and background information
- Send e-mail to your favorite authors
- Meet the Kensington staff online
- Join us in weekly chats with authors, readers and other guests
- Get writing guidelines
- AND MUCH MORE!

Visit our website at
http://www.kensingtonbooks.com

WOLF MOUNTAIN

L.J. MARTIN

PINNACLE BOOKS
Kensington Publishing Corp.
http://www.kensingtonbooks.com

PINNACLE BOOKS are published by

Kensington Publishing Corp.
850 Third Avenue
New York, NY 10022

All Kensington Titles, Imprints, and Distributed Lines are available at special quantity discounts for bulk purchases for sales promotion, premiums, fund-raising, educational or institutional use. Special book excerpts or customized printings can also be created to fit specific needs. For details, write or phone the office of the Kensington special sales manager: Kensington Publishing Corp., 850 Third Avenue, New York, NY 10022, attn: Special Sales Department, Phone: 1-800-221-2647.

Pinnacle and the P logo Reg. U.S. Pat. & TM Off.

First Pinnacle Books Printing: April 2004

10 9 8 7 6 5 4 3 2 1

Printed in the United States of America

Terry C. Johnston . . . too soon gone.
But if I know Terry, and it was my great pleasure,
he's blazing trail for the rest of us.

Chapter 1

October 22, 1876

An early and particularly bitter wind howled down the aspen-filled hollow from the fresh snow-covered rock escarpment above. Wisps of snow-powder lifted off the ridge and bent the trees below. The freak October storm did not bode well for the coming winter.

The sharp crack of a rifle again punctuated the wind's moan, and splinters rained down from fallen aspen.

"Kev, if the bloody dogs get above us to the top of the ridge, there'll be hell to pay."

"That's no problem, Colin. Let Dugan and me circle over to that cut, and we can flank them and pull their teeth as they try to cross the clearing."

"What the hell are the Hunkpapa doing this far west? Damn the luck."

Hunkered behind a blown-down aspen in late morning, Colin McQuade and his younger brother Kevin lay pinned down by a band of Hunkpapa Sioux, some of Sitting Bull's band. Since their great victory at the Little Big Horn, the Sioux and the Northern Cheyenne had become bolder. Miles's 5th

Infantry had routed Sitting Bull and the Hunkpapa at Cedar Creek and again at Ash Creek, destroying their lodges, and split them into roving bands of warriors. Miles had accepted the surrender of two thousand Hunkpapa, Minneconjou, and Sans Arc Sioux, over eighty percent of Sitting Bull's entire war strength. They were now on their way south to the reservation under the armed guard of Lieutenant Forbes and a strong force of the fighting 5th.

But there were still plenty of hostiles out there between Bozeman and the Missouri River.

Worse, half of the McQuades' herd of over five hundred head of summer-fat cattle milled just beyond the aspens, nervously stomping and bellowing, jumpy from the howling frigid wind. It was a wonder they hadn't stampeded with the first shots the Sioux had flung at the group from a distant stand of lodgepole pine.

Colin and Kevin knew the Indians were more than likely merely hungry and were hoping some of the cattle would bolt and stray from the herd, but the McQuades owed the bank, and every beef was critical to their survival. Even the family was eating elk, venison, and antelope, keeping every head of cattle for the few dollars they would bring.

"No, Kev, me lad. It's a fine idea, but I'm sending Petersen with Dugan. Let's keep yer ugly hide in one piece."

Kevin sighed deeply, running his hand through his thick black hair, feeling a little heat on the back of his neck. At ten years younger than his older brother, he was seldom able to try his wings at anything if his brother had anything to say about it, other than rounding up and branding stray steers, or haying. Yet he was a full-grown man, and better at many things than his brother.

But he'd promised his ma—on her deathbed—and his da that he'd listen to Colin, and he'd been taught to honor his promises. His ma had gone to her reward ten years ago, when Kevin was fifteen, and Colin had raised and guided him these ten years hence. His father had been near all that time, but hadn't been right in the head for many years. Kev clenched his jaw and slunk a little deeper behind the blowdown as a big .45/.70 slug slammed into the aspen, kicking up bark.

Many Sioux were armed with Springfield Army Cavalry carbines, thanks to Custer's brashness, but unless there were a dozen or more of them together, they couldn't throw as much lead as the McQuades, with their lever action Winchesters and Colt revolvers.

"Damn the thievin' redskins," Colin snapped. "If we're gonna get out of this, we'd better get our heads down and tails up and get on with it. Dugan! Petersen!" he shouted to the other two hands he'd hired to help bring the cattle down from the high mountain before the snows came in earnest.

From a spot in the aspens thirty yards away, a gravely voice rang out over the wind's moan. "I'm here, Boss."

"Take Petersen and work your way up to the end of the grove, then follow that cut up a ways to keep them from crossin' and getting atop the ridge."

There was silence for a minute; then Petersen's voice rang out, "Let them have the damn cattle—"

"The hell you say. This is damn nigh half our calf

crop and some of our best cows. If they get atop the ridge, there'll be hell to pay."

"Then we should light a shuck."

"I'm going," Kevin said, rising.

"No." His larger and older brother grabbed Kevin's wolf-skin coat and jerked him back down. "Petersen!" Colin shouted, shoving his brother low below the log pile.

"We're headin' out," Petersen answered as the wind quieted, his voice on the timid side, "before they figure out they can cut us up from atop the ridge. You boys is on yer own."

"If you do, then keep going, you damned cowering dog! Don't be stoppin' at the home place for your pay."

"A few dollars don't do a man no good if he's toes-up."

The McQuade brothers could hear the two drovers clamber away through the timber, then saw the flash of their horses' rumps as they mounted and gave them the spurs, galloping away from the ensuing battle.

"The bloody Dugans always was a sorry lot," Colin groused. "An' so's that squarehead. I shoulda given them a bullet in their backside."

"Now what?" Kevin asked.

"Hell, I wish I knew."

"Those Hunkpapa keep throwing lead, they'll have our horses down and there won't be much for us to do but wait till they get the angle on us. Come on!"

This time Colin didn't get a hand on Kev, who broke at a dead run toward where they'd tied their two mounts. There wasn't much to do but follow, so

Colin did, even though the woods up the hill exploded with gunfire. He sprang to his feet, ducked low, and charged after his smaller but much faster brother. By the time he reached the animals, Kevin was already mounted. The shallow earth around them was kicking up plumes of snow and mud as big slugs slammed aground.

Just as Colin swung into the gray's saddle, a bullet smashed into his thigh and blood splattered across the gelding's flank. "By the saints," he cried out, his eyes wide as blood gushed.

"Can you ride?" Kevin yelled.

"Have to."

"Then follow me."

Kevin slammed his booted heels into his big buckskin's side and the horse leaped forward; not away as Colin had anticipated, but toward the herd.

Colin sheathed his Winchester and grasped the horn with one hand, reining with the other, and giving the heel of his good leg to the big gray he rode. The gelding had already leaped after Kevin and the buckskin.

Kevin McQuade, Colin thought as his horse charged behind his brother, *you're a crazy lout, crazier than yer daft da. I'm shot all to hell. . . . If we live through this day. . . .*

Before they reached the herd, Colin realized what his wild little brother was up to. The nervous cattle had spun and changed direction, and were already moving by the time Kevin, drawing and firing his side arm into the air, reached the tail of the herd. Colin saw him motion to take the right flank, as Kevin took the left, turning the now-galloping herd toward the lodgepole pines where the Hunkpapa had laid up to ambush them.

It was slightly uphill to the grove, but the herd was moving hard and fast and hit the tree line like a high-mountain avalanche, crushing boughs out of the way and trampling everything in their path.

A couple of shots rang out from the lodgepoles, but then Colin could see Hunkpapa scramble for their horses. Some of them made it, a couple didn't, taken under the pounding hooves of the stampede.

Kevin broke through the trees and came alongside his brother, shouting, "Keep going, run them all the way through."

When they broke out the other side of the copse of lodgepole, most of the cattle were still ahead of them, and all of the Indians behind. Kevin looked back over his shoulder as they galloped on up a little creek bed. No Indians followed.

Again he reined his horse over to his brother's side. "You gonna make it?"

"Don't slow down. Run them all the way to the ranch."

Kevin needed little encouragement. They continued to work the cattle, slowing to a trot, but moving them far faster than they normally would. He knew this would cost them plenty of weight, but better a little weight than the whole herd; better the whole herd than their skins.

It was most of an hour before they came out onto the flat above the Yellowstone, where the ranch house and small outbuildings sat. They moved at a slow trot, and when they came alongside the main corral, Kevin reined up and eyed his brother, only a few strides behind.

Blood covered his pants leg, and had gone brown on the flank of the dappled gray. Protruding flesh poked its way through the hole in his tight buckskins. His leg dripped bright red, but his face shimmered with a pallor white as a lizard's belly.

Colin managed to rein up beside Kevin; then, as if a curtain was pulled down in his eyes, he lost consciousness. Slipping from the saddle, he slammed face-first into the mud. The cattle milled around the corral, but fought shy of where Colin lay. Kevin didn't bother to dismount, but rather spurred the buckskin to a gallop toward the house, only a hundred yards away. He slid the big horse to a stop near the front door.

"Brigid! Brigid, boil some water and get some clean bindings. Col's been shot in the leg."

Before he'd finished, the door swung aside.

"What happened?" Colin's wife asked, her bright blue eyes wide as she dried her hands on her apron.

"Damned Sioux hit us while we were comin' down the mountain." Before he'd finished the sentence, Kev reined the big horse around and gave him his heels back to where Colin lay. He heard her call out as he galloped away, "Sean, Patti, come quick . . . your da's been hurt."

It was no easy chore, as big as Colin was, but in a few minutes Sean, Colin's fourteen-year-old son, Pattiann, his eleven-year-old daughter, Brigid, his wife, and his younger brother Kevin had him in his bed. Brushing her coal-black hair out of her eyes, Brigid quickly stripped away the buckskins, then cleaned his wound while Kevin applied a tourniquet to the leg. Colin's face was peaceful bliss, as he'd regained consciousness, then again passed out moments after they'd hoisted him up and plopped him on the bedspread.

"Did it get the bone?" Kevin asked.

"Maybe," Brigid answered, now sewing the wound. "But no bone splinters in the exit wound. Let's pray not." She paused from her work long enough to cross herself and mutter a small prayer. Then she glanced back at Kevin. "Damn, if those bullets don't demand a terrible toll. He's lost flesh half the size of your fist where that bullet left his leg. All I could do was pack it with sackcloth; there was no closin' the wound."

Colin awoke for only a moment to mumble. "Feed the bloody cattle so they don't wander off," he instructed the ceiling, then slipped back into blissful sleep.

Kevin glanced up to see his father, white beard to mid-chest, mottled face, watery eyes, and dour look, negotiate the doorway into the bedroom, a willow cane in each hand.

"Well, you damn fools did it again, didn't ya?" he mumbled, then cackled as if he found the scene funny. "That's a drumstick what might as well be in the bone pile."

Brigid and Kevin ignored the old man's caustic and thoughtless remark, but he wouldn't be ignored.

"I got me a crosscut saw out in the barn. We can lop it off'n him, you say the word, daughter."

Brigid glared up at him. "You get back to your rocker, Da, or there'll be no dessert for you this night."

The old man cackled again with his toothless mouth, but turned and hobbled out of the room. A soft dessert was the highlight of his day; Brigid's threat was not one to be taken lightly.

Kevin rose to head for the corral, where a huge stack of meadow hay was separated from the cattle by a surrounding fence. He paused at the front door. "Is soup made, Brigid?" he asked.

"There's venison stew, and biscuits as soon as I finish this chore." She flashed her brother-in-law a tight smile.

"That's good. We ain't fed since daybreak, and we probably oughta get some of the broth down Colin."

"You worry about the cattle, Kev McQuade, and I'll do the nursin'. Now get on with ya."

Kev knew how worried she must be. They were a long way from a doctor. And if the wound went green . . .

"I'll be an hour or so," he assured her. "Sean, get your coat, we got some hay to fork," Kev yelled at his nephew.

Sean glanced over at his uncle, then looked to his mother. "Do I have to, Ma?"

"Do as you're asked."

Kev shook his head, a little disgusted at his nephew, then turned his attention back to his sister-in-law. "Brigid, if you need me, yell out." He left with his nephew trailing behind to tend the cattle, the wind howling around them as if summoning the hounds of hell.

When Kev unsaddled Colin's big gray, he found a flattened bullet buried in the leather saddle skirt.

At least the horse had been saved.

He couldn't help but lament as he worked that

Colin's wound was *his* fault. If Colin should lose the leg, Kev would be heartsick for all his days.

The reason for the early roundup was a contract with the Army. Two hundred head of cattle had to be delivered to the Tongue River Cantonment two hundred miles down the Yellowstone, and they had to be there in a month's time.

Two hundred head, sold at a price that would repay the bank, a note that had already been extended.

Good God, two hundred cattle two hundred miles through hungry bands of Hunkpapa and Northern Cheyenne. And only Kevin and his fourteen-year-old nephew to face the chore.

It would be a long row to hoe, with just the two of them . . . if they lived through to the end of it.

Chapter 2

The ranch house had started out as a soddy, built into the side of the hill; its rear walls and half the side walls of the dugout were the hill itself, the rest blocks of sod, its roof lodgepole-pine rafters covered with smaller willow branches, then with sod. That part of the house was now divided into two small rooms, one for Sean and Pattiann, the other shared by Kev and his old father.

Over the years Brigid had made a catch-curtain of sewn-together flour sacks, which hung under the sod roof catching the stray bit of dirt that continued to fall from time to time.

The rest of the McQuade house was made of logs, and roofed with split-cedar shingles—it had been Colin's intent to roof the soddy this year, but other chores had prevented it. A generous living area five paces deep by ten paces long was kitchen and common area, with a fireplace so large one could almost walk into the firebox, which also served as a cooking area with an arm of cast iron that one could use to swing a hanging pot over the coals.

There was also a small cast-iron woodstove nearby with a stovepipe run into the rock flue of the fireplace, and with an oven big enough to bake two pies at a time. Pots and pans hung from the wall between fireplace and iron stove, and a pie safe rested nearby.

The rest of the main room was filled with furniture, constructed for the most part by Colin from sawn timber, or bentwood willow. But it had a caring woman's touch. Gingham curtains decorated the two modest waxed-paper windows in the room, and hoop rugs adorned both the sawn-timber floors in the log cabin area and the hard-swept and pounded-smooth dirt floors of the old soddy. There were framed samplers adorning the walls, brightly colored hand-stitched lamp mats on the tables, and seashells, books, and china vases sat here and there.

On the side of the living area opposite the soddy was a generous room shared by husband and wife, which boasted a small sitting and sewing area and its own window filled with the only four panes of real glass the ranch house enjoyed. A white counterpane and white lace pillows adorned the bed, and a prized Irish lace coverlet lay folded neatly across the footboard. The dressing table sported a pink pincushion surrounded by dainty toilet things including a tortoise-shell comb and brush set. A small white china bowl and pitcher adorned with painted flowers rested on one end.

There was a heavy plank door leading out the back, but it actually was an access to a stairway down into the root cellar, dug into the hill behind the house; it also served as a safe-room, a room of last resort should the house be overrun by savages, be they rogue-white or Indian.

Later, after supper, they all sat around the big table Colin had built from hand-sawn fir, Kevin at the foot of the table, Brigid just to the right of the head, now vacant, as it would be for a good long while before Colin retook that seat. Sean, Colin, and Brigid's oldest surviving son sat across from his mother, his grandfather to his left. Pattiann sat next to her mother. The long table had been built to accommodate ten, with four on each side and one on each end. But the firstborn, Sean, had been drowned while bringing a load of supplies down the Yellowstone from Big Timber during a spring thaw, and Tobin, who'd been born two years after Sean and about the same before his sister, had been thrown from a rattler-spooked horse when only nine, and broken his neck.

Montana, a ruthless handmaiden, had extracted much from the McQuades, and it looked like she might demand even more.

Brigid had taken a long while making sure the semiconscious Colin partook of a full bowl of the stew's broth before she turned herself to the chore of feeding the rest of the family.

But Montana had also been generous. The huge bowl of venison stew still bubbled in the center of the big table, a plate of more than two dozen palm-sized biscuits sat to one side of it, honey filled a small earthenware crock, and a platter of pickled cucumbers, beans, and beets adorned the other side. A half-gallon hand-hewed wooden pitcher of buttermilk rested in front of Kevin, and one of fresh cold spring water was in front of Colin's empty place.

Brigid, in Colin's absence, said the grace, a particularly long and poignant one that night.

* * *

Supper was finished. The old man put to bed. Pattiann stood at the kitchen cabinet washing and drying the dishes with a ragged flour sack. Sean lay in front of the fireplace doing the penmanship lessons Brigid had assigned him. Kev's normally objecting sister-in-law surprised him by breaking out a small corked crock of store-bought whiskey. Occasionally they partook of a dollop of rhubarb wine after dinner, but whiskey was a rarity. She poured them each a generous three fingers.

"I think we'll be needin' this," she said with a deep sigh, then took Pattiann's seat at Kev's left, handing him his mug. She toasted him. "Well, brother-in-law, here's to you as you're to be the man around here all by your lonesome until Col's back on his feet. Just what in the Good Lord's name are we going to do now?"

Kevin gave her a reassuring smile. "Col's got the sale to the Army sewed up, and I can get the herd there. Didn't that Sergeant Starkey leave a deposit with Col?"

"He did. He stopped by on his way to Fort Ellis, near Bozeman. Fifty dollars, as deposit on two hundred head at seven dollars per, delivered to the Tongue River Cantonment. He said he'd stop back by to see how the roundup was coming, but not to wait if we wanted to strike out before he returned. The deposit is what we've been living on this past couple of months. Thank merciful Jesus, I still have the most of it." She took a long draw on the mug she held. "But it's a good long piece to the Tongue from here. You can't do it, Kev. Not without help you can't." For the first time since they'd brought Colin into the house, a tear formed and streaked her cheek. "And we owe the bank in Bozeman over four hundred. That piggish banker, Tolofsen, would much prefer to foreclose on the ranch than have his money."

Kev, with an unusual show of emotion, reached out and covered her hand with his as his voice softened. "I can take Sean, and we can go over the mountain and find Two Feather's band. He'll lend me a brave to help out, or we can give them a barren cow and with that hire a couple of his men for the drive downriver."

Sean had obviously been eavesdropping. "I can't be going downriver. I got to stay here and help Da."

"You mind your studies," Brigid snapped. "You'll do as you're asked. And it's 'I *have* to stay,' not 'I got to stay.'"

She turned back to Kev. "It's over two hundred miles to the Tongue. Can't you get a couple of the Dugan brothers, or Petersen, or someone else from Big Timber or Bozeman?"

"Hell, half the country's run off to some new gold strike over in the Flint Creek country, and Norval Dugan and Petersen turned tail, as I told you. They won't never show their faces around the Sweet Grass again. It's one or two of Two Feather's men, or nothing. Besides, I need to get the cattle moving long before I could get to Bozeman and back again."

"Sean's too young, Kev."

"Sean's as old as I was when we drove the seed herd here all the way from Minnesota. Colin was driving the wagon, and Da and I did the droving. Twenty head of cattle, some damn nervous sheep, and a milk cow. Sean's a fine hand, Brigid, as tough as I was at his age . . . even if he's a mite unwilling and his ma thinks he's still a pup. Maybe this trip, without you to coddle him, is just what he needs."

"He is a pup . . . and I don't think I coddle him."

"A damn-nigh-grown pup, with the teeth and snarl of a he-wolf," Kev said, and laughed and punched her gently on the arm.

She wiped away the tears, and smiled with confidence she didn't feel. "I know he's got far too sharp a tongue. I don't know about teeth." She glanced at her son, doing his lessons in front of the open hearth by the light of the fire. "He's a slight one, takes after me and not his father, and I fear for him."

Kev said, "He's got plenty of bark on him, Brigid. Sean and I, with damn little help, can get the two hundred head downriver before the snow flies in earnest. I'll start cutting out the yearlings in the morning, and we'll corral them. When that's done, we'll round up the others up Monument Butte way, and I'll keep an eye out for Two Feathers. Right now, I'm going to check the herd one more time before turning in."

He rose and downed the last of the whiskey, then stooped and grabbed his hat up from where he'd stowed it under his chair. In four strides he was at the door, pulling his wolf-skin coat off its hook. As he pulled on the heavy coat, he paused and gave her a wink.

"It's downhill all the way, and an easy trail along the river bottom. We'll be back in four or five weeks, six at the most, with a sack full of Army gold coin."

"If you aren't back by Mr. Lincoln's new holiday, Thanksgiving, bless his soul, then the bank will be wanting a reckoning."

"We'll make it just fine, Brigid." Kev glanced away, not meeting her eyes. "Besides, it's my fault Col got shot up. If'n I hadn't charged in like Custer's off ox . . . You go curl up beside Colin. He'll rest better, knowing you're near."

"It's the fault of this damnable country," she said, but moved away toward the bedroom door.

The wind had quieted some by the time Kev closed the door behind him. He took a deep breath and pulled the high collar of the coat up around his ears until it nudged the wide brim of his hat, glad he had the whiskey warming his gullet. *Well, at least I talk a good tale*, he thought. Two hundred miles through hostile Indian country to the Tongue River Cantonment and the Army corrals, and it was unlikely they'd see a white man along the way, except possibly at Big Horn City or John Sarpy's trading post at about the halfway mark, and the last he'd heard, Big Horn City and Sarpy had about folded their tents and left the country.

With a half-pint boy at his side, and maybe a couple of Indians who'd as soon ride off chasing the first buffalo they came across, or more likely slit his and Sean's throats in the night. Hell, it might as well be two thousand miles to the Tongue.

But hell or high water, he'd make it.

He had to make it.

Chapter 3

A stiff breeze blew down the canyon, causing fluttering whitecaps in the half-mile-wide river. The weather had a bite to it, but it still was not cold enough that a man could see his breath. A murder of crows sailed on the wind, their wings set, their raucous cries heard even above the clatter of lines and creak of winches and the shouting and swearing of hardworking soldiers and boat crew.

Lieutenant Frank D. Baldwin sat astride the varnished taffrail of the river steamer *General Meade*, watching his contingent of 5th Infantry troops depart the gangway. He smiled tightly, scratching his cheek through pork-chop sideburns, glad to be rid of this boat even though his next bivouac would be on the ground while on a forced march, as an infantry officer's should. He adjusted his chapeau, and picked a bit of lint off his uniform dress coat, both donned in honor of the fact they were arriving this day. The double-breasted coat boasted seven gold buttons on each side, the mark of an officer of a rank lower than colonel, and a pair of stripes, chevrons, on the cuffs, each chevron trimmed with one-eighth inch of red indicating service in wartime. Above those, the sleeves had a number of service chevrons, each indicating an honorable term of enlistment.

However, due to circumstance, Captain Polkinghorn and his greeting party stood on the other side of the river, their fort band drumming, fifing, and trumpeting a welcome. Baldwin, being a practical man, saw no reason to depart the boat on the north side of the river, as they'd just have to cross to the south for their march to and up the Yellowstone, where they'd cross that more shallow river to the north side to follow the wagon track that served for a road upriver. Despite donning the dress uniform for his arrival, Baldwin wasn't a man to stand on ceremony, or waste effort, even if not doing so might rankle Polkinghorn.

As an old hand at Indian fighting, Baldwin wasn't particularly proud of this assignment—shepherding the band, additional staff, and a few enlisted men replacements to join the rest of the fighting force—but someone had to do it. Across the river, Fort Buford squatted behind the greeting party and the small floating dock that would have made disembarking slightly more desirable—but not so desirable that it offset having to cross the river later with the whole troop.

In the distance, the American Fur Company's derelict Fort Union overlooked the canyon.

Just upriver swirled treacherous whirlpools, resulting from the confluence of the Yellowstone and the wider Missouri, up which they'd been traveling for three weeks. Up the Yellowstone 150 miles was their destination—the Tongue River Cantonment, Colonel Miles, and the rest of the fighting 5th, six companies of the 22nd, and two of the 17th. From here on, it was shank's mare, as it should be for a tough well-trained infantry force. Only one short layover at Camp Glendive, sixty miles up the Yellowstone, the last real outpost of civilization between the Missouri and Bozeman. Baldwin smiled, wondering how tough these staff personnel and band members really were.

One hundred and fifty miles, and his instructions were to get there posthaste. If he knew Colonel Nelson A. Miles, the man wouldn't tarry long before he would be harrying the remaining groups of hostiles, particularly Crazy Horse and the Lakotas, Sitting Bull and the Hunkpapa, and Dull Knife and the Northern Cheyenne. Baldwin knew Miles had promised General Sherman that he'd bring the hostiles into the fold of reservation Indians before the snow left the Montana plains, and Colonel Miles always did what he promised. God willing, the weather would not delay the apprehension of the Sioux and their compatriots—then again, the hostiles would suffer even more than the Army should the weather soon be plagued by Canadian winds and heavy snowfall. The Army had the new cantonment to resupply them; the Hunkpapa and other hostile bands had to live off the land.

Baldwin's men wore their fatigues, as their day was hard labor.

At the bow of the boat, deckhands assisted by soldiers were unloading supplies and equipment with a swinging boom that barely reached the shore. A donkey steam engine huffed and puffed, driving a winch that off-loaded heavy bundles and pallets. A squad of soldiers calf-deep in the cold river received the loads and passed them from hand to hand to where they were being stowed ashore. The gangplank, amidships, was being used by disembarking troops, each carrying his personal gear, weapon, and whatever else he could manage.

One of the band members stumbled on the gangway, lost control of his load—with a drum case balanced atop his personal belongings—and juggled, then dropped the drum case overboard.

"Get in after it," Baldwin yelled, but the man looked at him as if he was as crazy as Crazy Horse was reputed to be.

"I can't swim, sir," the drummer shouted.

The drum case and its contents were bobbing away down the Missouri.

Fifty feet aft, a young redheaded corporal Baldwin didn't know well yelled, "Lieutenant, if I may?"

Baldwin glanced back to see the young man stripping away his blouse, then kicking off his brogans.

"Permission granted, Corporal," Baldwin shouted, and before the echo stopped, the corporal was on the rail, then arched into the air over the frigid river, plunging headfirst into the water.

Ordnance Sergeant John O'Connor, his uniform piped in bright crimson, stepped up behind Baldwin. "That's Brian McGloughlan, sir. Bigger balls than a six-pounder."

Baldwin smiled at the grizzled old sergeant. "Need more like him."

The young corporal stroked like a man with a swamp gator on his tail until he caught up with the bobbing drum case, captured it, then seventy-five yards below where the *General Meade* was secured to the south bank, made shore. The young soldier shook himself like an old hound, then trotted back upriver until he reached the gangplank. He handed the drum to the embarrassed band member, then continued up the gangplank to the applause and hooras of the rest of the men.

"Well done," Baldwin said as the young man, his red hair still dripping, hurried past to recover his blouse and brogans.

"Thank you, sir," the soldier acknowledged, then stopped short. "Anything more I can do for you, sir?"

"Get dry. Don't get the croup."

"Yes, sir," he said, flashing Baldwin a smile, then moving on.

O'Connor cleared his throat, then said in a low voice, "Beggin' your pardon, Lieutenant, but you might consider getting McGloughlan out of the quartermaster's clutches. He's too good a man to be coddling rations."

"All in good time, Sergeant, all in good time."

"Of course, sir. Still and all, he's a willing sort."

"We'll all get our chance to shine, soon enough. Watch your footing, man!" Baldwin yelled at another infantryman who'd stumbled. "By all that's holy, some of these recruits are as clumsy as cavalry afoot. Let's be done with this so we can get to *stumbling* up the Yellowstone."

"Yes, sir," Sergeant O'Connor said, then bellowed his own encouragement. "You soggers get moving, before I plant my shinny new campaign brogans where the sun don't shine." He glanced back at his lieutenant. "We've still got the wagons and two dozen mules to off-load . . . and your horse, sir." O'Connor started to move away, but was stopped short when Baldwin spoke.

"And my horse, Sergeant. And be damned careful with his unloading." He started away, then paused. "On second thought," Baldwin asked, "can McGloughlan cipher?"

"He's educated so's you'd think he was a officer, Mr. Baldwin."

"Then at the end of the day send young McGloughlan to me. I'm looking for a personal man, an enlisted adjutant if you will, and he might just do."

"Yes, sir," O'Connor snapped, and gave Baldwin a snappy salute. He was glad to see McGloughlan get a leg up, and this just might help do it.

From a spot on a high ridge above the Big Dry River a few miles south of the Missouri River, near the summit between the Missouri and the Yellowstone, a few Hunkpapa Sioux sat near a tall needle rock. Due to the cold, the men had mostly set aside their breechclouts and were wearing buckskins, but some had only blanket leggings; most had buffalo robes wrapping their shoulders.

Among them was their young leader, Sitting Bull. In the distance, a group composed of Cheyenne, Oglala Sioux, Brule, and more Hunkpapas rode quietly to Finger Rock, the meeting place.

Sitting Bull and his Hunkpapas had recently been routed at Cedar Creek and again at Ash Creek, with only him and four hundred of his followers left, and his people were divided, his forces split and wandering.

When the various groups arrived, they dismounted and gathered around the fire, almost fifty strong. Sitting Bull, Gall, Roman Nose, of the Lakota Sioux; White Bull and Black Moccasin of the Cheyenne; and many others. All men of stature, all men who hated the walks-a-heap, as they referred to the Army Infantry.

Sitting Bull—his face with its prominent nose and continence as if it had been chiseled from red rock, his powerful squat physique always as if in a crouch ready to pounce—harbored even more hate than most of them. He spoke first. "Roman Nose, you have been to where the walks-a-heap gather on the river of the elk. What news do you have?"

Roman Nose came to his feet. "They are of the same number, they linger about the camp like women. They have few horses, and hunt seldom. They have cattle, but no more than the days between the full moons, and if they continue to butcher them, they will soon have none . . . then I think they must leave that place."

"Much work has been done?" Sitting Bull asked.

"They have many low lodges, made of the shaped pieces of trees. Yes, much work has been done, but there are no more of them than the last time I was there. And it is not like other gathering places. Small lodges only, none of the lodges where men walk above other men . . . where fighting men have the advantage of height."

"Good," Sitting Bull said. "Now, who has seen the *tatanka*?" He waited patiently while reports of sightings of buffalo were relayed. They must have more buffalo if they were to make it through winter, particularly if they had to move to avoid the walks-a-heap.

And the reports were all bad.

But surely the walks-a-heap would hole up for the winter. Men afoot could not survive a winter on the move. If they came to where the people would winter, then they must be destroyed, just as Yellow Hair, the horse soldier, had been.

The war chief, Gall, rose from the cross-legged position, and let his eyes drift from man to man. Finally, he spoke, his deep voice resonating. "It is time we struck the walks-a-heap. Time we wiped out their camp on the river of elk, and sent them back to their lodges beyond the morning sun."

Sitting Bull rose also, his hate tempered with a wisdom beyond his young age. "No. Soon there will be no forage for our horses. Already they are in bad shape. Let the walks-a-heap run out of their cattle. Without cattle, and with the *tatanka* moving south, they will begin to starve, and when they become hungry, they will leave. Then we will burn their camp on the river of elk."

Gaul was disgusted with their inaction, but merely stared at Sitting Bull, saying nothing.

"Our time will come again," Sitting Bull said, but most of the men looked unconvinced. He rose. "My lodges will go north, to Fort Peck. We need ammunition and blankets, and we may be able to get them there."

Gall too rose. "I thought we'd agreed to go south, where we might fill our bellies with *tatanka* and our lodges with hides."

"You go south if you wish. We are going to Fort Peck."

Gall stomped away, and the other leaders seemed angered also. But Sitting Bull, always his own man, merely moved calmly to his mount. He didn't look back as he rode out of sight.

For the next three days Kev and Sean moved up and down in the saddles of the Monument Butte country, east of the ranch. By the end of that time they had gathered almost another three hundred head, and as importantly, found Two Feathers, an Assiniboine Indian whose small band lived in the Sweet Grass during the late summer and early fall. Many years ago Colin had made friends with the band, and helped feed them during one particularly hard winter. Since that time each man had called on the other many times.

For the gift of a barren cow, Two Feathers agreed to lend Kev two young braves for a month, for the drive to Tongue River. Sleeps-in-Day was a large young man with the girth of a bear, and most of its strength. He moved slowly, but deliberately, and talked not at all. Badger-Man stood tall and thin, and moved quickly. He rode like he was one with his paint horse, and when he was afoot, the animal followed him faithfully like a dog. He and the animal seemed to communicate without any formal motions or movements on the part of the man. The animal seemed to respond to the Indian's thoughts. Badger-Man never spoke to the horse, at least not verbally. A willing man, he responded quickly to any request Kev made. Both of them would be handy to have along.

The drive back to the ranch went quickly, with three men on the flanks and one riding point. The Indians camped in the barn, more than content with the forequarter of whitetail deer Brigid had given them.

Colin, to Kev's dismay, had worsened. He was feverish and still unable to leave his bed. Brigid was exhausted, her eyes deeply sunken, her complexion sallow.

After supper, over another dollop of whiskey, Kev expressed his worry.

"Do you think we should load him in the wagon and take him to Bozeman?" Kev asked Brigid.

"You have to take the herd the other way, and you must leave in the morning. I'll tend to Col."

Kev was silent for a moment. "I fear for him, if that wound turns . . ."

"And I fear he wouldn't make it to Bozeman, should we take him out in this cold. I'm watching the river, should someone come along. I'll get help, if he gets worse. You've got to go on, Kev, or we'll lose everything."

Kevin rose and walked over to stand with his back to the fire. The youngsters and the old man were already in bed. Finally, Kev addressed his worry. "Can you take the leg, should it go green?"

A single tear found its way down Brigid's cheek; then she wiped it away. "I can, if it has to be done. Pattiann and I, we can do it."

Kev walked over and placed a hand on her shoulder. "Should you begin to smell it, and it begins to streak up his leg, then you've got to do it. If it gets in his belly, it'll be too late. Feed him a pint of that whiskey first. . . ."

Brigid rose, and for the first time ever, put her arms around her brother-in-law and gave him a firm hug, then turned and headed for the bedroom she shared with Colin. She stopped in the doorway and surveyed Kev with gentle eyes. "I'm strong enough to stay, Kev, and you've got to be strong enough to go. I'll be packin' your panniers before sunup, and I'll have Sean ready."

"Then I'd best turn in," Kev said.

"Best," she said, and quietly closed the door.

The old man was snoring loudly when Kev folded into his bed under a frayed but still serviceable feather-filled cover, the last night he'd spend enjoying it for many cold nights to come.

With the sunrise he was to set out across two hundred miles of Montana. With winter nigh upon them, with the probability of several thousand hungry and angry redskins between him and his destination, and with his only help a whelp of an unwilling boy and a couple of braves who might change sides at any moment. And with the attraction of two hundred head of prime cattle thousands of redskins would kill to have.

He was sure he'd faced worse, but at the moment he couldn't think of when.

As hard as he tried, sleep just wouldn't come.

Chapter 4

With Kevin riding point well in the lead, a bell cow following with 220 eight-hundred-pound-plus steers and heifers trailing her, Sleeps-in-Day and Badger-Man on the flanks, and an ever-complaining Sean riding drag and leading a pair of pack mules, the herd began to stomp trail shortly after dawn.

Kev carried a Winchester in his saddle scabbard and his Colt on his hip. Sean also had a saddle gun, but rather than a rifle, his was a twelve-gauge shotgun, shoved into a scabbard Kev had slit down a foot or so to make the wide double fit. He also wore a side arm; an old .36-caliber Navy Colt converted to percussion.

Brigid walked to a rise and watched them until they were out of sight. Colin was getting no better; now his brow lay hot to the touch.

A sullen steel-gray sky lay like a blanket over the land, but the wind was only a whisper and the cattle seemed content.

Each man had a spare mount, and the little four-horse remuda made their own way, content to stay at the point near Kevin's buckskin or at drag near Colin's big gray, which Sean now rode. The Indians sat their own personal horses, a paint and an Appaloosa, but had been provided back-up mounts by the McQuades.

The mules' panniers carried spare weapons and ammunition; jerked meat; lard; flour; baking powder; coffee; a bag each of carrots, onions, and potatoes; a couple of handfuls of sugar; utensils and tools; the McQuades' bedrolls; and a small Goodyear rubberized tent that would just hold the four of them should they cozy up like sardines-in-a-can if the weather turned bad. The Assiniboine each had a buffalo robe tied on behind their sparse saddles.

As the day wore on they rotated positions in a clockwise direction, with the man in drag taking the loaded mules to lead. As soon as they were a couple of days from the ranch, the mules would be freed from the lead and allowed to wander on their own, only to be hobbled at night.

The first night they camped in a wide meadow with plenty of feed poking through a two-inch blanket of snow near Reed Point, not far below Monument Butte, where they'd earlier collected some of the cattle. A line of evergreens flanked them on the uphill, and a line of yellow cottonwood on the down. The snow already blanketed the peaks in the distance, but was no impairment to the forage here. The Indians made their own camp, not far from the McQuades.

After a simple stew of boiled jerked venison and potatoes, Kevin leaned back on his bedroll and eyed his young nephew, who was untying his.

"You did just fine today, Sean." The boy didn't respond. "What's galling you?"

"I started out on drag, and ended up there. That

means I rode it more than you and those redskins. Ain't fair."

Kev took a deep breath for no other reason than to keep from snapping at the boy, then said in a quiet voice, "There ain't no dust, so drag's just another spot on the compass—"

"That ain't so. Drag's got to tow them knot-headed mules."

"It'll all even out. Tomorrow you'll start out on the left flank, and if it goes as it did today, you'll end up there."

"Ain't fair . . . and there ain't no dessert," he mumbled, unrolling his own bedroll.

"Complaining don't make the day go any faster, Sean. Why don't you learn to whistle?"

"I can whistle," he snapped at his uncle.

"Good. I'll be happy to hear you whistling a soothing tune, as all your complaining makes the cattle nervous."

"Cattle don't give a damn if I complain."

"Yes, they do, and your ma gives a damn if you curse."

"You gonna tell her?"

"Not if you shut up the complaining. You're doing a man's job, and you can talk as you like so long as you are, but complaining is not man's work . . . it's worm work."

"Worms don't complain." Sean said, missing the point, then crawled into his bedroll and had nothing more to say.

Kev lay quiet, watching the stars come and go through the cloud cover, happy to be seeing them as the day had been solid gray with a bone-soaking, silent, unmoving cold, until they made camp. The wind had risen. The trees were black skeletons dancing against the night sky, with the wild howling between them.

He closed his eyes, knowing that Badger-Man, who was riding nighthawk, would come for him in less than four hours. Until they got a couple of days to the east, only one man would be with the herd at night. After that, as they got deeper into Hunkpapa country, two would ride, two would sleep. Maybe, with a little luck, Sean would be too tired to complain after a few nights of that.

If Sean ever got too tired to complain.

Among Kevin's last thoughts, before he earnestly tried to sleep, were hopes Sean would grow into a man even half as fine as his father, Colin.

Unless they were real lucky, this trip might not bode well for any of them getting any older.

On the ridge above, a pack of wolves lamented the night, mimicking the moaning wind, and somewhere in the distance a grizzly snorted his displeasure at their serenade. The snort was a sound that always chilled Kev.

The cattle bawled, braying to those they'd left behind.

Sleep came, but fitfully.

Brigid awoke to the putrid smell of rotting meat. It turned her stomach as she left the bed she shared with Colin and went to make coffee. Only after a cup of black brew did she venture back into the room to remove the blankets and then the bandages from Colin's putrid leg.

It must be done today . . . no, this morn, as soon as pos-

sible, she concluded with a shudder, then went to the kitchen to begin boiling water for the task. Thank the Lord, Colin was unconscious, his breathing labored, but even her shaking him had not awakened him.

The old man had hobbled to the table in his nightshirt and taken a seat, awaiting the cup of coffee heavily laced with cream and sugar she always made for him. She served him hurriedly without comment, and even as daft as he was, he seemed to sense the gravity of the morning, making none of his normal inane remarks. Pattiann hurried through the living area in her nightshirt, and headed out to the privy. By the time she returned, Brigid had stoked up the fire and had a large pot full of water swung into the firebox, and another on the iron stove.

Pattiann looked at Brigid with fear in her eyes when she realized it was not breakfast her mother was preparing. "Do you have to do it?" she asked her mother, her voice wavering.

"No, *we* have to do it. I'll need your help, young lady, so as soon as this water's hot, I'll want you to be boiling all the toweling we have."

Pattiann's face lost all color as her mother began sharpening their largest butcher knife on the kitchen whetstone. While she worked, she spoke softly to her daughter. "Your pa has a small handsaw out in the barn. Fetch it for me."

Her daughter took a racking breath, and stood frozen in her tracks. "I . . . I can't."

Brigid quietly set the knife aside and walked over and took Pattiann in her arms, then whispered in her ear. "We can ignore this task, and your father will surely die. And he will die a terrible painful death. Is that what you want, Pattiann?"

All she received in return was a series of racking sobs.

She hugged her daughter even more closely. "Get it all out, then we must set to the task." Brigid waited until the sobbing stopped, then held her daughter firmly by the shoulders at arm's length. "Now that that's settled, go to the barn and fetch me your father's handsaw."

Pattiann nodded her head, and Brigid released her. The girl spun on her heel and ran for the door, threw it open, then screeched at the top of her lungs. Brigid had turned away, but spun back to see a hulking, hairy shape filling the doorway.

A gravely voice rang out. "Sorry to startle the little lady. I was about to knock."

Brigid released a deep breath she'd been holding, then managed, "Sergeant Starkey."

"Orin Starkey, at your service, ma'am."

"My God, we're glad to see you. I don't imagine you have a surgeon with you?"

"Hardly, ma'am . . . six soldiers and a pair of wagons full of vegetables from up near Bozeman. We come by to see how you was comin' with the cattle . . . came in late and spent the night in your barn, hopin' you don't mind."

"Of course not. Have you seen a surgery, Sergeant?"

Starkey raised a hand to his face and scratched the bushy dundrearies he wore—side-whiskers hanging below his chin. "I been in the field for the better part of twenty years, Mrs. McQuade. Ain't much I ain't seen . . . and I seen a dozen surgeries or more."

"Well, sir, we've got a rotten leg to take off of Mr. McQuade. Could I employ you to help in that task?"

Starkey reached inside his blouse, pulled out a twist of tobacco, and bit off a little. He tucked it in his cheek with his tongue, then answered with a deep sigh. "Not my favorite way to start out a day. We was hopin' for a little breakfast, but I guess that will have to wait."

"Thank God," Brigid said, handing him the knife.

The weather had warmed, and the shallow layer of snow was going to mud.

The cattle had bedded down in a wide meadow, but were now on their feet as the sun rose over the low mountains to the east, grazing toward the Yellowstone and water.

Kev sliced a little side-pork and fried it up in its own fat in a cast-iron pan while Sean gathered and saddled their mounts. As Sean returned to the campfire, Kev dropped some hard biscuits in the hot pork fat.

"That's breakfast?" Sean asked.

"That is breakfast," Kev said, frowning at his nephew, who stood with a disgusted look on his face. "You wanna do the cooking?"

"Nope. I guess you didn't bring no eggs?"

"Eggs don't pack so well, as you damn well know, Sean. You don't want this, I'll be happy to eat your share."

"No . . . I mean, yes, I want it."

"Good, then eat and you scrub out and pack this skillet. You take the mules and drag this morning."

"The hell . . . it ain't my turn."

"Every time you bellyache about something, you're taking the mules and the drag. You understand?"

Sean said nothing, just stared at his uncle, then spun and walked away to roll up his gear.

Kev wolfed down his breakfast, then yelled at his nephew. "You want this grub?" Getting no answer, he ate Sean's share, cleaned and packed the skillet, then went to roll up and pack his gear.

The two Indians sat their horses on a nearby ridge, watching the cattle. Kev reined over to them. "Sean's starting out on drag this morning."

Badger-Man pointed to a distant ridge. "Man on horseback."

"Hunkpapa?" Kev asked, concerned.

"No. White man."

"He coming this way?" Kev asked, trying to spot the man.

"No. He just watch."

"Well, to hell with him. We got cattle to move." Kev gigged the buckskin toward the cattle and the Indians followed.

Except for his grousing nephew, worry about his brother, and the stranger on the horizon who hadn't bothered to ride in, it was a fine morning.

It was midday before Brigid and Sergeant Starkey stood in the main room, where, after both of them had scrubbed up, Brigid was brewing coffee.

Colin lay quietly in the bedroom, his leg gone to eight inches below the crotch, leaving just more than enough room to apply a tourniquet while the surgery was under way.

"You were a real soldier in there, Mrs. McQuade. Most of my men would have lost their breakfast, having to do what you did." Starkey stroked his whiskers as he spoke.

"You did most of the work, Sergeant—"

"Don't suppose you'd call me Orin."

"Orin. You did most of the work."

"Well, you did a fine job of sewing."

"I wouldn't have known to leave so much to fold over, had you not come along. I don't know what I'd have done." She wiped her hands on a towel for the thousandth time, then turned, apologetic. "I just don't know if I can face the stove and cooking you and your men a meal. My stomach . . ."

"I'd surely settle for a bit of the barleycorn, should you have a dollop."

She smiled wearily, then went into the bedroom and to the door to the potato cellar, and disappeared inside. She returned quickly, with a gallon-sized corked crock.

"That should do just fine," Starkey said.

She placed the jug on the table and fetched a pair of cups.

He guffawed. "Well, now, I'm proud to see yer a drinkin' woman."

"Not normally, Sergeant, but this is a day that seems to call for a little calming."

"I'm proud to have you join me."

Brigid turned to Pattiann, who had been allowed to remain outside while the operation was performed. "There's another crock in the cellar. Take it out to the men in the barn."

"Yes, ma'am," she said, and hurried to her parents' bedroom and into the cellar to perform the task, happy to then have the excuse to leave the house.

The old man had sat quietly in his rocker the whole morning, not complaining about anything. Sensing, if not knowing, what was taking place. For the first time all morning, he spoke. "Biscuit, please."

Brigid rose from the table, went to the pie safe, and fetched him a couple of day-old biscuits. He sat quietly gumming them, rocking.

Orin Starkey was a large man, wide of shoulder and thick through the middle, but none of it was fat. He sported a full head of coal-black hair and pork-chop dundreary sideburns peppered with gray. Other than the huge sideburns, his face was shaven clean, except for a two-day stubble.

Brigid stopped at three fingers of the hard throat-scorching brew, but Starkey drank on. Occasionally, she would rise and go to the bedroom to check on Colin, but he continued to sleep.

Finally, at mid-afternoon, Brigid had calmed enough to cook. She fetched a forequarter of venison and some vegetables from the root cellar, stopping only long enough as she passed to stoop and kiss her husband on the forehead, then began a stew. Starkey continued to drink, and talk. The more he drank, the more loquacious he became. But by the time the stew was finished, he had drunk himself into a sullen silence.

Brigid heard a low moan from the bedroom, and quickly filled a bowl with broth from the stew and went to her husband's bedside. He was fitfully conscious. She tried to pull him into a sitting position so she could get some of the broth down him, but he moaned so loudly she feared she was hurting him. She stepped to the door and called to Starkey.

"Orin. Could you come give me a hand?"

He eyed her, then mumbled, "I done enough for the bugger," and went back to his mug.

She returned the stare, for the first time, with some trepidation.

Turning back to the task, she closed and latched the door behind.

Chapter 5

Frustrated and concerned about the man she'd invited into her home, she struggled to set Colin upright. It was a long time before he opened his eyes; then she began to try and spoon in some of the broth. He managed to get a little down, then set his lips and shook his head. Again, she fought to get him laid flat so he could sleep. In moments, he was breathing deeply.

She too took a deep breath before she unlatched the door and returned to the main room.

But when she entered, Starkey had a smile on his face. He wasn't an unpleasant-looking man.

"Been talking to yer pa," he said, his speech only slightly slurred.

"That's fine," Brigid said, and was a little disconcerted to hear Starkey laugh, a little too loudly, and a little sarcastically.

All day, the old man had quietly rocked in his chair. When Brigid returned, he managed to get his canes under him, and made his way to the room he shared with the now-absent Kevin. He disappeared inside, but left the door open. It was normal for him to nap in the afternoon, so Brigid barely noticed.

What she did notice was the fact that Starkey's eyes

now followed her wherever she moved, as he stroked his whiskers and tongued the chaw around his mouth, and it was beginning to make her nervous, particularly after his refusal to help her with Colin. Pattiann had spent most of the day outside, for a change not having to be reminded to do her chores.

Brigid ladled Starkey up a bowl of the stew, and cut off a generous slice of bread from one of the loaves she'd baked just the day before. She moved over and sat it in front of him, but as she moved away he roughly grabbed her by the wrist.

"You be a fine-looking woman, Mrs. McQuade. You got a given name?"

"It's Brigid," she said, staring directly into his eyes, but her look was now anything but friendly. "But I think, Sergeant Starkey, that you should be callin' me Mrs. McQuade. Now, let me go, so I can take some stew out to your men."

"To hell wis . . . with them. They got their own grub."

He was beginning to slur his words, and she was beginning to become sincerely concerned . . . as he had not let go of her wrist.

"Release me, Sergeant, so I can take out some stew to your men."

He swiveled in the chair, then dragged her into his lap, holding her firmly there with an arm around her waist and a hand still clasping her wrist.

She did not panic, but rather looked him directly in the eye, her face only inches from his. "I appreciate your help, Sergeant Starkey. But all you'll be getting for your trouble is that jug of whiskey, which you've had far too much of, and that bowl of stew. Now if you'll be letting me go . . ."

The hand around the waist slipped up to grab her by the back of the neck, and he pulled her face to his, smashing his lips into hers in the semblance of a kiss. To his surprise, she allowed it. He stood, slipping her off his lap, and she melded herself to his body, feeling his growing hardness press into her.

Gaining confidence, he slid his tongue into her mouth, and she parted her lips to receive it . . . then viciously bit down, sinking her teeth deeply into his tongue, grabbing him by the whiskers with each hand, and jerking his head back.

He tried to wrench away, but she held him. He slapped her viciously, knocking her away from him and onto the ground. Stumbling back, both hands to his face, he tasted his own blood. He backhanded his mouth, and his hand came away crimson and dripping.

"You bloody bitch," he screamed out. Then he reached down and snatched her up by the blouse front. She was still groggy, but came to life as he ripped away the cotton garment.

She screamed, then yelled, "No, Starkey, take your hands off me. Damn you, damn you," but his fist knocked it from her and she went limp. He had her flat on the floor, her ankle-length gingham skirt up around her shoulders, when he felt the blows raining down on his shoulders. It was the old man, beating him with one of his canes. Starkey leapt to his feet and smashed a meaty fist into the old man's red mottled face, knocking him senseless and into a pile in the corner of the room.

Before he could get back to his task, the door flew open and the daughter ran into the room.

"What's the matter. What have you done to my ma? Is Pa . . . ?"

Starkey reached past her and slammed the door, just as she saw her grandfather also on the floor, then the blood streaking the soldier's face.

Her cry became a croak when he reached out and grasped her by the throat with one hand, then with both, and in moments she was on the floor unmoving. Only then did Starkey return to the task at hand.

Something awoke Colin. He'd lain for a moment, hearing something in the other room, something that drove him to pull himself out of the bed, crashing to the floor. He pulled himself nearer to the door, then passed out, unable to go further.

Later, Orin Starkey went out to the barn, where the men were sleeping off the crock of whiskey. He kicked them out of the hay and to their feet.

"You hitch up and get on. I'll be catching up later tonight. I still need to give Mrs. McQuade a hand." He was slurring his words, not only from the whiskey, but from a tongue badly injured and swollen.

"What's the matter with your face?" a soldier, Corporal Donklin, asked.

Starkey backhanded his mouth, and again pulled away a bloody hand. "Hot stew. Burned me good, then I damn near bit my own tongue off," he mumbled.

Donklin shook his head, thinking it a strange way to bloody your mouth, then asked, "Sarge, why don't we spend another night here? Hell, we'll only be making two or three miles afore it's too dark to go on. I'll bet that stew was fine, and maybe she'll be sharing a bit with all of us."

Starkey tried to give Donklin another kick, but the soldier dodged him. "By the Good Lord you'll be obeying me, or I'll have you horsewhipped," Starkey said.

"Yes, sir. But it don't make no sense."

"It don't have to make sense to the likes of you."

Grumbling, the men hitched up and whipped up the teams, soon disappearing over the horizon.

It was the better part of two hours later when Orin Starkey went to the pump outside and cleaned his knife; then he returned to the house and poured coal oil everywhere inside. Convinced that his men were far enough away so they could not see the flames, he went to the stove and used the prod to throw out a few embers onto the oil-soaked floor. As an afterthought, he turned back to the pie safe, reached in, and fetched out an apple pie he'd been admiring, then picked up one of Brigid's seashells from a nearby shelf. It was a brightly colored thing, with alternating stripes of red and purple. He smiled, shoving it into his pocket; it would be a thing by which to remember this day.

Then he headed for the door, only then realizing the growing flames across the hooked rug had ignited his trousers at the cuff.

He must have spilled some oil on his pants. Dropping the pie, stumbling out the door in a panic, he madly beat at his flaming cuff with his hands, searing his leg and badly burning his left hand, but getting the fire out.

By the time he stumbled toward the barn, the flames behind were driving him away.

"Damn," he said aloud. He searched the barn until he found an old shirt used as a rag, then some axle grease to dress the wound. Carefully, with teeth and his one good hand, he bound the blistered left.

Even with that small trouble, he rode out content that the McQuade homestead was well afire, and all evidence of his deed would burn with it.

Happy with the knowledge that the carnage he'd left behind would be most likely blamed on Indians, he never looked back, riding out with the house roaring in flames behind him.

Lieutenant Frank Baldwin sat his big dun on a ridge overlooking a creek and its confluence with the Yellowstone. So far, the march had been uneventful, with the exception of one sighting of a small band of Indians and their pursuit. By the time the force assigned to the job had traveled three miles afoot, the mounted Indian band was well out of sight, and the pursuit abandoned.

The journey had begun with inclement weather, but it had warmed, and only the high ridges were now dusted with snow.

They had made fine time, almost twenty-two miles a day if Baldwin's calculations were correct, and should be more than three quarters of the way to the cantonment.

Baldwin paused a moment before he gigged the dun back down the slope to where the column was marching upriver a mile below. He eyed the column of just over a hundred troops, followed by the cook's wagon, a supply wagon, then by a half-dozen pack mules. He hooked a leg over the forks of the saddle and sat quietly. They were out of the barren plains, and the hills across the river were timbered, but only with low cedars. As they got nearer the cantonment, Baldwin knew they'd begin to see lodgepole pines interspersed with the lower cedars. The high ridges were dusted with snow, and the sky was spotted with clouds puffy as high mountain bear clover and even less threatening. In the distance, a herd of over a hundred antelope grazed away from the column below, their white rumps matching the snow they climbed to meet. Across the Yellowstone, Baldwin counted a dozen dark spots in an arroyo only he could see, hidden from the troops below. It was the first buffalo they'd spotted, and these seemed to be moving south. All in all, it was a beautiful day and had been a good march.

God willing it would remain as such until they reached the Tongue River.

Young Corporal Brian McGloughlan broke ranks as he saw Baldwin coming down the slope, and walked away from the column to meet him.

"Sir, Grigsby just rode in."

"Drop back and tell him to ride up alongside for a while. I want to hear his report."

Grigsby had been gone overnight, scouting ahead, hunting for camp meat, and generally doing his assigned task.

Barton Grigsby was the scout Baldwin had employed back at Fort Buford. It was not that Baldwin thought he couldn't find the way to the cantonment. There was a road fifty to one hundred paces wide leading the way, the Yellowstone, but it was always good to have a man along who knew the country, and the savage. Grigsby, even though as young as any man in the column, should know both, as he was born in the Judith country to a

Crow woman and a trapper from St. Louis. He dressed half Indian and half white, wearing moccasins, blanket leggings, and a store-bought cotton shirt and twill coat. A tomahawk hung stuffed on his right side through the red sash tied about his waist, and a wicked knife, an Arkansas toothpick as long as his forearm, through the left . . . and he carried a Sharps rifle in .40/.90 as well as a Springfield carbine in .45/.70 in an Army-issue scabbard on his saddle. Tied behind that saddle was a buffalo robe. He constantly smoked a carved pipe, its contents a mixture of bark of the red willow, kinnikinnick, and larb . . . Indian tobacco.

And he'd served under General Hallick in the West during the recent rebellion when barely old enough to enlist.

So far, he'd proved his worth time and time again. Part of it was because of the money he earned, but more so because of a natural inbred hatred of the Crow's lifelong enemies, the Sioux.

As Baldwin took his place at the head of the column, Grigsby reined up alongside. "Sorry, Lieutenant, I was delivering a fat whitetail to the cook's wagon."

"One whitetail won't go far."

"I'll be back out this evening."

"I saw a few buffalo over that rise from up on the bluff. One of those fat critters should last us the rest of the way to Tongue River."

"As you wish, sir. With this Sharps, if I can see it, I can kill it."

Baldwin smiled. Modesty wasn't one of Grigsby's faults. "So, anything interesting up ahead?"

"Plenty of track, and I don't mean buff. A hundred ponies, north to south, crossed the Yellowstone up ahead at what we call Stony Flat. Didn't see no drag marks, so they weren't no women and children. I'd say it was a party with mischief on its mind. We might have to kill us a few Sioux."

"A hundred or more mounted braves. Could make for an interesting day tomorrow."

Grigsby's look turned a little more serious. "God willin' they're on their way somewheres and have no mind of us."

"Tomorrow will tell, I'd imagine. You do your hunting this evening, then take my man, Corporal McGloughlan. I'll issue him a head of the wagon stock. I want the both of you out front at least two miles ahead of us tomorrow, riding the ridges on both sides of the river. I'll brook no surprises."

"Yes, sir. If I could take him with me on the hunt, along with a couple of pack mules, it might save me coming back to fetch someone to tote meat."

"Done."

As he rode away, Baldwin surveyed the country ahead. A series of cedar ridges dropped away to the river in deep arroyos. There were a thousand or more places for a hundred men to hole up, and worse, to have the high ridges looking down on a column of marching men.

The coming one could be a most interesting day.

Chapter 6

Like Baldwin, Kev McQuade sat surveying the country ahead.

On a high ridge, a quarter mile or so above the herd, a lone rider sat with a leg hooked over the saddle horn. Kev could see he was no Indian. He wore a floppy-brimmed hat and a white shirt, and the big bay he sat was well trimmed in a high-cantled saddle that might have come up the Bozeman Trail from Arizona or New Mexico. A long gun rested across the saddle.

Kev decided it was the same man they'd seen yesterday, and it made him nervous. The man clearly was not trying to hide his presence, but it wasn't right, a man just sitting and watching. He had to have something on his mind, and it was probably something foul, otherwise he'd hail them and ride up alongside.

The herd was moving quietly and the country ahead was unimposing, so Kev decided he would find out what this stranger was all about. He moved along quietly on the left flank of the herd, until he came to a deep and well-sheltered ravine, edged over to it, then when he dropped low out of sight of the stranger above, reined into the bottom of the ravine and moved up. Up to where he might come face-to-face with the watcher.

He rode far up along the bottom of the ravine, constantly climbing, until he estimated he might be even with where the stranger had sat, then reined up out of it. Another hundred yards through the cedars, and he reached a high barren ridge and the spot where he thought he'd seen the rider.

Moving up then back down the hog-back, he finally located a set of tracks, but no rider. He stood in the stirrups, holding a hand over his eyes to shelter them from the sun, and studied the direction the tracks led. No one in sight, but the cover was thick with hawthorn and chokecherries. He decided to track the man a while, since his trail led the same way the herd was moving.

When he was deep in a copse of cedars, a voice rang out behind him.

"You looking for me, friend?"

Kev spun in the saddle, resting a hand on his Colt but not drawing. There was no one in sight, but he answered nonetheless. "I'm looking for the man that's been spying on my trail herd."

"Didn't know watching a few cattle meander along was against the law." As he spoke, the man moved out onto the trail behind Kev.

"Ain't, but it ain't real sociable neither."

"So, where you fellas off to with that herd? Miners are all the other way, and the rail at Cheyenne is a hell of a trip in the coming winter."

The man, Kev guessed in his forties, now wore a well-tailored coat and waistcoat over the white shirt. The waistcoat sported a watch fob and chain, and the pocket opposite where the watch was tucked showed the ends of four fine cigars. His trousers were also sewn by a fine hand, probably a city tailor. He had hard-edged features, and eyes the color of amber. *Cat eyes,* Kev thought. The rifle now hung loosely in his left hand, leaving his right free to draw the low-slung butt-forward revolver on his left hip. The rifle and revolver both gleamed, and the cartridge belt and holster were hand-tooled and shimmered of polish. Kev appraised him carefully before he answered. "You got a reason for askin'?"

"No special reason, just making conversation. Where you fellas from?"

"Rocky Butte Ranch, down near Reed Point on the Yellowstone."

"Don't know the place."

Kev was silent for a moment. "So, you alone."

"Alone enough. I wouldn't mind coming on down to your camp, come supper time."

"You'd be welcome. Better than having you sit atop some ridge just watching. It gives a fella the willies, being watched like that."

The man smiled, then stepped forward alongside the buckskin and offered his hand. "I'm Chadwick Steel. Heading east from . . . from Helena."

Kev didn't like the way the man hesitated about where he was coming from, but took the hand and shook anyway. There was a passel of fellows in Montana who didn't want you to know where they were from or where they were headed.

"Nice to make your acquaintance," Steel said, then asked, "Where you headed?"

"I'm Kevin McQuade, from the Rocky Butte Ranch, like I said. These cattle are sold to the Army, and we're headed to the cantonment at Tongue River."

"Then I might just ride along for a ways, you don't mind."

"Pleased to have the help. You been a drover before?"

"Hardly, Mr. McQuade. I run a gambling establishment in St. Louis, and I'm heading back there. Hope I'll catch a paddle wheeler going downriver, once I get to the Missouri."

"Good chance you'll do just that. You're welcome to share one meal, maybe two, but then on if you eat, you work, so long as you understand that. You gonna follow me back?"

"Nope, got other business before I ride in. See you when you've made camp."

"Fair enough," Kev said, and gigged the horse as the man called Chad Steel doffed his hat, exposing a full head of steel-gray hair to match his name.

A strange fellow, Kev thought as the buckskin picked his way down the slope, but he'd found that city folks often were a mite strange and St. Louis was a big city, or so he'd heard. Still and all, he'd welcome the help, particularly if it only cost a little bacon and beans.

Norval Dugan spent several days shamed by the fact he'd let his worthless cousin, Oscar Petersen, talk him into running out on the McQuades when the Indians had attacked the roundup. Finally, it was his brother, Patrick, who'd convinced him that the only right thing to do was to go back to the McQuade place with hat in hand and try and make amends.

So he and Patrick had set out for the three-day ride from their place just above Big Timber.

When they rounded the last bend in the river before the Rocky Butte home place, Norval pulled rein and eyed the scene on the plateau, atop a rimrock, a half mile up-slope from the riverbank. Where the McQuade place normally stood was a wide vacant spot. He thought he could see the roof of the barn beyond, but no house. A pile of rubble that might have been the chimney was the only remnant in sight.

"What the hell, Pat. I believe the house is done gone."

"Houses don't get up and go, you damn fool."

"Well, this one has. It sets up there atop that rock face, overlooking the river, but she sure as the devil ain't there now."

"Let's get up there," Patrick said, and they whipped up their mounts.

It was a half mile up a ravine to the plateau, then another quarter along the rimrock to the pile of rubble that had once been the McQuade ranch house on the Rocky Butte Ranch.

When they reined up, the horses were worked into a lather. They sat them a minute and let them blow, just staring at the jumble of burnt and tangled logs.

Finally, Norval spoke. "You don't suppose those damned Hunkpapa followed them all the way back here and burned them out?"

Patrick dismounted. "Don't know, but I doubt it. We'd had a hell of a snow, and a rain down lower that day. It would have been real soft out here in the yard. All the tracks I see hereabouts are shod horses. Let's pick about and see if we can pick up any sign."

He moved into the rubble as Norval dismounted.

"My God, they's bodies in here. Burned till you don't know who's who or what's what, but they's bodies all right."

Norval joined him, and they stood staring at the prostrate burnt mounds among the tangle that had once been the McQuade family.

"That small one there, that's probably the little girl. That'n over there has what looks to be a cane at hand. That's bound to be Old Man McQuade, and this'n here is the missus."

"No sign of Col or Kev. You suppose them redskins hauled 'em off?"

Just as he finished the sentence, they heard a low thumping and a primal scream.

Norval jumped back as if the angel of death had tapped him on the shoulder. "What the devil."

"Shut your face so's I can listen."

Patrick walked to what had been the bedroom, then across it to where a heavy plank door had fallen out against the rock face of the slope that part of the house was dug into. The heavy planks were scorched and blackened, but not burned through. He bent nearer and listened.

The knocking grew louder.

"Who's there?" Patrick shouted.

"It's the by-God devil hissef." Norval stumbled back away from the bedroom.

"It's somebody, or something," Norval said, "that's for damn sure." Then he reached down and worked his fingers under the edge of the remnants of the door, and jerked back. But got little movement. "Norval, damn it, man, help me."

Reluctantly, hesitantly, Norval moved to his brother's side. Together, they jerked the door away.

From the darkness the gaunt eyes of a man stared out at him until the man covered his eyes with a scorched hand.

"Who . . ."

"Too bright . . . Colin . . . Colin McQuade," the apparition whispered in a tone so low Patrick had to bend forward.

It was a half hour before they had Colin lying in a pile of straw in the barn, and had gotten some water down him.

He explained, as best he could in his emaciated condition, that he'd been awakened by something—he vaguely thought it was Brigid's screams—but by the time he'd managed to fall out of bed and crawl to the door, the door itself was smoking so badly he knew it was about to burst into flames, and the roof over his head was afire. He remembered crawling to the root cellar, pulling the heavy door closed, and tumbling down the stairs inside, before he lost consciousness. For the last several days, he'd lived off the vegetables in the root cellar and drunk the juice from canned peaches and beans. He was not strong enough to shove the heavy door away, and had decided he would just die there when the food ran out.

They left him alone to sleep while they found a tarp, then returned to the house to scoop up the remains of the McQuade family, then bury them in the plot that already contained three markers: Maddie McQuade, Colin's mother, who'd taken a fever and passed on when Colin was sixteen; Sean Mc-

Quade, Colin and Brigid's nineteen-year-old son who'd drowned; and Tobin McQuade, their twelve-year-old son who'd been horse-thrown and broken his neck.

When they returned to the barn just as the sun was setting, Colin seemed better, and they got him to sit up. Colin's horse had kicked his way out of a stall in the barn when he'd decided no one was bringing him any hay, and the remnants of the gate were used to build a small fire.

"Who was the burying for?" Colin asked in a low, almost mournful tone.

Patrick cleared his throat before he began. "I think it was Da McQuade, Brigid, and your daughter."

"Did you mark the graves?"

"We did."

"I'm forever obliged to you."

Patrick Dugan and Col McQuade sat in silence for a while as Norval had gone to gather more firewood.

Finally, it was Colin who spoke. "Kev and Sean, I'm hoping they've gone to deliver the herd to the Army. Don't suppose you've heard anything of them?"

"Sure haven't, Col. We just rode in from over at our place. Norval wanted to let you know it was Petersen who wanted to run out on y'all at the Indian fight . . . when you was gatherin' up the herd. You know, you can pick your friends, but you can't help who you're related to."

"That's old business."

"Still and all, he felt he had to make sure his cousin got out."

"Old business. I got other things on my mind."

It was later, after they'd sat by the fire built in the

middle of the barn floor where they'd cleared out the straw, when Patrick got around to asking Colin, "How'd it start?"

"What?"

"The fire. How did the fire start?"

Chapter 7

Colin took a deep breath before he began, and waited for Norval to stack the firewood, then join them. "Don't rightly know how it started. I was in bed. Guess they'd just lopped this leg off'n me, and the next thing I knew, Brigid was screamin' at the top of her lungs. Somebody else was here, but I just can't remember . . ."

"And the leg?"

"Gunshot. Damned Hunkpapa. Went green on me. Brigid and this other fellow, whoever the hell it was . . . They took the saw to me. But I'll be damned if I can remember. What I don't understand is why none of them got out."

"Don't matter now," Patrick offered in a low tone. "They're all dead."

"Not Kev. Not Sean," Norval said, then was silent for a moment. "Sorry about you gettin' shot, Colin. I never shoulda followed that yellow-bellied cousin of mine out of there."

"Old business, Norval, don't speak on it again. I'll be forever obliged for you two coming on back and taking care of Da, Brigid, and Pattiann. Little Pattiann, my God, that is . . . was . . . one beautiful child. I knew it, knew they was all dead . . . lying there in the damnable darkness. I knew it, but I still think I might just die from the pain of it." He shuddered, covered his face with both hands, but did not sob.

"Didn't have no Good Book, Colin," Patrick said. "Someone should read over them sometime soon. You want a chaw?" Patrick fished a twist out of his pocket, changing the subject, fearing that Colin was about to break down in tears.

"No. Fact is, I want my wife and daughter back."

There was an awkward silence, then Patrick offered, "Tomorrow, we'll saddle up and take you back to our place."

"No. No, I'm staying right here. Most of my kin is over in that plot . . . my child . . . my children . . . my wife and da and ma . . . and all we've worked for is here. It'd be like turnin' tail on all of them should I leave now."

"You can't tend no cattle," Norval said, "with one damned leg."

"It's *damned* sure enough, but not so damned as the one got threw away," Colin said. "I'll manage here. I'd appreciate it if one of you would carve me a crutch. I know the 23rd Psalm, and I'll say it over them as soon as I can hobble over there . . . and face it."

Patrick rose and stretched. "Guess we can hang around for a couple of weeks and see you get on your feet . . . er, get that good leg under you."

"God willin', Kev and Sean will be back by then. I . . . I'm obliged to the both of you."

The campfire had burned down, so they found some horse blankets to cover Colin with, rolled out their bedrolls, and slept where they lay.

*   *   *

Chad Steel rode into that night's cow camp just as Kev was dishing up some stew from the Dutch oven, and just as the sun touched the mountaintops to the west.

For the first time since they'd left the Rocky Butte Ranch, Sean showed some interest in what was happening on the drive. He arose from the log upon which he had perched himself and eyed the dismounting fancy-dressed man.

Kev too stood from his perch on a rock. "Mr. Steel, grab a tin there and dish yourself up some stew. There's coffee there." Kevin's tone turned a little sheepish. "I ain't much at biscuits, but there's a bit of hardtack in that sack."

Steel walked over to a pannier near the fire and fished out a tin cup. He poured himself a cup of syrupy coffee from the pot on the fire, then turned to Kev. "Before I get a plate of food, I should tell you I've got another mouth to feed."

Kevin eyed him suspiciously. "Just one?"

"Just one. An a small one at that."

Kev relaxed a little, thinking he had a child with him. "Well, fetch 'im on in. It's better than having him watching from out there in the shadows."

Steel walked to the camp's edge and whistled.

The hawthorn brush a few paces away rustled, and a mounted rider pushed through.

Kevin and Sean stared at the rider, and even Sleeps-in-Day and Badger-Man, who shared a fire twenty-five paces from the McQuades, rose and watched with interest.

The rider sat sidesaddle, her face hidden under

a wide-brimmed bonnet with a scarf tied around her head, anchoring the bonnet but effectively hiding her face in shadow.

Steel met her, reached up and took her by her narrow waist, and helped her down. She stood brushing her long shimmering skirt back into some semblance of order, then reached up and untied the scarf from under her neck, removed the bonnet, then untied a bow at her neck and let her wrap fall away. Her white blouse was trimmed in lace, and well fitted.

Kev and Sean stared even harder as she shook out long blond tresses across her shoulders. Chad Steel took her by a fine, long-fingered hand and led her forward.

"Gentlemen, this is Caitlin Steel."

Kev managed to set his coffee cup aside and move forward. He doffed his hat, standing with hat in both hands in front of him. "Pleased to meet you, Mrs. Steel."

She laughed, and Kev blushed. Then she spoke. "It's actually Mrs. Tolofsen, formerly Miss Steel."

Kev couldn't help but notice the hard look the man gave her, but she seemed to shrug it off. Kev was still trying to figure out their relationship. "Then you're . . ."

"I'm Mr. Steel's daughter." She affectionately placed a hand on his shoulder as she related this, then stepped closer and nodded. "It's nice to meet you . . . Mr. . . . ?"

"McQuade, Kev McQuade. And this here's my nephew, Sean."

Sean had retaken his seat, and blushed as Kev had, cutting his eyes away without greeting her.

Ken continued. "And that's Badger-Man and Sleeps-in-Day over there by the other fire. Get to your feet, boy," Kev chastised his nephew. "This is Mrs. Tolofsen."

Sean stumbled to his feet, spilling his coffee and managing another blush as he brushed it off his trousers. "Nice to make your acquaintance, Mrs. Tolofsen."

"My, that smells good," she said, stepping into the firelight. "It's been some time since we've dined."

In the last glow of sunlight and with the glowing embers below, Kev could see that she had her father's eyes, amber cat's eyes. With the blond hair, and complexion perfectly tanned from days in the sun, she was so strikingly beautiful she took Kev's breath away . . . and she was young. Younger than Kev.

He finally managed, "I'm sorry, ma'am. Let me fetch you a plate."

"You finish your supper, Mr. McQuade. I'm perfectly capable. In fact, I understand we're to ride along with you to the Tongue River. If it pleases you, I'll do the cooking and camp work until we reach there."

It was a hard picture for Kev to contemplate, this beautiful woman doing camp work, but he managed, "That would be just fine, Mrs. Tolofsen, if that pleases you."

"It does. Now let's eat. I'm famished."

As she got even closer to the fire, Kev could see that she was not quite perfect. A crow's-foot scar showed in her left eyebrow, still a little red and angry, maybe only a few weeks old. But it was a tiny flaw, and she was still by far the most beautiful woman Kev had ever seen.

If he could even imagine the deed, it looked as if she'd been struck in anger with a fist.

Who could be so low as to hit a woman, particularly a woman this perfect? He eyed the tall gray-haired man with her for a moment, thinking the worst.

Convinced he was mistaken, he went back to his supper while she dished up a plate for her father, then one for herself.

She smiled at him as she took a place on the log next to Sean, and managed to say just before she took the first spoonful, "Tomorrow evening, we'll have biscuits, if you have the makings."

To Kev's surprise, all the pair had for bedding was their saddle blankets. He offered the lady his bedroll, but she refused, so he fixed them both up with pack tarps from the mules, and left them to camp alone in the hawthorns.

Lieutenant Frank Baldwin, Scout Barton Grigsby, and Corporal Brian McGloughlan knelt by a roaring fire, taking a late supper. Grigsby and McGloughlan had returned to camp with mules loaded with buffalo meat, and would have to return to the kill site in the morning to pack in the rest of the load. But the best of it, the tongue and the hump, were turning over the fire in front of the three as they spoke.

Cold-induced steam rolled from Grigsby's mouth as he spoke. "I hope it stays this cold, so's this meat lasts until we reach the Tongue . . . unless you got time to sit about and jerk a couple a hundred pounds." Grigsby leaned back and packed his pipe with more Indian tobacco. Its poignant odor permeated the night as he lit up.

Baldwin glanced up at the stars. "It's cold enough, but I imagine it'll warm up again tomorrow. It's clear as a high mountain creek."

"We'll be out before light, Lieutenant," Grigsby said, "and recover the rest of the meat before you soldiers is packed up. Then we'll lope on up ahead of you on the point."

"You've done a good job, Barton," Baldwin said, complimenting him.

"You should have seen the shot that took this old bull down, Lieutenant," McGloughlan said, obvious admiration in his eyes. "Four hundred fifty yards if it was a foot, and that big bull dropped in his tracks. I'll bet that forty-ninety could reach out a half mile."

"Made one over six hundred yards one time," Grigsby said, not boasting, merely stating a fact.

"And the rest of the herd," McGloughlan continued with the same enthusiasm, "didn't run off. In fact they seemed to be trying to get the old bull to his feet, using their heads to butt him up."

"That normal, Barton?" Baldwin asked.

"Buff's a funny creature. Nothing much they fear 'ceptin' prairie fire. Makes them an easy hunt, if'n you come on them."

"Well," Baldwin said, "this one will last us till we reach the cantonment. Glad you didn't take another."

"Never take nothing I don't eat or can't sell," Barton said. "Less'n, of course, it's a Sioux."

"And that's a grudge thing?" McGloughlan asked.

"Guess that's so, but it's been that way long as I can remember."

"Well, sir," Baldwin said, "you may get your chance to settle a little more of your grudge before we finish this march."

"If'n I do, I do; if'n I don't, I don't. If'n they come our way, I'll take my share."

"I'm sure you will," Baldwin said, his tone a little sad. Then he lightened up. "Looks like it's about time to share that ol' waggle tongue, don't you think?"

With that, Grigsby pulled the stake skewering the peeled tongue away from the fire. "Done to a turn," he said, and began carving it up with the large Arkansas toothpick he wore on his hip.

Kev was surprised to find Caitlin Steel Tolofsen up and tending the fire when he awoke, just as the sun's first rays pierced the eastern sky over the low hills.

Kev quickly pulled on his boots and rolled up, then went to give her a hand. He could see she'd rifled through the stores. "You need more wood, Mrs. Tolofsen?"

"I could use a little, and it's Caitlin if you would."

"Caitlin then. I'll fetch it."

"And a little coffee water if you'll wander down by the creek."

"I can do that."

The mud was gone, but the ground was well frosted, and what was left of the coffee in the half-gallon pot had frozen. He had to bang the pot on a rock to shake the remnants free before he could wash it out and fill it with fresh water.

By the time he'd returned, his arms full of wood

and the pot dangling from a hand, the rest of the camp was stirring. She had sliced a slab of bacon and had it frying, and had something else cooking in the Dutch oven.

Her father joined him without comment as he rounded up the hobbled horses and mules, brushed them, and saddled up.

Just as they'd finished and had them staked out to a line tied between two cottonwoods, the man finally spoke. "I don't mean to be burdening you with a woman, Mr. McQuade, but I have to get my daughter back to St. Louis."

Kev merely nodded. "She's hardly a burden, Mr. Steel. She had the fire stoked when I climbed out of the canvas. And whatever she's cooking smells like home."

Steel pulled him up short before they got within earshot of the campfire. "She had some trouble in . . . back up the trail. I came all the way from St. Louis to fetch her home."

"Her eye—"

"That, and other things. I beat the son of a bitch who marked her, maybe a bit too much of a beating. I don't know, as we had to light out of there."

"Well, it looks to me like he had it coming . . . whatever happened."

"That's kind of you to say, McQuade. Still, I don't want to bring trouble down on you and your herd. They may be coming after us to bring me down. And to take her back to him, if he's alive. He had friends. . . ."

"Was this a husband of hers?"

"If you can call the bastard that."

Kev stared away at the line the sun was forming

over the distant hills for a moment, then turned back to Steel. "Anyone who'd be a friend of a man who'd strike a woman as beau . . . A helpless woman—they won't be friends of mine, Mr. Steel. You're welcome in this camp. All I ask is you pull your weight while you're here."

"Both of us will."

"Then it's enough said."

With that, they made their way to the campfire, where Caitlin was forking big fluffy biscuits out of the Dutch oven.

After Kev had finished his bacon and biscuits, and as he and Steel were retracing their steps to the horses, he gave the tall gray-haired man a smile. "It'll take a whole lot of that old boy's friends to drag her out of this camp, even if she wasn't a lady mistreated. I thought those biscuits were gonna float off'n my plate."

"She's a fair hand, Mr. McQuade, at a lot of things."

"We'll be at the Tongue River before you know it, and you can probably catch an Army escort on down the Yellowstone to the Missouri, and maybe still catch a steam wheeler on down to St. Louis."

"I appreciate your help, Mr. McQuade. I won't forget it."

"Kev, if you would, sir."

"Then Kev it is, and I'm Chad. We'll be out of your hair before you know it."

Kev merely nodded, then suddenly had the thought that it would be a sad day when Chad Steel rode on downriver with his daughter. A sad day, married woman or not.

Sean was already at his horse when Kev arrived.

"Sean," Kev instructed as he strapped on a pair of elk hide bat-wing chaps, "you're not riding herd the rest of the way."

"Why not?" he demanded. Kev had noticed that since Caitlin had arrived, Sean had been a different boy. He was up and at it early, impressing her with his willingness to do whatever needed doing.

"Because I have more important work for you." The sour look left his face.

Kev continued. "I want you to stay with Mrs. Tolofsen, as sort of an escort. Make sure she gets along all right, and make sure the remuda and mules keep up. It's rough county up ahead, deep with buck-brush and tangles, and I don't want her too far from the herd. Mr. Steel will take your place in the rotation."

Sean couldn't contain his smile. "If you say so, Kev. I should ride right alongside her?"

"Don't let her out of your sight."

"Yes, sir," Sean said, addressing his uncle politely for the first time since they'd left the ranch.

Kev started to ride away, then as an afterthought, suggested, "You keep that old shotgun at the ready. Mr. Steel has some worries about someone coming to carry Mrs. Tolofsen off, and we wouldn't want that."

"You want I should fill 'em fulla buckshot—"

"I want you to fire a shot in the air so we know there's trouble about, and can come at the run."

Kev smiled inwardly as he rode toward the grazing herd. *Maybe there is more than one way to turn a boy into a man. Maybe having a beautiful woman around is a lot more effective than having a grumpy uncle.* Kev laughed out loud, then gigged the buckskin into a lope to take the point.

As he rode abreast of the herd, he realized something was wrong and drew rein. On the far side of the herd, Badger-Man and Sleeps-in-Day sat their ponies, staring off up a ravine. Not strange in itself, but the fact the whole herd had their heads up, standing stark still, staring in the same direction, was more than strange.

Something had their attention.

Kev hit the buckskin with his spurs and galloped around the herd until he reached where the two Indians were studying the cut.

"What's up?" Kev asked after he slid to a stop.

"I think bear. Maybe cougar, maybe bear. Big bear," Badger-Man said.

Chapter 8

"Will he come down and pester us?" Kev asked, surveying the hillside, searching for any sign of cougar, wolf, or bear.

"No. He wait for stray or . . . Whatever he is, he act strange."

"Well, keep a sharp eye. Let's move 'em out." With that, Kev gigged the buckskin and took up the point.

The herd seemed more than eager to move away from the deep cut that had had their attention.

The sky ahead was lead gray, and dappled. A sign of changing weather.

It was late in the day, and it had been a long one for young Corporal Brian McGloughlan. He'd started well before dawn with a trip back to the buffalo kill site with the scout, Grigsby, and returned before the other soldiers had taken their morning coffee. He and Grigsby had delivered the meat, grabbed a cup of coffee and some hardtack, then ridden out so they'd be at least a mile ahead of the marchers on the right and left point. Grigsby had taken up the right, across the Yellowstone, and Mc-Gloughlan the left.

McGloughlan was daydreaming in the saddle of the pack mule he rode when a shot rang out, snapping him to instant attention. He couldn't zero in on its source, until the second rang out. Reining up, he shaded his eyes and looked across the river until he located Barton Grigsby, standing in the saddle, madly waving his rifle.

He was pointing to something up ahead, but the cliff-side was almost at water's edge and McGloughlan couldn't see what he was motioning at. As excited as Grigsby was, it couldn't be anything good.

It was only seconds before the young corporal heard the pounding of hoofbeats, then another shot from Grigsby. McGloughlan spun the mule in his tracks, facing back the way they'd come, but continuing to stare back over his shoulder, and it was lucky he did so. Less than a hundred yards behind, a group of pounding riders, Sioux riders, rounded the cliff.

McGloughlan didn't wait to find out how many they were, but dropped his head low and madly quirted the mule into a gallop.

The mule wasn't particularly fast, but he was steady and Brian figured he had at least seventy-five yards on his pursuers. He glanced back as the mule pounded into a copse of river willows, to see a dozen of the riders break off from the group and plunge into the river, Brian presumed to pursue Grigsby, who continued to fire.

Willow boughs slapped at him, trying to drag him out of the saddle. He slunk lower in the saddle and pounded on. Brian knew there was a bog ahead, and tried to remember how many yards he'd slogged through it, and beyond that there was a point where he'd had to swim the big mule around . . . then decided he'd lose too much time and the Indians would close on him if he tried to go that way, so he veered right up a ravine that he prayed would take him to the top of the plateau overlooking the river.

Grigsby fooled the dozen attacking Indians by not spurring his horse away and fleeing. Rather, he leaped from the saddle, both rifles in hand, and sunk to a flat-topped rock to begin a barrage of fire. Before the dozen had reached the middle of the broad river, three of them had been knocked out of the saddle.

The mule was strong and sure, and pounded up the ravine until he reached a long shale slope. But McGloughlan knew he couldn't tarry, and had no choice; he gave the mule his heels and quirted him at the same time. Thank God he was game, and took off up the slope, gaining three strides, losing one.

The Indians closed ground, firing so that heavy slugs slammed into the loose shale splattering rock around mule and rider. This encouraged the big mule more, and he seemed to gain new fervor.

Brian topped the slope, still in one piece, the mule breathing heavily. He hoped the big mule would hold out, then realized that the Indians too would have spent horses by the time they reached the top of the shale escarpment. He reined the mule back into a comfortable lope, then suddenly jerked rein, bringing the big animal to a sliding stop.

Brian sighed deeply. Not over a hundred yards ahead was a column of at least fifty Sioux. To his right, the plateau rose into a thickly wooded slope, to his left was the cliff over the river, but somewhere beyond that was his column of comrades.

Only hesitating for a moment, he jerked rein to the left just as the Indians ahead of him caught sight and gave heels to their own horses. Brian glanced left, and the original pursuing group was topping the slope not more than fifty yards behind, and to his right, another band was screaming, firing, and pursuing from a slightly longer distance.

He hunkered low in the saddle and pounded toward the cliff over the river, thinking he had nothing to lose and would jump the mule into the void, praying that the river would be below to receive them. Whatever faced him, it couldn't be worse than what was behind.

The original group of Indians was closer, and he felt slugs cut the air overhead. Only another forty yards until he'd either jump to his death, or into the Yellowstone below.

The big mule stumbled, but recovered his footing, and pounded on, twenty yards, ten yards, then suddenly the animal balked, refusing the jump into nothingness and setting his forefeet, at the same time lowering his head and humping his back.

Brian flew out into the void alone, the reins jerked free of his hands. His arms outstretched, his legs akimbo, he plunged downward. Water, it was water below, rushing up to meet him? Now how deep?

Slamming into the surface, expecting a final slam into a body-crushing rocky bottom, he went down and down.

Then he fought the dank darkness until he surfaced, surprised he was alive, spitting and gag-

ging—then the water's surface began to explode
with slamming lead. Not wholly recovering his
breath, he nonetheless dove under the surface as
shells snaked through the water around him, and
stroked downriver with the current. He'd made at
least a hundred feet in the fast-flowing water before
he feared he'd black out and had to break surface
and gasp for breath. This time only a couple of
shells popped the surface, but again he plunged
under the water and stroked downstream.

Across the river, Grigsby was now firing at only a
half-dozen retreating Indians, accompanied by the
same number of rider-less horses, madly retracing
their tracks to their original position across the
river from where Grigsby had set up his deadly field
of fire.

He dropped one more before they disappeared
into the cottonwoods and willows lining the broad
river.

The next time Brian McGloughlan surfaced, it
was to the pleasant sound of a column of 5th Infantry soldiers a hundred yards downriver, one
group in the kneeling position, the group behind
standing, firing alternating volleys at the Indians
four hundred yards away atop the plateau. In seconds, the Sioux disappeared, and all was quiet.

McGloughlan made his way to shore, stumbling
to where Lieutenant Baldwin met him and helped
him to a rock, where he flopped down.

"You didn't lose my mule did you, Corporal?"
Baldwin asked.

Between gasps, the corporal managed to look up
to see his lieutenant smiling at him, then realized
the question had been a joke.

"I'm . . . afraid . . . I did . . . sir. Damned if that . . . tough old ground-pounder . . . won't make a stringy dinner for those redskins." He managed to finish, then put his head down between his legs and tried to catch his breath. He again sat up, then held his hands out and realized he couldn't stop them from shaking. He slipped one under each arm and clamped down on them to keep his lieutenant and comrades from seeing his fear.

Baldwin again smiled at him, and laid a hand on the younger man's shoulder. "At Vicksburg I couldn't stop shaking for most of a week. Don't worry, it'll pass."

McGloughlan attempted a smile, but then was afraid he was going to lose what little breakfast he had, and again put his head between his legs, then as quickly raised it again, wide-eyed. "Grigsby, he's still out there."

"He's making his way back along the far shore. He picked them off like they were pigeons on a fence rail. He's fine as Sunday morning."

"Good," McGloughlan said, returning his head between his legs. "Sioux picked a hard row to hoe if they went after Barton," he mumbled from his head-lowered position.

"I got another mule, you ready to get back out there?" Baldwin asked.

Again McGloughlan raised his head, hoping to see another smile on Baldwin's face, but he looked dead serious.

Then Baldwin smiled. "Actually, we're making camp here tonight, Corporal. Tomorrow's another day."

"Good . . . tomorrow." And the head went down again.

The next three days passed uneventfully on the McQuade cattle drive, with the weather remaining the same, overcast, gray as lead, with the sky dappled.

Each day Caitlin Tolofsen endeared herself more and more to the McQuades, and even to Sleeps-in-Day and Badger-Man, inviting the Indians to share some of what she cooked.

The weather had worsened, and each night had brought a rain squall, but little or no snow. The country was becoming sparser and sparser, and the eight to ten miles they tried to make every day became easier and easier.

Even so, the cattle remained nervous, and twice Badger-Man had reined off up hillsides and to investigate ravines, wondering what had them so ill at ease.

For the last three days, Caitlin had continued to veer off the trail, collecting edibles from the riverside, until Kev had begun to wonder what she was up to.

He had purposely steered clear of her and had refrained from riding alongside her. Not because he didn't value her company, but because he feared he might value it too much, and she was, after all, a married woman—even if unhappily so.

When the cattle were circled for the night, with a fine small stream feeding out of a ravine heavy with hawthorn and lined with mountain ash covered with red berries, into a meadow with plenty of grass, Kev made his way into where Sean and Caitlin had begun to make camp.

Just as he arrived, he saw his nephew and the woman wander off into the undergrowth.

He thought nothing of it, and found a place to roll out his bedroll, flopping down to rest a minute and shake out the kinks of a long day in the saddle, without even bothering to remove his chaps or boots.

Chad Steel rode up, dismounted, and walked over to stir the fire. He glanced around the camp, then turned to Kev. "Caitlin and Sean?"

Kev lifted his wide-brimmed hat off his eyes before answering. "Wandered off toward the river just as I rode up. Must be fetchin' water."

Chad walked over and flopped down in the grass beside Kevin. "I've been saving these like they were the queen's jewels, but I think it's time we shared a smoke." He removed paper-wrapped cigars from his waistcoat pocket, bit the end off one, and handed the other to Kev.

"Never had the pleasure," Kev said, "but don't mind if I do. You bite the end off?"

"Yep, won't draw if you don't."

Chad removed a small metal container from a pants pocket, pulled out a sulfur-head, and struck it across the metal cylinder's bottom. It flared, and he lit up, passing his lit cigar over to Kev, who used its glowing end to light his.

"Been a fine trip so far," Chad said, expelling a billow of smoke.

Kev lay back on his bedroll, took a deep draw on the cigar, and nodded in agreement.

Chad too lay back in the grass.

* * *

Sean had taken up the habit of following Caitlin Steel wherever she went, unless she informed him her business was personal. All along the trail, she'd been spotting elderberry bushes, and those not already stripped by the bears or elk she'd attack until she had a bonnet full.

She'd seen a likely spot down the slope toward the river when they'd picked a campsite. One more bonnet full, and she'd have enough to cook down for a pie. If these men thought her biscuits were good, they would absolutely die and go to heaven over her elderberry cobbler. And there was just enough day left that she could get the chore done before she had to have a plate of supper in front of the men.

The hawthorn and buck-brush were at least six feet high, but the elderberry she'd spotted was four feet taller than the other brush, high enough that even the elk couldn't reach the tops, although they'd stripped all the leaves off the bottom of the branches.

She turned to Sean, who had a bucket in one hand and his shotgun in the other. "I'm going to fill my bonnet from that elderberry bush over there, and have some personal business to take care of. Why don't you wander on down to the river and fill the bucket."

"Yes, ma'am," Sean said, then pushed through the brush. She waited until he was out of sight and earshot, then spread her skirts and knelt in the grass to relieve herself. When she was finished, she rose and started to move to the elderberry, then froze in her tracks.

Well above the six-foot underbrush, she could see the huge head and shoulders of the bear.

Chapter 9

The grizzly's massive frame seemed as wide as a wagon as he reached up at least ten feet, bent an elderberry branch down, and stripped away the berries. Bulging muscles rippled in his shoulders and broad back.

Figuring she was no more than twenty-five paces from the huge animal, Caitlin began to carefully back away, afraid to take her eyes off him. When she'd backed away a dozen feet, her skirt caught in a snag and she cried out softly.

The big griz snapped his head around, snorting his displeasure.

Screaming when his beady black eyes centered on her, Caitlin turned and ran, leaving a torn piece of her skirt in the underbrush.

With the scream and roar of a bear coming from no more than fifty or sixty paces from where they lay, both Chad and Kev bolted to their feet, trying to ascertain from which direction it had come. Then Chad charged toward the direction Kev had earlier told him Caitlin had gone. He was armed with nothing but a side arm, and jerked it from its holster as he clambered into the undergrowth.

Kev took time to run to where he'd tied his horse

and grab his Winchester from where he'd placed his saddle across a log, then sprang after Chad Steel.

Caitlin bolted back up the trail, brush grasping at her, running as she'd never run. She could hear the bear smashing through the brush behind her.

Before she'd covered twenty paces, she saw her father coming.

The trail was too narrow for both of them, and as he reached her, he swept her aside with a powerful arm into the underbrush. He'd no more than done so when he and the bear met. It was no contest, a ten-foot bear and a six-foot man. She heard the pistol he carried discharge as she tried to dig herself deeply into the brush.

Kev was no more than three dozen paces behind Chad, but heard the roar of the bear and the pistol shot and thrashing underbrush before he could see what was taking place. As he neared, he could see that the bear had something or someone under him, and was ravaging whoever it was. He got within a dozen paces and dropped to one knee, not wanting to risk firing down on the bear and hitting what he could now see was Chad Steel.

Chad and the bear were both roaring, with Chad trying to cover his throat with one arm and trying to get the pistol in position with the other.

As quickly as he could lever in, Kev fired three shots into the bear at point-blank range. The bear rocked back and forth, snorted, then rose on his hind legs and stood, facing Kev, who fired again into his chest, then began backing up, levering and firing. The bear took a half-dozen steps forward, then spun, went down to all fours, and charged down the trail away from Kev, running over an unmoving Chad again as he did so.

Kev ran up to where Chad lay, now still, and fired again at the retreating bear, then realized that Sean was coming up the same trail. The bear slid to a stop and again rose on his hind legs, facing the boy.

From less than ten feet, Sean let both barrels go into the massive face of the grizzly.

Sean screamed over the roar of the bear as the huge animal, now a mass of blood and mangled flesh above the shoulders, charged forward. Sean stumbled and fell to his back, still trying to aim and discharge the now-empty shotgun.

Kev charged up from behind as the bear tumbled forward. It fell directly down on the boy, but also on the upright barrels of the shotgun, bending them at a ninety-degree angle. Sean screamed, then "ooffed" loudly as the bear fell partially upon him, but the shotgun barrels had deflected the bear enough that Sean was not subjected to his full weight.

Sean knew he was dead, but in fact, it was the bear that was dead. Sean had finished him with the shotgun, blowing away half his thick neck.

Kev ran alongside and kicked the bear with all his might in the ribs, knowing he was causing no damage, but merely making sure the animal was finished. Then he touched the bear's open eye with the muzzle of his rifle. Getting no reaction, he quickly set the Winchester aside, dropped down beside his gasping cousin, and put a shoulder into the bear's side and pushed with all his might, until Sean could scramble out from underneath the dead weight.

Both of them sat still for a second, then between gasps, Kev managed, "Caitlin?"

Both got to their feet and charged back up the trail. Sean paused to pick up the shotgun, only then realizing it had been bent nearly ninety degrees by the weight of the bear. For some strange reason, he found it funny, and began to laugh and tear up at the same time as he ran along behind Kev.

By the time they reached Chad, Caitlin was bent over him, also with tears streaming down her cheeks, trying to stop the bleeding from deep rakes in her father's chest and shoulders. His coat, waistcoat, and shirt lay in tatters.

Just as they were trying to lift him to carry him back to the fire, Badger-Man and Sleeps-in-Day ran up. Together they managed to get the severely wounded man next to the fire, and onto his bedroll.

Kev and Caitlin began to work on him, applying compresses and bandages torn from camp rags and spare shirts. Caitlin found a needle and thread in the reticule she had tied to the back of her saddle, and spent a hour sewing up her father's wounds as best she could. She had to stop and unravel thread from the hem of her gown in order to continue, as she quickly used up all she had with the needle.

Chad only opened his eyes once, and that was to mumble, "Is it dead?"

"He's dead, Sean finished him, and Caitlin is fine," Kev managed, but barely got it out before Chad seemed to pass out again.

The McQuades and Caitlin ate cold food while watching over Chad Steel. He'd lost a lot of blood, but seemed to have no broken bones, at least none they could discern.

Sleeps-in-Day and Badger-Man built a fire near

the dead bear, roasted bear meat, and spent over an hour skinning out the huge animal.

When they came back into camp, they informed Kev that the animal had been sporting an old and very deep wound in its upper back, probably a rifle shot, and it had festered and must have been driving the animal wild. In addition, he carried eight fresh wounds, five in the chest and three in the back.

The huge bear had taken a lot of killing, but it would worry the cattle and the drovers no more.

Then the McQuades and Caitlin, while standing around the fire drinking coffee, determined they must stand watch over Chad, and decided to sleep in shifts. Sleeps-in-Day and Badger-Man would take four-hour shifts with the cattle, and would have the next day to themselves.

Kev informed her he could wait two days, but only two days. They would build a travois in the event Chad could not sit a horse by the time the herd had to push on. They did not discuss the other possibility, that Chad Steel might have found his final resting place in this riverside meadow.

"Wait," Caitlin said as the two McQuades started toward their bedroll. It had been decided that Caitlin would take the first watch. Walking over to Sean, she wrapped her arms around him and whispered, "Thank you." Releasing him, with his face reddening, she moved to Kev and did the same, holding onto him for what seemed a long time. He felt her body jerk once, then once more.

When she let him go, he realized tears coursed down her cheeks.

"Everything will be fine," Kev managed, then

reached up with a calloused thumb and wiped away the tears.

She covered her lowered face with both hands, speaking through them. "My father came to help me. He didn't want me to marry . . . that man . . . that animal. I defied him, now look what I've done."

This time it was Kev who wrapped his arms around her as she began to sob and mutter, "It's all my fault."

"It's no one's fault. No one's. A bear is a bear, and he was just doing what bears do."

"But my father wouldn't have been here."

"Then he would have been in his gambling house, which I'd guess is a lot more dangerous than out here on the trail."

That brought a small smile to her face, and the sobbing slowed. "That's the same thing he told me not but a few days ago."

"Now," Kev said, holding her by the shoulders at arm's length, "the best thing we can do for your father is for us to get some sleep while you watch over him, then we'll take turns. Wake me when"—Kev looked up at the moon, which had just begun to rise—"when that moon reaches about ten o'clock in the night sky. Tomorrow we'll decide what we're going to do."

Later, when Kev lay in his bedroll beside his nephew, he praised him. "That was a brave thing you did, Sean, standing up to that bear."

"Not much choice, Uncle Kev."

"You'll find that's what life brings us . . . little choice. Still and all, you did a man's work today . . . maybe a man and a half."

"Thanks."

But at that, none of them slept well, as Chad often moaned in his sleep, and the wolves kept up a constant bone-chilling serenade. By morning, Chad Steel seemed feverish.

To add insult to injury, it snowed in the night, and morning found three inches covering everything.

It was late afternoon when they spotted the approaching wagons, after they'd spent a day rigging a tent from pack covers and blankets, a tent that would shelter a fire and hold at least four of them. Badger-Man and Sleeps-in-Day made a shelter from river willows covered with boughs that would keep the snow off and a little heat inside.

For the first time since they'd met, Kev had been forced to stay near Caitlin Steel, and they'd had a real conversation. Sean would not be constrained by the tent, and spent most of his time checking on the cattle, or climbing a nearby hill. Kev discovered Caitlin was not only a beautiful woman, but a fascinating one. Kev had never met a woman like her. She spoke French and Spanish. Knew more about politics and what was going on in not only Montana, but the country and the world, than any person Kev had ever met, much less any woman. She had some radical ideas, that women should vote, that women should be equal to their men in all ways. Ideas about which Kev merely shrugged his shoulders when she talked of them, as he'd never thought on them before. It did make him think of Brigid, and somehow, he thought her equal to the McQuade men in every way, if different in what she contributed.

While they talked, her father stirred, then awakened. They managed to get some broth down him, before he again fell into a deep sleep. His fever seemed to come and go, and sleep was furtive.

It was Sean who ran into the tent to announce that the Army had arrived, at least a few soldiers and a pair of wagons.

A sergeant led the six soldiers who manned the wagons. Kev had never met him as he'd been up the mountain when the sergeant had come by Rocky Butte Ranch and made the deal with Colin for the two hundred head they now drove to the cantonment. But Kev recognized the name when the sergeant extended his hand.

"Proud to meet you, Sergeant. As you can see, your cattle are well on their way."

Starkey turned and scratched at the dundreary whiskers adorning his face, then spat a long stream of tobacco as he surveyed the herd, quietly grazing, quietly pawing at the meadow to expose grass now covered with snow. "They look fine, just fine. But they'll be the Army's cattle, and you'll have your money, when they're safe in our corral. Not until. The risk in getting them there is all your'n."

Kev nodded, as he well knew where the risk lay. "Tell your men to climb down, Sergeant. We've got coffee on, and would be proud to share with you fellas."

Caitlin stepped from the tent and was introduced to the big sergeant. As soon as they'd exchanged pleasantries, Caitlin said, "You've got a fine pair of wagons, Sergeant. My father and I are on our way downriver, and he's been mauled by a bear. Could you make room—"

Starkey seemed to think on it for a long moment,

then shook his head. "We don't haul civilians, ma'am. And these wagons are plum full of vittles."

"Then I guess we'll have to wait until he's a little better."

"Guess so," Starkey said. "Graze looks fine and the cattle could probably use a day or two of rest."

"Looks like you've had an accident too," Kev said, noticing the sergeant's wrapped left hand.

"I . . . I fell in the campfire."

Corporal Jason Donklin, the second in command on the vegetable expedition, had climbed down from the wagon and was near enough to hear. He centered ice-blue eyes on Starkey, and scratched prematurely gray hair as he questioned, "I thought you said—?"

"I fell in the campfire," Starkey snapped.

Donklin shrugged his shoulders and moved to unhitch the team.

"Leave 'em hitched," Starkey snapped. "We're moving on. We've got to get these vittles to the cantonment."

"But I thought you said—"

"Leave 'em hitched."

Again Donklin shrugged his shoulders. "Can the men get down for a stretch."

"Just that," Starkey said, returning his attention to Kev and Caitlin. "Damn worthless trash we get in the Army nowadays."

Kev ignored his remark, then asked, "You must have stopped by the Rocky Butte. How is my brother doing?"

Chapter 10

When he answered, Starkey cut his eyes away in a manner than bothered Kev. "Passed by, just long enough to pay my respects."

Kev was insistent. "And how was everything? My brother's leg?"

"Everything seemed fine," Starkey replied, suddenly giving Kev a wide grin, after glancing back and making sure Donklin was out of earshot.

"Good. I've been worried."

Starkey started away, then stopped and turned back with a wry grin. "You folks could probably stand a few vegetables. We got carrots and turnips and potatoes and some greens."

"That would be very generous of you," Caitlin said, moving forward.

Kev could not help but notice the way Starkey looked her up and down as she passed him on the way to the wagon. It was unseemly, and even though the heat raced up Kev's backbone, he said nothing. It wasn't his place, unless Starkey actually said or did something untoward. Besides, it was this sergeant who'd made the contract with them, and Kev felt it would be this man who he'd have to satisfy before he got paid. It wouldn't pay to get on this man's bad side. Instead, Kev ignored him and moved over to help Caitlin load up with bounty.

In moments, to the grousing of the soldiers, the wagons had moved on, now leaving definitive mud tracks in the shallow snow.

Starkey sat his horse, watching the wagons move away, seeming reluctant to leave. He was still eyeing Caitlin in a manner that offended Kev.

Kev snapped at him. "I hope you've put up a pile of hay. Won't be long before you'll be having to feed these cattle."

"We'll have another warm spell before we got to feed 'em much. You just get them there in good shape, McQuade. The Army will take it from there."

"They'll be there. Thanks for the vegetables," Kev said, as Starkey reined away and gigged his horse to catch up with the wagons.

As they stowed the vegetables, Caitlin commented, "That was nice of the sergeant to share these, even though he couldn't seem to make room for my father in those big wagons."

"Neighborly," Kev said, but then added, "but there was something about that man that raised the hackles on my back. No matter what he did, he don't seem the giving type unless he's got a reason other than Christian charity."

"Well, we have the vegetables, and he's on his way. And all he got out of it was a cup of coffee. I'd say that was Christian enough."

Kev studied her amber eyes for a moment, then added, "I'm not disappointed that you folks didn't go with him."

Caitlin's tone became placating. "I'm only thinking of my father, Kev. Don't think for a second that I don't appreciate your letting us—"

"One more day, Caitlin, then we have to move on. God willing, Chad will be ready to travel. I'll build a travois, and you'll see, it'll move soft as a feather bed through this light snow and he'll be far more comfortable than if he was in one of those jolting wagons, laying on a bumpy pile of spuds."

"I hope so," she said, giving Kev a tight, worried smile.

"I promise so," Kev said, giving her a reassuring smile in return. "We'll push hard and have him mending in a warm Army hospital in less than a week."

The next morning, a hundred miles downriver, a tired but still diligent column of men marched up the Yellowstone. They'd crossed to the south side at a shallow known well to the riverboat men as Thompson's Riffles.

They'd been on the trek a day short of two weeks when Lieutenant Frank Baldwin, riding ahead of the column, noticed Corporal Bryan McGloughlan, who was riding the left point a half mile ahead, top a rise and rein up, then stand in the saddle. Spinning his mule, he came back at a lope.

He jerked rein beside Baldwin, collected himself, then snapped a salute. "Cantonment ahead, sir. About a mile across a river beyond that rise."

Even though it was a cold crisp morning with diamonds of ice coating the grass and brush, Baldwin had left his buffalo-hide coat and fur cap with his other gear, and wore his blue coat, with its sky-blue braid, and black fatigue hat. He thought that this would be the day when he would no longer be the officer in charge. With luck, Colonel Nelson Miles would be in camp, and Baldwin's duty would no longer be to serve as nursemaid for a troop of replacements. He looked forward to action against the Sioux and Northern Cheyenne, and to ending this cold campaign. Not only for the country's sake, but for the sake of the Indians. Baldwin knew the more the country became populated, the worse it would be for the red man. He was actually an admirer of the Indian, of any man who could make a life in this rough country. But he knew that the country would fill with whites, and he'd seen in Texas what that would mean to the Indian. And he, and the 5th, had their orders.

He took a deep breath of relief at ending this march without serious event, particularly without the loss of a man, and turned to his corporal. "Tell the men to take a short break and sharpen up. I'm going on ahead and expect you to follow, by the twos, in fine fettle with the band announcing your coming. When you get in front of the fort, it's parade rest until I come to dismiss you to your new quarters . . . understand?" He got a prompt nod. "You've done good work on this march, McGloughlan." With this he got a nod and smile. "Now, return that mule to the hostler and join your men."

"Yes, sir," McGloughlan gave him another snappy salute and grin, then gigged the mule back toward the trailing column.

Baldwin passed a woodcutting crew dragging pine timber down a slope to the meadow below, where more men sawed and stacked cordwood, as he loped his big horse over the rise and down a long gentle slope to the confluence of the Tongue and Yellowstone—to his colonel and the makeshift fort of the U.S. Army, District of Yellowstone.

The Tongue, flowing almost due north, wound out of a long low valley covered with cottonwoods. As Baldwin neared, he realized he'd have to cross the muddy Tongue, now slushy with ice almost the consistency of wet snow. Navigable, but nonetheless an uninviting exercise. It was impossible to tell how deep the Tongue ran, as it was so muddy you couldn't see your boot toes six inches under the surface, but the lay of the land said it should be wide and shallow. Thank God they didn't have to cross the Yellowstone, as it looked deep where it cut into a bank cliff-side, uninviting, and full of even more freezing slush than the muddy Tongue.

Baldwin was pleased to confirm that the water was shallow, and he was only soaked to mid-thigh by the time he made the crossing.

Now at a cantor across a long pasture near the fort, he noted that fewer than a dozen cattle pawed through the snow grazing on the stubble they exposed. In the distance, three huge meadow haystacks rose out of the pastures, protected by tall fences. A hundred times more hay than these few cattle would need.

He reined up and saluted the guard, asking, "The general's quarters?" Out of courtesy, Miles's troop referred to him by his late Civil War rank of brevet major general, even though, like many who'd elected to remain in service, his actual rank had been reduced.

"You'll see the headquarters sign over the door where the two wings join, sir. Welcome to the fort."

"Thank you, soldier." He again gigged the horse and reined up in the crotch of the simple L-shaped structure, dismounted, tied his horse to the hitching rail, and entered.

An orderly greeted him, walked to an inner office and announced his arrival, then waved him on.

Nelson Miles was the epitome of a classic Army officer, ice-blue penetrating eyes, tall, wide-shouldered, erect, trim, handsome if hawk-faced. He had what the old Prussians referred to as the "look of eagles." The ultimate warrior's compliment. A heavy bearskin coat hung from the uprights of the chair he occupied, a coat that had resulted in the name given him by the Indian hostiles, Bearcoat.

He rose from a table made of a wagon tailgate and extended his hand. Another man in civilian buckskins sat across the table from him, both of them with a plate of food in front of them. "We're taking a late breakfast, Frank. Would you like to join us?"

"I've eaten with the troop, sir."

"Then sit and have coffee, unless you'd rather stand in front of the fireplace and warm up. Those wet trousers don't look too comfortable. This is Luther Kelly, chief of scouts." Kelly made a half effort at rising, gave a perfunctory nod, then turned his attention back to a plate of flapjacks, a fried loin of venison, and a couple of hen's eggs.

Baldwin took a chair to the general's right.

"Your march went well?" Miles asked as the orderly sat a tin cup in front of Baldwin.

"Fine as frog's hair, sir. We saw only two groups of hostiles. Sioux, or so my scout Grigsby said."

"Barton Grigsby?" Kelly asked without looking up.

"One and the same," Baldwin replied.

"Good man," Kelly mumbled.

"And you would be the one referred to as Yellowstone Kelly?" Baldwin asked.

"One and the same, but don't believe all you've heard," Kelly said with a chuckle.

Baldwin smiled. "Glad to hear it from your lips, Kelly. You'd have to be six men if all I've heard was true."

Miles turned to a shelf behind where he sat and retrieved a large object, then turned back and dropped it on the table in front of Baldwin with a wry smile. "This was Kelly's calling card when he rode into camp. It's a bit shriveled at the moment, but still impressive."

The object was a dinner-plate-sized bear paw, with four-inch-long claws now marking the tabletop.

"I suppose you wrestled him down an' chawed that off'n him?" Baldwin asked, the corner of his mouth turned up in a half smile.

Kelly looked up to make sure he wasn't being made fun of, then satisfied that Baldwin was only repeating stories he'd heard, commented, "Actually, Lieutenant, I shot him a half-dozen times after a Army woodcutting crew had already shot him the same. Still and all, he was a tough customer, and I'm proud it's not my paw he's showing off." He went back to eating.

Baldwin drained his cup. "With your permission, sir, I'll get back to seeing my men properly bivouacked?"

"Do that, Frank, but first get some dry things on.

The quartermaster will issue you some trousers if your spares are still with the column. Can't abide by a sick lieutenant coming into this campaign. See to your men, then come back and let's talk a little about the coming exercise."

"Yes, sir."

Four riders, each wearing an ankle-length duster, sat their horses on a ridge high above the snow-covered meadow dotted with cattle. The horses' breath roiled in the cold air, matching that of the men who'd made a hard ride up the slope behind where they rested on the crown of a ridge.

A tall broad-shouldered man with a well-waxed handlebar mustache wore a heavy double-blanket coat under his open duster, both over a shirt crossed with a pair of bandoliers of bullets. He removed his broad-brimmed black-felt hat and studied the camp below through a small brass telescope. When his hat was pulled away, it revealed, under shoulder-length sandy hair, the fact he was missing most of an ear; jagged remnants showed it had been bitten off. In his saddle scabbard rested the Sharps-Borchardt hammerless rifle, the latest in long arms, that seated each of the two-dozen cartridges the bandolier carried. On each hip he wore a Starr double-action .44 revolver, butt forward. He spoke without dropping the glass. "By God, there be a woman in that camp . . . a trim woman. I believe our journey is about over."

"How many men?" the thick-built full-bearded man beside him asked. He, like the first, carried a pair of revolvers, but his, each with elk-horn grips, rested in saddle holsters on either side of the saddle horn. The other two, both tall and angular, sat their horses quietly studying the scene below; they were equally well armed.

"Looks like only two white men, and that Indian out there with the herd. So I make it three, but that's shorthanded for so much stock."

"Is one of them Steel?"

"Can't tell from here. Could be. Shall we shoot them all down?"

"No. We don't know who those fellows are, and where those cattle came from. This is a far piece east for a cattle herd, but they're likely innocent . . . not that it matters much if'n they got a fleein' felon traveling with 'em. And we need to make sure the woman is Tolofsen's. We'd hate to shoot a bunch of fellas down for having their ugly sister with them." The other three guffawed as the bearded man turned to face the first man, smiling like a cat after a canary. "But hell's bells, man, who wouldn't give Mrs. Caitlin Tolofsen shelter, should she come calling."

"So, how do you want to play this? I got a plump dove in a warm bed waiting for me back in Bozeman, and I don't want to waste no more time. I can pick 'em off from that point over there with this here Sharps."

Chapter 11

The four duster-clad, well-armed men sat high on a ridge, surrounded by undergrowth, overlooking the pawing cattle, the tents, and the few people moving about the camp and cattle.

The heavy built black-bearded man spoke patiently to his impatient friend. "You're being well paid, Brennen. We all got things to do back in Bozeman. But remember Tolofsen's words . . . no woman, no pay. And it's double pay if we bring Steel back alive so Tolofsen can see him hang."

"Then let's go down there and sack 'em up," Brennen snarled. "You're carrying a badge, McTavish, and that should scare off a couple of cattle prodders and that redskin, even if this Sharps and these Colts don't."

"Badge never scared no redskin before," the one called McTavish said, still patient. "Badge don't mean nothing to them, and we don't know who those other fellows are, just that they're giving aid and shelter to fleein' felons, if that be the woman . . . so let's wait for dark so we can creep up quiet-like and see for sure. 'Sides, if the fools can read, they'll see that this here badge says Guard, not Sheriff."

"Fine. Let's get back over the hill so's we can sit by a fire and wait."

"No fire, we're too close and they'll see the smoke and might send someone to see what's afoot. This is about done and I want it done right, and us with our pockets full of double eagles."

The broad-shouldered man harrumphed loudly, but reined away toward the hilltop behind them, mumbling as he pulled a square quart bottle of Duffy's Malt Whiskey from his saddlebag, "I got me a way to keep warm."

A hundred paces away, deep in the shadows of a tangle of fir, Sleeps-in-Day sat his pinto, watching the group of riders. He'd come up a deep ravine tracking four steers that had wandered.

Now he ignored the animals, gathered behind him, grazing quietly in the deep grass surrounding a small steaming hot spring, and studied the riders. When they reined away, he spun his horse and dropped back to the bottom of the ravine behind him, but he didn't begin pushing the cattle back to camp. Rather, he turned up the ravine wondering what the white men were up to. He'd at least know where they were headed before he returned to the herd. One thing he'd learned long ago. He didn't like white men at his back.

Chad Steel was awake and his fever was down, even though his wounds were red and already showing pus in spots. Caitlin was on her knees at the side of his bedroll, holding his head up, giving him a drink of water from Kev's canteen. After he waved her away and laid his head back down, he asked about the bear and Kev related the whole story to him. Sean returned to the tent as Kev was finishing.

"Sean," Chad said in a low weak voice after hearing the boy praised by both his uncle and Caitlin, "if you'll look in that canvas roll behind my saddle, you'll find a fine Parker shotgun wrapped in oilcloth. I'd be proud if you'd make it yours."

"Mr. Steel, that shotgun I used on that ol' bear was my father's. It wouldn't be fittin' for me to take yours for his—"

"I'll be sending you home with a ten-dollar gold piece for your father. He can buy a brand-new scattergun with that. It's you I want to have my Parker, for lookin' death in the face and not wavering. For killing that big ugly beast."

"Uncle Kev?" Sean asked, wanting confirmation that he should accept such a fine gift, a firearm such as he never in his life expected to own.

"If Mr. Steel wants you to have it, Sean, you should. You stood up to that bear as brave as any man, and you should have a long arm the rest of the way to the Tongue and back."

Sean excitedly spun and ran from the tent to find the Parker.

Chad centered sunken eyes on Kev. "McQuade, am I holding up your cattle drive?"

"You have, a wee bit, but no harm done. I'm going to rig a travois tomorrow, and you'll hold us up no longer."

"I can ride. . . ." He tried to rise, went white in the face, and settled back to his pallet.

"Tomorrow, on a travois, Chad. You've lost a lot of blood. It's soon enough. We passed Pompeys Pillar just a couple of miles back, and we'll be at the

Big Horn River and Big Horn City after another day or two, and either there or beyond at Sarpy's trading post, we'll get you some good care . . . at least some store-bought medicines."

"Now," Caitlin said, "I want to prop your head up so I can spoon some broth down you."

"I am famished," Chad managed, allowing his head to be placed on a rolled-up coat.

"That's the best news I've heard," Caitlin said with a laugh.

Kev, realizing Sleeps-in-Day and Badger-Man stood outside the tent, quietly waiting, excused himself and stepped out into the failing light.

Night was almost on them again, and Colin McQuade was as frustrated as a woodpecker working a tin roof.

Colin could not put the slightest amount of weight on the stub of his right leg, and wondered if he would ever be able to. Then again, it was still scabbed over, and one shouldn't be able to put weight on it until it was well healed . . . probably another month or more.

The strange thing was, the toes on the missing foot itched him something terrible, and there were no toes to scratch. He wished he had some other fella with a missing limb to ask about that, if it was a normal thing or not. Damned if it wasn't the most irritating thing.

Norval Dugan had stayed with him, while his brother Patrick had returned to their small place to get it ready for the coming winter. Dugan had busied himself building a small cabin inside the barn, a shelter inside a shelter, including the construction of a stone fireplace, and laying up wood for the coming cold. The woodpile the McQuades had gathered during the summer had been stacked against a side of their ranch house, and most of it had burned with the house. Dugan had dug a privy right in the middle of the barn floor and built a seat over it, wondering why he hadn't done the same at his place. He'd constructed a crutch for Colin, and a peg leg, but the stub was far too tender for the peg, and without a knee joint, it was doubtful if the long rigid peg would ever be much use.

Dugan had kept busy, doing a month's worth of work in two weeks, and kept Colin's mind off his troubles and onto the day-to-day business of getting by in a tough country with an even tougher climate.

One thing Dugan was very good at was saddle making, having apprenticed at that trade before he'd run off from Pennsylvania and joined his cousin, and the most useful thing he'd made from scraps he'd gathered around the barn was a crude saddle maker's draw-down table. They'd carved a saddletree out of chokecherry using the crude implements gathered from the barn, with Colin doing most of that work, and Dugan had begun to teach Colin the intricacies of saddle making.

And Colin had been an apt student, when he didn't fall into a deep depression, which he was doing less and less as the days wore on. It was now only hourly when he seemed to stare off into the mountains and wonder why.

At the moment, he was high on his new art, and watching intently while leaning on a crutch as

Dugan glued a newly cut layer to the saddletree they'd constructed.

"Okay," Dugan said, "that's it for a while until this dries. I think I'd better get back to finishing the fire flue, before we really get some cold."

"I can pass you the rock, and mix the mortar."

"Good. You're getting on fine, Col. An' that's good, 'cause in a week or so, I think I'd better head for the home place to see what needs doin', if'n you think you can get on."

"I'm surprised you've put up with me this long—"

"I owed you. I can leave you with a full larder if I can knock down another whitetail. Then I can be back in a couple of weeks to make sure you're making out all right. It should be easy getting a big buck as they'll all be doe-crazy right now."

"Hell, Norval, Kev and Sean will be back in three weeks or less. No reason you should be coming back at all."

Norval Dugan guffawed loudly. "I got to teach you how to trim out that saddle. You don't keep busy, you'll have a miserable winter."

Colin suddenly looked as if he'd been kicked in the stomach. "Don't see how it could be anything else." Then his face brightened. "But that ain't your worry, Norval. You've been a godsend. I don't know how . . ."

"You'll do fine, and come spring, you'll be tellin' Kev how to run the ranch and selling saddles all over the countryside . . . now, let's get that stack up so that fire'll draw."

* * *

A half mile downriver from the McQuade cattle herd, another group of men, twenty-four strong, sat their hard-ridden, well-lathered, ponies high on a flat-topped ridgeline above a sandstone cliff in a grassy flat backed by a thick forest of fir, overlooking the Yellowstone and, much more interesting to the hungry men, the McQuade cattle herd.

Their leader sat resplendent in yellow and red war paint, as did all of them. His face was solid red, with eagle feathers hanging from a wolf-skin headband, as he rose in the saddle and studied the scene below.

One of the braves beside him offered encouragement. "The white men are few, but not so few as the *tatanka* we've seen. I prefer the buffalo, as we all do, but the people must have meat. Those scrawny cattle will do. And they must not reach the walks-a-heap down the river. These are enough to feed them into the birthing moon."

The Sioux war chief, Gall, turned to his group of warriors. "If we move quickly, we can strike from the trees between the river and the meadow where the white man's herd grazes, and drive many of them into the hills before they know we're there . . . then darkness will be upon us, and they will not follow. They are few and we are many."

As he spoke, he gave heels to his pony, and moved to a cut in the cliff-side, where he knew he could descend to the river below. Before he started down the steep incline, he again turned to his men. "Are your ears uncovered?" They all turned their attention to the impressive Gall, quieting their mounts. "I know we set out to kill the walks-a-heap, but this is better for our people. Kill any white-eye who gets in your way, but remember, it's the cattle our women and children need, and keeping the cattle from the walks-a-heap is what we must do. Forget your war paint. We are not here to count coup, not with these beasts offered to us by the Great Father, but now we have the opportunity to bring food to our women and children. There will be another time to dry the scalp of the white-eye on your war lance."

With that, he plunged down the sandstone slope, his horse sliding with feet planted, and Gall pitched so far back he was almost lying flat against the carved saddle and the horse's rump.

The McQuade tent rose at the west end of the long meadow where the cattle pawed at the snow-covered grass. To the north of the meadow lay a hundred-pace-wide grove of towering cottonwood, now almost barren of leaves, with undergrowth of patches of river willow. A bald eagle sat attentively atop one of the cottonwoods, clearly seen with the lack of vegetation. He would soon be flying south, as the river was covered with slush ice and in days, if the cold held, he'd be relegated to lowly carrion and his talons would find no fat squirming cut-throat trout.

On the north of the meadow, partially up-slope, a line of fir sheltered the mountain that rose in folded cedar-covered ravines over a thousand feet to a flat ridge. McQuade's was an ideal camp and meadow, protected from the wind, deep in grass under the shallow snow, with a fine small stream cutting across the meadow to join the river—and the stream was still unfrozen.

But, as Kev noticed, it would not be so for long. As he spoke with Badger-Man and Sleeps-in-Day, he noticed it was growing even colder.

He eyed his Indian friend, who'd come back into camp with interesting news. "So, you think they are up to no good?"

As always, Sleeps-in-Day remained silent; it was Badger-Man who shrugged his shoulders. "Sleeps-in-Day say they watch camp from a dark place, then go over top to gather in ravine and wait. Cold, but they make no fire. No fire means they not want to be seen. If not trouble, what then?"

"Good question. Maybe what they wait for is to do some mischief in darkness." Kev turned back to the tent flap and called inside. "Caitlin, when you're finished, please step outside for a moment."

"Just about there," she called out.

Sean walked over from where he'd been sitting on a log, shining the beautiful Parker that he'd recovered from behind Chad's saddle, having joined barrels to stock. "I've never seen anything as handsome as this," he said, stroking the gun as if it were a new speckled pup.

"It's a fine weapon, Sean. As fine as any made. You may have a chance to try it out real soon."

As he explained the situation to the boy, Caitlin stepped from the tent, wiping her hands with a camp cloth. She listened, then shook her head worriedly.

"It's Terrance McTavish, if he had a full black beard. He's nothing but a bank guard for my husband, but he's a hard man, been known to kill a man with his bare hands, and he'll have hard men with him. McTavish does other things for Mark . . . things he won't discuss with me, and that I'd rather not know about. I knew that Mark wouldn't let this lay."

"Mark?" Kev asked.

"Mark Stanley Tolofsen, my husband, and the man my father beat to a pulp before we left Bozeman . . . in a hurry, I might add, before he had a chance to put this bunch of hooligans on us."

Kev stood studying the dark fir forest in the distance, and the ridge-top beyond. "If they come, they'll most likely come down that cut, where the stream comes off the top of the mountain. That fir and lodgepole forest is too full of windfall to make any other way practical. We should be waiting for them where they don't expect us."

Caitlin placed a warm gentle hand on his shoulder. "Rig that travois and I'll get out ahead of them, Kev. This is not your fight. You've got cattle—"

"Enough! Caitlin, you're in my camp, and your father is injured and in our care. No one's going to take anyone out of my camp, sure as hell . . . pardon my mouth . . . sure as heck, no one's going to take you or your father out of my camp, unless you're wanting to go."

Her eyes misted. "I do, Kev. I want to go. I don't want you and Sean—"

"Do you actually think I'd let you go out into that Indian-filled wilderness alone? Get inside that tent and watch over your father. The four of us will take care of this. Four of us, and four of them, and they don't know *we know* they're coming . . . if they're coming. Don't worry, Caitlin, you just watch over Chad and we'll watch over the both of you."

She eyed him a moment, her eyes warming, then

spun on her heel and headed back in the tent, while Kev called his three healthy male compatriots together for a palaver.

Chapter 12

Colonel Nelson Miles, three of his senior staff, and newly arrived junior officer Lieutenant Frank Baldwin sat around Miles's wagon-hatch table. The supper tins had been cleared and replaced with a map spread flat on the tabletop, where cups, each with a generous dollop of brandy, helped hold the map flat. Standing nearby, both in buckskins, were chief scout Yellowstone Kelly and his new employee, scout Barton Grigsby. Four other scouts, Clubfoot Boyd, Liver-eating Johnson, Charley Bass, and half-breed Billy LeBeau, waited outside, sipping coffee, awaiting orders reputed to be coming this evening. Back in their own camp, a dozen Crow scouts, historic enemies of the Sioux, waited around a campfire for orders from Bearcoat, to be delivered by Yellowstone Kelly.

"So, gentlemen, if the replacement contingent saw hostiles almost one hundred strong, could it be Sitting Bull and the Hunkpapa, or Crazy Horse and his band? North and east of us, on the Yellowstone? Grigsby?"

"Well, sir, it was sure as the sun sets in the west it's the bloody Hunkpapa. I got three new scalps out there among my folderol a-hangin' on my saddle. Hunkpapa, sure as hell's hot."

Miles ignored the reference to the scalps Grigsby had taken. It was the way things were in Indian country, and the white mountain man would take a scalp as quickly as an Indian. "Then we've been on a blind-man's folly, thinking they were north of us between here and the Missouri."

"Sir?" Baldwin said.

"Go ahead, Frank."

"They are a highly mobile force. They could be damn near anywhere by now. We need the snow to pin them down, weaken their horseflesh, and put them afoot. They can't trail their women and children nor haul their lodges if they're afoot and the weather worsens. They've got to hole up. If we bide our time—"

"True enough," Miles interrupted. "But if the weather worsens, we need to know where to find them. We can't scout effectively in four feet of snow, and if we don't know where they are, we can't harass them into submission, and that's my plan. The Fifth must march them into submission, drive them until they're eating their horseflesh, and when their horses are no longer a factor, they'll be at the mercy of the Fifth. Pray for adverse weather, gentlemen."

"Amen," several of them chimed in.

Miles continued. "But we must know where to find them. Kelly, split your scouts up and cover six points of the compass. We must know where the main band of Sioux and Cheyenne are located, so we can harass, harass, harass, until they are out of food, out of strength, out of will."

"Yes, sir," Kelly said, then added, "You know, sir,

we'll be hamstrung also, so far as scouting far and wide, when the snow hits, if it hits. We'll all be afoot if'n we get a real norther."

"Then let's find them first, before we too are limited to a day's march rather than a day's ride. Each of you take a soldier with you, as I want two of you together so if one man goes down, the other may still be able to report back, and I want the scouts spread as far and wide as possible. Send your Crow scouts wherever you think best serves us."

Kelly nodded. "We'll be off before first light."

As they walked out, excused by Colonel Miles, Grigsby, packing his hand-carved pipe, said to Kelly, "I want to take Corporal McGloughlan along with me. He's green, but he listens and he's got plenty of bark on him."

"You choose who you want; you'll get no argument from Miles."

"Then McGloughlan it is. We'll head west, upriver, if'n that suits you. I got a hunch. . . ."

"I'll set the others to other points of the compass. Keep your hair."

Grigsby laughed. "Hell's fire, Kelly, there ain't no Sioux alive can take my hair."

"God willing an' you got a fast horse," Kelly mumbled as Grigsby went to find McGloughlan to tell him it was McClellan saddle and mule-back for him again.

After he'd excused the scouts, Miles rose and began to pace. "Gentlemen, it's been a little more than a year and five months since the Lakota and the Northern Cheyenne dealt their devastating defeat to my old friend Custer and the 7th Cavalry, and the Cavalry has not been able to avenge that catastrophe. It's up to the us, the infantry, the fighting 5th, and those of the 17th and 22nd." He waited until the calls of "Hear! Hear!" quieted before he continued. "As you know, General Terry follows that same old and well-worn belief that white men can't survive in Montana Territory cold without a well-prepared shelter and wood for a full winter. I disagree, and I pray to prove that pure folly. We *will* prove that belief is, in fact, folly.

"What I'm going to tell you will not leave this room. Agreed?"

Miles waited until each man gave him the nod.

"Sheridan gave this job of driving the savage back to the reservation to General Alfred Terry, and I came here only to support his effort. Well, Terry wandered up and down the Yellowstone for the better part of a year while we were shuttling supplies, and made no substantial advance against the Sioux and Cheyenne. Sheridan ordered him out, and left us only as an occupying force, with the job of constructing this cantonment. But we are a thousand strong, with companies of the 5th, the 17th, and the 22nd. I'm not satisfied with our being only an occupying force. I did not join this man's Army to be a supply officer, and I plan to show the Army what a dedicated force of infantry, fighting infantry, can do in harsh winter.

"We are well prepared, and as tough or tougher than the red man, clothed well enough to take on the Arctic, much less Montana. Unlike the red man, we have a well-stocked cantonment to fall back on. We can, and will, march him down, in his own element, until he is subjugated. We have vegetables on their way, and a beef herd should be

here in days. We'll immediately jerk enough meat
so we have ten pounds per man, while filling the
men for a week or so with hardy beef stew . . .
putting a good layer of fat on them. Make sure your
men have their winter gear in perfect repair. Then,
when the Hunkpapa are located, we will harass
them on foot, doggedly, day in and day out, until
their backs are against the wall and they turn and
face us. The result of that battle will be a long
march to the reservation . . . for what's left of them.

"Here's to success, gentlemen. Here's to Sitting
Bull and Gall on the march to the reservation. And
soon." Miles raised his coffee cup and toasted.

Kev left Sean near the tent in a stand of river willow with a clear view of the meadow and with strict
instructions not to fire at anyone, unless he knew
they were being fired upon.

Kev, Sleeps-in-Day, and Badger-Man—the Assiniboine with bows and arrows and old trade rifles as
well as handguns—spread themselves out in the
fir at the foot of the slope that he figured the in-
truders must come down in order to attack the
camp. Kev placed himself near the toe of the slope,
close to the stream, and adjacent to the major game
trail that the men would probably follow. As he
waited for twilight to fade, Kev hoped they were
worrying about a group of men who simply had no
interest in coming into a strange camp . . . but
Caitlin's description of the man with the beard so
closely matched that of Sleeps-in-Day's that he was
sure the men were here for Caitlin and Chad.

He had a momentary but almost overwhelming attack of guilt, knowing that his family's ranch depended upon him getting the herd to the Tongue River Cantonment, and anything that jeopardized that effort was not something he should be participating in, but then again, Col and Brigid would be the first ones to offer sanctuary to someone in need.

No, he had to do this; besides, his feelings for Caitlin were growing to the point that he couldn't fathom letting anything happen to take her out of his life, and her father was helpless, unable to defend himself, much less Caitlin. He shook thoughts of Caitlin off, as they were indecent ones to have about a married woman, even one who'd informed him that she intended to seek an annulment as soon as they got back to Missouri.

The first rider was upon him in the failing light so quickly, he knew he'd been daydreaming. There are times when a woman on a man's mind . . . will get his throat cut. He slunk deeper into the brush, and waited as the man approached, carefully picking his way down the trail beside the crashing stream.

The first rider passed, then another. The first had not been the bearded man, rather a tall broad-shouldered man with a Winchester across the saddle horn and a pair of revolvers butt-forward on his hips.

Nor was the second the bearded one; rather he was tall and sharp-featured, riding easily on a Canadian rig, wearing a fur hat with ear flaps and a coat fashioned from a Hudson's Bay blanket.

They were twenty yards down the trail, almost to the meadow, when Kev realized they were not followed by their compatriots. The other two must have gone another way.

Kev, his Winchester cocked and ready, stepped

out onto the trail and closed the distance between himself and the man in the Hudson's Bay coat.

They reined up at the meadow's edge. The man in front turned to speak to the other as Kev was almost at the horse's tail.

"Frenchy, remember, no shooting unless McTavish gives the signal. He wants to make sure it's the Tolofsen woman, and if so, that these cowmen won't give up her or her father without a fight."

Kev stepped to the side so the man in front could see him, leveling the Winchester on his belly.

"Not likely, friend," Kev said in a gruff voice.

"Damn!" the one in front yelled.

The one following, who'd been called Frenchy, spun his horse in the narrow confines of the trail, almost knocking Kev down. Then Kev purposely dropped to his back as the front man brought up his rifle and fired. The bullet cut the air over Kev's head, but Kev's eyes were centered on the one called Frenchy, who drove his heels into his horse's side, in an attempt to run the animal over Kev.

Kev swung the rifle and fired, blowing Frenchy out of the saddle. The horse wheeled back, away from the muzzle blast. Frenchy, now pitched off the horse into the brush, and his horse were between Kev and the first rider, and by the time they'd cleared, the man had given heels to his animal and they'd bolted out into the meadow. There was just enough light so as Kev got to his feet and scrambled forward, hoping for a shot at the fleeing man, he could see the arrow strike the rider between the shoulder blades. He pitched forward in the saddle and Kev's shot flew over his back. Reining the horse to the side, charging directly into the cattle herd, the man disappeared.

Kev ran into the open, only to see two other riders charge out of the cottonwoods—one of them the black-bearded man—on the far side of the herd. Kev dropped to his knee to get a sure shot at the men, who'd joined up with the one with the arrow in his back, when he was surprised by a dozen more riders breaking out of the woods, whooping and hollering.

Hell, Kev thought at first, there are a lot more of them, then realized that the second, larger group was firing at the same men *he* was firing at, who were now pounding ground to get back to the line of fir trees. Perplexed, Kev clambered to his feet, only to see that the second group were Indians, Hunkpapa or Lakota if he knew his Indians. As they charged into the herd, they lay low in the saddle but drove the cattle in front of them.

My God, Kev thought, they're not after Caitlin, they're after the cattle.

Again he dropped to a knee, and this time began firing with some accuracy. But he was only able to hit one of the Indians, who merely pitched forward in his carved saddle.

Almost as soon as it had begun, it was over, with almost half of his herd driven off in front of the pounding riders and into the firs and cottonwoods at the east end of the meadow.

Kev gathered himself and ran for the tent, in the heat of the moment almost firing at Sleeps-in-Day and Badger-Man, who ran from the fir to join him.

"Let's check on the others," Kev yelled as soon as he recognized them.

He yelled out as they neared the tent as it was growing very dark, and he didn't want to get two barrels of buckshot in the face from his nephew's new Parker. But Sean met them near the low fire they'd purposefully left burning to make the invaders think it was a normal camp.

"What happened?" Sean asked. "The cattle are on the run?"

"Saddle our horses," Kev snapped, "while I check on Caitlin."

She met him at the tent flap, her father's Colt hanging loosely in hand at her side. "We're fine. Go get your cattle."

Kev needed little encouragement, and in moments the four of them were in the saddle and scouring the underbrush for cattle. Only half the herd was milling about the meadow, but Kev thought some were working their way back out of the trees to rejoin those who had nervously gone back to grazing.

The moon rose, but the cloud cover kept it dark, with only intermittent brightening when the clouds parted. By midnight, Kev had done all he thought they could until they got some decent light.

He'd found twenty-five or so more head in the copse of fir. God knows where the rest were. He presumed a good number were in a Sioux camp somewhere. Damn the luck.

He was back in the camp when he remembered that he'd shot a man out of the saddle, and he might still be in the brush, wounded or worse.

In a few minutes, they'd found the one called Frenchy, who was moaning softly and more than willing to give up his weapons, if only they'd tend to his wound.

They got him back and laid him on a pallet near the fire. When Kev inspected the gaping hole in the man's stomach, it was fairly obvious to him that the man would probably not last the night. The Winchester slug had entered just under the rib cage on his left side, and exited out his back on the right.

All they could do was make him as comfortable as possible. And question him. For the cheap cost of a few sips of water, they learned that due to Tolofsen's broken ribs and slight concussion from the severe beating given him by Chad, there was a price on Chad and Caitlin's head; Chad dead or alive, but Caitlin only if returned safely. They learned that McTavish was the man leading the group, and that he had two others with him . . . one of them a renowned shootist who went by the name of Nobel Brennen, the other another French Canadian named Andre Toulouse—and that the Indians who'd come out of the cottonwoods after the cattle were a surprise to all of them.

On hearing this, Kev smiled inwardly. Hell, the Hunkpapa had cost him some cattle, but they might have saved him a major gunfight with some hard men including a skilled shootist, and worse, the possibility of losing Caitlin and Chad to some hard men with evil intentions.

Morning dawned cold to the bone with lightly falling snow, and with Sean and Kev digging a grave for the man known only as Frenchy. Kev had shot at a lot of men, mostly Indians, and didn't know quite how to feel about burying a man he *knew* he'd killed. He knew it hadn't been the Christian thing to do, but then again, it was kill or be killed. Still and all, it was a hard thing. He said some of what he thought were the proper words, and finished the task as quickly as he could.

When that unpleasant job was finished, Kev made a quick count of the cattle. There were 177 head, if his count was right. Still more than enough to get the money to pay the bank and have a goodly amount left over. It was then that he realized that his brother Colin had said it was a man named Tolofsen to whom they owed the money. It must be Caitlin's husband, Mark Stanley Tolofsen. My God, they were indebted to the man whose wife he was squiring away down river, and Kev had just killed one of his employees.

To state the obvious, that probably wouldn't set well with the banker. Kev couldn't help but chuckle. Getting a loan extension had probably gone downriver with the wife.

Oh, well, the die was cast.

But maybe, just maybe, he could recover some of the lost cattle. He was going to need every dollar.

Chapter 13

Over the ridge, back in the ravine they'd waited in the evening before, three men huddled by a generous fire.

"If you hadn't a-hogged down all that whiskey" McTavish said, pulling at the beard with one hand while probing the wound in Brennen's back with a finger of the other. Six inches of a broken arrow shaft protruded into the air.

"Damn it, man, quit poking at the damn thing and get the blade and dig it out."

The arrow had hit one of the bandolier straps crossing Brennen's wide back, and only penetrated the flesh a little past the arrowhead. It was pure luck, as it was just left of the backbone, and would have been a heart shot had the thick leather not slowed the projectile. Brennen's shirt had been removed, the bandolier cut away, and the shaft broken so there was just enough left to be able to grip.

"It's gonna pain you some."

Brennen lay on his belly on a bedroll near a roaring campfire. McTavish and the French Canadian known as Andre hunkered down on their haunches studying the wound.

Andre pulled his knife from the fire where he'd

been heating the blade. He eyed McTavish. "You pull ze arrow, and I will seal ze wound. *Sacre bleu,* all in one motion."

"Just do it," Brennen snapped, "so I can heal up and get back to killing those sneakin' cowmen."

"We'da had them," McTavish said, "had it not been for those damn Sioux pickin' just that time to raid the herd."

"Pull the damned arrow out," Brennen said, "or it won't be just the cowmen I come huntin'."

With that, McTavish eyed Andre and got a nod, then jerked the shaft, eliciting a loud bellow from Brennen, then another as Andre hit the gash with the hot knife blade. Brennen bucked, throwing both his benefactors aside. "Jesus Lord," Brennen shouted, rising and moving around the fire, looking for some relief. "Jesus Lord, am I gonna kill somebody for this!"

"Anybody in their camp," McTavish cautioned, "or the Sioux's, but not the woman."

"No," Brennen said, slowing his trek around the fire. "Not the woman. But I may show her what a real man is like before we haul her back to that worm of a banker she's married to."

"No, you won't, Brennen, not if you want to get paid. Tolofsen said unharmed. And it's unharmed we'll return her."

"Humph," was all the big gunfighter said, then feeling the blood tracking his back, he turned to Andre. "Get a bandage on this damn thing so it don't bleed me out."

"*Oui,*" Andre said, smiling.

"You think this is funny?" Brennen asked, his eyes narrowing, his fists balled at his sides.

"*N'est-ce pas?* You don't think so?" Andre rested his hand on the hilt of the knife shoved through his belt.

"You two knock it off. We'll need each other before this is done," McTavish said, his tone hard and demanding.

"Just bandage the damn thing," Brennen said. "There will be time for you too, Toulouse, after this is done."

"Anytime, *monsieur,* anytime," Andre said, his voice low and sinister, but he went to find something to use to bandage Brennen's wound.

Seventy-five miles up the Tongue River, south of the cantonment, near the confluence of Hanging Woman Creek, at a higher elevation where over two feet of snow already covered the ground, the Sioux chief Crazy Horse sat on a ridge overlooking the creek bottom, satisfied that his tactics had worked. Next to him, Dull Knife sat his pony, likewise surveying the wealth of lodges and manpower below. It was not Crazy Horse's tactics against the walks-a-heap that he was thinking of, but his tactics to compel his own people to stay off the reservation and fight for what the Great Father meant to be theirs.

Below him in the creek bottom lay a village grown to nearly eight hundred lodges. The Lakotas and Northern Cheyenne who'd fled the reservation were living alongside Sans Arc and Minneconjou lodges, and one hundred lodges of other Lakota tribes.

Among the prominent men in the encampment

were Dull Knife, No Water, Bull Eagle, The Yearling, Fat Hide, Lame Red Shirt, and Bad Leg.

When any of his own band had weakened and attempted to return to the reservation, Crazy Horse and his warrior society, the *akicita*, had destroyed the belongings and horses of the perpetrator. No one had left. No one would leave.

Now they were at strength again. Now, if just the winter would be kind, by spring they would be able to face the walks-a-heap and destroy them as they had Yellow Hair.

Right now, it was this early winter that was the real enemy.

As he eyed the camp below, he saw another group approach. It was Sitting Bull and the Hunkpapa. They looked haggard and worn, about done in. It was obvious they had found no *tatanka* in the north.

Kev, Caitlin, Sean, and Chad finished their breakfast while Badger-Man watched the herd. Sleeps-in-Day had ridden out with first light to scout and see if Frenchy's friends had left the country, or were still in the neighborhood.

They'd found a steer that had been killed by a stray bullet, and would butcher it before they set out to leave this place that had seemed so ideal, but had been such bad luck. They also had a travois to build. Sean left as soon as he'd finished his plate to let Badger-Man get something to eat. Then he would help him butcher the steer.

As Kev helped Caitlin clean up and pack the

camp, he was surprised to see Chad walk out of the tent, fully dressed.

"Father, you mustn't. . . ." Caitlin said, stopping her work to stare at him.

"Yes, I must. I'm on my feet, dressed, and I can ride, so let's hear no more talk about a travois."

"You sure?" Kev asked.

"If I can walk, I can ride."

"Caitlin?" Kev asked, not wanting to agree unless she did.

"It would be better if he could ride. So if he thinks so . . ." she said, but her look belied what she was saying. She was obviously worried.

"Then it's settled. I'll saddle the horses," Kev said, and went to do so as Caitlin began folding up the canvases they'd used for the tent.

Just as Kev returned, Sleeps-in-Day rode back into camp. "Black Face Hair and two more camp over ridge."

That took Kev aback a moment, as he'd hoped they'd ridden out of the area. Now it was either face them down, or move out and worry about them being at his back.

He knew one of them had been wounded; watched the arrow strike his back. Maybe they'd made camp until their cohort died or got better. Maybe they too were laying up while one of their own healed well enough to travel. One thing he was sure of, they were only two, plus one carrying an arrowhead, so they were not the threat they had been—of course, they might be carrying a real grudge, now that one of them had been killed. Revenge was a great motivator.

He decided to ride on, and avoid another run-in if he could.

While Sean and the two Assiniboine worked on butchering the steer, Kev managed to round up another ten cattle; now he figured he had 185 or so. That would do, if only the Sioux left them alone from here on in.

As they pushed the cattle out of the meadow, he dropped back to ride beside Caitlin and Chad. As he had a worry at their rear, he'd asked Sean to take the point.

"Do you think this McTavish fellow will leave things be?" Kev asked the two of them.

"Caitlin knows them better than I," Chad said. "I didn't learn too much about those Bozeman boys during my short time there." He smiled as if it went without saying.

"I wish I could believe we'd seen the last of them, but I fear not," Caitlin said, shaking her head worriedly.

"Then come mid-afternoon, I'll drop back and see if they're dogging our trail," Kev said, as much to himself as to Chad and Caitlin.

"I can ride a flank," Chad said, "so long as I don't have to chase some stray though the underbrush."

"And I can watch the pack mules and the remuda," Caitlin said.

Kev smiled, studying her. Still in a flail dress, even soiled and smudged, she looked like the last one you'd expect to see wrangling a few head of stock on a wild trail down the Yellowstone River, with some fellows who were little more than bandits dogging their tail and the hills full of wild Sioux waiting to take some scalps, or a woman captive.

"You're a case," Kev said, and got a smile from her.

"A good case or a bad one?" she asked, a light in her eyes.

"One that could use a hot bath," he said laughing, teasing, then added, slightly embarrassed at his forward comment, "Of course, not so much as the rest of us." He punctuated that by rubbing a hand across the half-inch stubble on his chin. "And a shave, in my case."

"Your wish is my command," she said, the twinkle still in her eye.

"What?" Kev said.

"Tonight, when we make camp. Papa has a fine shaving kit in his pack, and he owes you the loan of it. I'll heat some water, and you'll think you were at a St. Louis tonsorial parlor when I finish with you."

Kev blushed, cutting his eyes away. "I never had no woman take a razor to me."

"Then you're about to be spoiled, Kev McQuade, like I've spoiled my father many times. Like I'm going to spoil myself with a hot bath and some lilac water when we get to Big Horn City."

"Tomorrow, or the next day, or day after," Kev mumbled. With that he merely shook his head. The thought of her as God had made her in a hot tub of suds was a little too much for him, so he gigged his horse to catch up to where he noticed some cattle begin to move away from the herd.

"Why, I believe you've frightened Mr. McQuade, daughter," Chad said with a guffaw, then a wince of pain at the effort.

"Not so much as I plan to," Caitlin said thoughtfully, then repeated her self-imposed promise. "Not so much as I plan to." With that, she turned to her

father. "Papa, what do you think about Kev Mc-
Quade?"

"Since when are you asking me about what I
think about some man that's turned your fancy?"
He laughed, and winced again.

"I didn't say he'd turned my fancy, I asked what
you thought about him."

"Well, he sure as hell isn't Mark Stanley Tolofsen."

"So, what does that mean?"

"It means he's a fine-looking young man with a
good heart, bark like an old oak, and not an ounce
of backup in him. In fact, none of the McQuades
we've had a chance to know have any backup. I'm
growing right fond of Sean McQuade as well."

She looked puzzled for a moment. "And that's a
good thing? No backup, I mean."

"Good as Sunday morning. And bad. It can get a
man in trouble, but most often as not, it will keep
him out of it."

She turned serious. "I tried to get him to let us
ride on when we knew McTavish was out there—"

"Like I said, not an ounce of backup."

She sighed deeply. "And me a city girl."

Again, her father laughed. "First thing we have to
worry about is getting you back to the city, and getting you annulled from that worm you thought was
so fine."

"True. Father?" He turned to her, noting that she
was now serious. "I'm sorry."

"About what?"

"About Mark. I should have asked, and then
taken your advice."

"Water way under the bridge."

"Still—"

His tone turned serious. "Caitlin, if anything happens to me, you stay close to Kev McQuade."

"Nothing is going to happen to you. Nothing more anyway. And I plan to stay close to Mr. McQuade nonetheless."

"He lives a long way from the city," her father teased.

"Then we'll just have to get him to ranch a little closer to one . . . maybe close to St. Louis. Then again, maybe he'd be interested in getting into the saloon business with a fine St. Louis businessman I know?"

Her father laughed and shrugged his shoulders, and winced again, as he moved away to take the riverside flank of the herd, leaving her to watch over the mules and horses.

Chapter 14

Sergeant Orin Starkey reined up, then yelled to the wagon drivers to do the same. His whiskers were even more unruly and hung past his Adam's apple, and were more tobacco-stained than usual. Big Horn City, or what was left of it, and a full quart of Pettibone's Rye Bourbon, was a full day behind them, and he expected to see no one until they neared the cantonment, at least three days ahead. But there up ahead, two riders approached, and one of them wore infantry blue. Starkey sighed deeply, hoping it was not a superior officer. He had a terrible hangover, and the last thing he needed was guff from some West Point shavetail.

As they neared, he realized it was a corporal and some damned civilian . . . probably some know-it-all scout on the Army dole.

"You'll be a welcome sight at the cantonment if them are vegetables under that tarpaulin," the corporal said as they reined up in front of them.

"A welcome sight . . . *sir*," Starkey snapped.

"*Sir*, sorry, Sergeant. The vegetables, I mean."

"We got mail too. So, I haven't seen you before, Corporal. Nor your friend."

"Yes, sir. I'm Corporal Brian McGloughlan, and

this is Scout Barton Grigsby. We're on special orders from General Miles himself, looking for sign of the Hunkpapa or other hostiles."

Starkey didn't answer, merely spat a long stream of tobacco into a patch of snow below where he sat.

Grigsby didn't like this sergeant's attitude, and decided he wanted to waste little time with him. A sergeant demanding a "sir" from a corporal out on the plain was pressing military protocol to an unnecessary hard edge. His patience was already worn thin with the man, who he studied carefully, and it was reflected in his tone. "So, you seen any sign of hostiles?" Grigsby snapped as he banged the tobacco out of his pipe against his saddle horn.

"Crossed a trail of twenty or more unshod horses the day before we rode into Big Horn City. They were headed upriver."

"Up the Yellowstone, or the Big Horn?"

"Big Horn."

"How old?" Grigsby asked.

"A day or two."

"Travois tracks?"

"I'd a told you, scout, if they was travois tracks."

Grigsby eyed him with a look that could melt bullet lead, but his tone remained even. "I'm obliged to ask, Sergeant. That sort of thing is what I'm paid for."

"So, if you two want to find some hostiles, I'd suggest you keep riding upriver." Starkey stroked his whiskers with his left hand as he spoke, and Grigsby noticed the hand was bandaged.

"We intend to. I got a message for Miles. We passed a track of over fifty hostiles ten miles back, headed south. You tell him that soon as you get into camp."

Starkey glared at the scout. "So, why ain't you following' that fifty. Too many to track, or are you afraid you'll catch up with them?" Starkey and his corporal, driving the front wagon, guffawed.

Again Grigsby gave him the lead-melting look. "Not that it's your concern, Sergeant, but we got our own counsel to keep and it's with four hundred, not fifty. You just tell Miles what I told you."

"Humph," Starkey managed as Grigsby gave him a snarl. Then McGloughlan followed Grigsby as he spurred his horse on by the wagons.

As they moved on upriver, Grigsby dropped back alongside McGloughlan. "You know that sergeant?"

"First time we've met."

"He don't set well with me."

"Must be a tough sort."

"Why's that?"

"Miles has him out here leaving tracks for a blind man to follow, and no troop with him. Only seven of them. I'd say Miles thinks he can handle himself."

Grigsby was silent for a long moment. "I think I met him one time, a few years back, when I was little more than a whelp."

"Really, where?"

"Kansas. During the war. I think he rode with Quantrill. I spent a little time with General Hallick's command in Missouri, and we came head to head with Quantrill's boys more than once. I know that ugly old boy who the Army done made a sergeant . . . he was one of those murderin' scum."

This time it was McGloughlan who was quiet for a while, then offered, "Well, he's Union Army now. We got a lot of rebels among us."

"And some of them murderin' scum."

"Probably more than we'd care to admit," Mc-Gloughlan said, then changed the subject. "How far we going?"

"Far enough," Grigsby said. Without further comment he gigged his horse into a lope.

The cattle drive enjoyed an uneventful day, with only a few flakes of snow and the occasional patch of warming sun. Kev had ridden their back trail after they were halfway through the day, back a couple of miles and even up on the ridge overlooking the river, and found no sign of any pursuit by the black-bearded McTavish, the gunman Brennen, or the remaining Frenchman.

The country was becoming sparser and sparser, with the firs and pines behind them and only a few ravines filled with cedars, as the junipers were commonly called. The river was lined with cottonwoods and slushy with ice, but nowhere near frozen over, so the cattle could drink, and the snow was very shallow so they could still paw and graze with little problem.

Before he caught back up with the herd, Kev came upon Caitlin and Chad Steel resting, sitting atop a large beaver-downed cottonwood, admiring the river and the cliffs across and fronting it.

He reined up and dismounted beside them. "You all okay?"

"Just resting," Chad said. "I get a little winded."

"I'll ride on ahead," Kev said, "and tell them to pull up. We've gone far enough for today."

"I don't want you to lose time," Chad said, rising.

"Rest a while. We'll have camp made when you get there." Kev remounted, then glanced back at them. "I didn't see anyone tracking us, but don't tarry too long, they could still be back there."

"We'll be careful," Caitlin said, then added, "You have Sean put on the big kettle. I want a lot of hot water tonight."

"Yes, ma'am," Kev said as he gave spurs to the buckskin and loped ahead.

"Do you think they're still after us, Father?" Caitlin asked.

"Yes, daughter, I do. I don't think your husband has the sand to make this chase himself, but he sure as hell has the money, and the anger, to have someone do it for him."

"Even Kevin killing that man?"

"Even that. They'll still be coming. I imagine there's a fine price on our head."

She thought about that for a long moment, then asked. "Then if you feel well enough . . . ?"

"Let's ride on," Chad said, and headed to where their horses pawed the snow and grazed.

As they let the horses move slowly up the trail, Caitlin quietly asked, "Do you think it was necessary, Kev killing that man?"

Chad studied her for a moment. "Sometimes a hard decision has to be made in the blink of an eye. Kev made one, and I trust that he made the right one."

Again she was silent for a long while, then added, "This is a hard land, full of hard men. I don't know that I could ever be really happy here. I know I've only known him a little more than a week. Do you think Kev McQuade could be happy in the city?"

Chad smiled. "Who knows? Sounds like he's got

family and a fine ranch back upriver. That might be a hard thing to leave."

She sighed, and they were silent the rest of the way to where Kev had selected a meadow to bed down the herd.

As soon as they reached the camp, Caitlin went straight to the fire and stuck her finger in the large pot of water there, then put it in her mouth as the water was already hot. Then she went to her father's bedroll and removed a small canvas bag. She found a log not far from the camp, came back to the campfire, and filled a small pot with the scalding water, fetched a camp towel, then walked over to where Kev was rolling out his own bedroll.

"Mr. McQuade, it's time for you to shed those whiskers you were complaining about."

He looked sheepishly at her. "I'm perfectly capable—"

"I offered, and I keep my promises. Besides, I'd like to see what you look like under all that black brush you're wearing."

Kev sighed deeply, but shed his hat and followed her. "Don't expect me to get much prettier," he mumbled under his breath.

She laughed, that lilting sound that had begun to make him uncomfortable because of the heat it brought to his loins, but he said nothing, only followed dutifully.

After a couple of soaks with a towel dipped in the hot water, while she stropped the razor on a small leather strap from her father's bag, she picked up a cup of soap and began brushing up and lathering Kev's face.

"You're not gonna cut my throat?" he said, only half-teasing.

"I have a woman's fine touch, Kev McQuade, and promise not to even nick you . . . God willing and you keep your mouth shut."

While she worked, Sean walked over and watched. Finally, he spoke, a little self-consciously, "I'm going to have to shave real soon."

They ignored him, so he said again, "I'll be real glad when I have to shave."

"The hell you will," Kev managed. "Up to now, shaving's been a real chore."

"Unless you want to lose a lip, you'll button it," Caitlin said, concentrating.

After she'd finished, and she'd used the towel to wipe away the remnants of soap, she stepped back and surveyed her work.

"You're right," she said.

"Right? About what?"

"You're not even a smidgen prettier." Both she and Sean enjoyed the joke, laughing loudly.

He reddened.

Then she added, "You are surely a good deal more handsome, however."

He reddened even more, and her amber eyes seemed to light with mirth.

She laughed again, then turned her attention to the fire. "How about a good beefsteak?" she asked no one in particular. "McTavish did us one favor when that steer caught a stray bullet." She glanced at Kev. "Sorry, Kev. We could have gotten by fine on venison."

He smiled at her. "I'd have traded a steer for that shave."

She flashed him an even bigger smile, then went to work. While she saw to that chore, Kev walked on down to the riverside, wet his hair, and smoothed it as well as he could with his five-finger comb. *My God,* he thought, *I'm getting real attached to that woman.*

He turned to start back to camp, and glanced up on the ridge behind them. The sitting sun nicely outlined three riders, not more than a half mile back.

Damn the flies, Kev thought. We're not shed of them yet. And that wounded man was not as wounded as Kev had at first surmised.

And now it looked like they were moving this way.

Chapter 15

Kev returned to camp to the welcoming odor of beefsteak sizzling in a cast-iron frying pan.

Chad was lying on his bedroll, his eyes closed; Sean was sitting on a log, shining the Parker; Caitlan stood over the fire, her hair a little disheveled, her attention on a pan of potatoes and the meat. The Indians were, as usual, in their own camp, awaiting a call from Caitlin, as they'd been invited to partake in the bounty of the accidentally killed steer.

Kev waved Sean over to where Chad Steel lay, then nudged Chad with a booted toe. "They're still dogging our trail," he said as Chad opened his eyes.

"Not surprised." He sat up. "How far back?"

"Half mile, maybe a little more, but they dropped off the skyline."

Chad yelled to his daughter, "How are those steaks coming?"

She had not overheard their conversation, and turned back to them. "Hold your horses. Steaks are off, but the potatoes are still a little crunchy."

Chad rose and walked to the fire. "We better eat them as they are. McTavish and his boys are not far back."

"Damn," she said uncharacteristically. Then she turned to Kev. "Father can ride now. We should go on—"

"I don't want to hear any more of that, Caitlin." He yelled at the Indians, waving them over as she dished up the feast. "Eat fast. We've got company coming, again. . . ."

Caitlin handed them a plate, but Sleeps-in-Day didn't take it; rather, he grabbed the steak up in one hand and headed for his horse. "I see," he said.

They wolfed the food down, then Kev sent the boy down to the riverside with an admonition. "You watch the water this time. If you see them coming, fire off a round."

"Shouldn't I wait until they get close, and pick one off?" Sean asked.

"I got lucky, Sean. These old boys aren't like that ol' bear. They'll be shootin' back. I couldn't explain to your mother that I had to plant you in the sod this far from home. You just fire off a round, understand?"

"Yes, sir," Sean said, and grabbed his coat up and headed for the riverside.

"Can you two find a hideout here close to camp?" Kev asked Chad and Caitlin.

"We can," Chad said, "but Caitlin's idea of riding out may be a better one. Big Horn City is not far. We can make it there, and wait there for you."

"You may be waiting for McTavish. No, it's better if we face up to this here and now."

"Then we'll hide out," Chad said without further argument.

Kev and Badger-Man each headed for separate ravines leading up and away from the meadow, between it at the ridge-top beyond. It would be dark very soon.

All they could do now was wait.

At the Rocky Butte ranch, it was snowing hard and the wind was moaning softly, but Colin McQuade was smiling. They'd brought the draw-down table into the small shack so he could work into the dark, and the saddle was coming along fine.

"Why, you know, Dugan, I'd pay as much as twenty . . . even twenty-five dollars for a saddle as fine as this one is turning out to be. Do you think a fella could make as many as, say, three of these in a month?"

"You get yourself another two or three draw-down tables," Dugan said with a wide grin, "and you get a dollar-a-day helper doing the cutting and carving, the rough work, and you could make six saddles a month. And a couple of bridles and and even chaps to boot."

"Sean could help."

"Sure, you and Sean."

Colin suddenly got a faraway look in his eye. "I wish Brigid could have seen this. She was always the one for admiring fine work."

Dugan changed the subject. "Now that you've got that fat whitetail hanging, and a half-dozen cords stacked in the barn, you think you could make out a while?"

"You get on back to your ranch. I can do just fine here till Kev and Sean get back. They've been gone a tad over three weeks, so a few days into the cantonment, then eight or ten days hard riding back, depending on the weather . . . "

Dugan laid a hand on Colin's shoulder. "Then I'll be riding out tomorrow with first light. I'll come on back in three weeks, if the snow don't keep me by the fire."

"I want you to jerk the fence down around the summer haystack, so the cows we got left can feed themselves."

"I can do that tonight."

"You've been a godsend, Norval. I'll make it right by you, come spring."

"The way this winter's starting out, let's hope all of us see the spring."

Colin stared off again. "Let's hope it's better downriver, and that the damned Hunkpapa and Cheyenne . . . " His voice trailed off to a mumble. "I don't know what I'd do if I lost Sean."

"Kev will take good care of Sean."

"And himself, God willing."

"God willing."

With the dawn, Colin found himself leaning on his crutch, watching Norval Dugan mount up.

In moments, he was alone, with only the remaining cows, and a fine herd bull, to keep him company.

Now, if the damned Indians and wolves let him be, all he had to do was work on the saddle, cook, haul in a little wood a few steps, all under the cover of the barn, and manage to hack an occasional piece of venison off the whitetail hanging under the hayloft.

That should be no hill for a stepper, even a one-legged one.

* * *

In spite of himself, Kev had dozed off a couple of times in the night, but was awake when the sun came up. The wind also was up and it was hard to hear, and to keep warm, even in his heavy wolf-skin coat. But so far, no shot had come from the camp nor from where Badger-Man had hidden.

With the first light, Kev worked his way back to the camp, where Caitlin already had a fine fire roaring, and beans in the pot. To his left, Kev could see Badger-Man also returning to camp. Caitlin had taken to wearing Sean's duster as the boy had another fine knee-length buffalo coat, and the duster dragged the ground as she worked. When Kev neared, he could smell biscuits in the Dutch oven.

Chad and Sean met him with a cup of coffee when he walked in. It was welcome, as he was chilled to the bone.

"Nothing?" Chad asked.

"Not a damn thing other than a bone-chilling cold, a couple of nighthawks, and an old hoot owl. I should have taken my bedroll out there."

Kev looked worried, directing his next comment to Badger-Man, who walked up, also being met by Chad with a hot cup of coffee. "Sleeps-in-Day should have come back in. I haven't seen hide nor hair of him."

"If not back by finish eating, I go look," Badger-Man said.

"I'll go with you. Chad and Sean can get the cattle moving. He should have been back."

They ate in relative silence, each of them worried about their comrade.

When finished, Kev took the most westerly way up the canyon wall, and Badger-Man the easterly. They figured they'd have a better chance of cutting Sleeps-in-Day's trail on top of the ridge if separated.

The wind was moaning in the canyon bottom, but banshee-screaming through the cedars by the time Kev reached the rimrock where the rolling hills stretched beyond as far as the eye could see. The country was grass-covered, now partially snow-covered, and it had again begun to snow. This time the snow was wet and cutting. With this wind and new snow, Kev feared they would not find any track—not of Sleeps-in-Day, nor of McTavish and his men.

Kev turned east on the rimrock, as the herd would be moving that way, and he feared that McTavish and his men might have, somewhere in front of him, made their way to the canyon bottom and be lying in wait for Chad and Caitlin.

He'd only gone a couple of hundred yards when he dropped into a ravine and spotted shod hoof-prints under a rock outcropping that had been protected from the snowfall. He dismounted and studied the sign. Three horses—one of them had thrown a shoe, and that track would be easy to identify again. All of the horses were mounted, as the tracks were deep in the mud. He was sure it was McTavish and his henchmen.

Damn the flies, the man hadn't been wounded badly enough to turn them back. And they were pressing on. That only meant one thing—Caitlin and Chad were still in danger, which meant all of them were.

Kev used all his skill trying to follow the track, but it was lost in the windblown snow of the upper rims. He did determine that they seemed to be staying back away from the rim, not bothering to keep the herd in sight—possibly wanting to stay out of sight themselves—confident that the way they were going, they would again be able to easily locate the herd, and Caitlin.

He hadn't gone more than a mile more when he spotted Badger-Man sitting stone-still on his horse, studying something.

As he neared, Kev could hear the growing echo of Badger-Man's mournful chants, then even closer, realized that he was looking at a lone pine on the rimrock. A pine that Sleeps-in-Day was tied to, a rope with many turns binding him tightly, the last turn around his throat. His lifeless eyes bugged out and his jaw hung slack. Spittle had frozen to his chin. A pair of hopeful crows rested in the tree overhead. His own knife had been driven through his throat and into the tree, and what little blood there was, was also frozen in grotesque worm tracks down his buckskins.

Kev dismounted and walked around the tree to see that a short limb had been used to twist the line until Sleeps-in-Day had choked to death. There was an indication of hoofprints in the muddy area under the pine that had not yet been snow-covered, including an odd one without the shoe.

There was very little blood from the knife, so Kev concluded that it had been driven into the man's throat as an afterthought.

Badger-Man continued his chanting as Kev, trembling with anger and frustration, removed the knife, cut away the bindings, and lowered the big man gently to the ground. Then he walked alongside Badger-Man's pinto and placed a hand on his buckskinned thigh. "I'm sorry. He was a good man, a fine hand, and a friend."

But Badger-Man did not acknowledge Kev's remarks, only went on chanting.

It was the most mournful thing Kev had ever heard. He found a log and sat, waiting for Badger-Man to finish lamenting to his god, or his ancestors, or whoever he wanted to hear his woeful dirge. Finally, after most of an hour, desperately worried about Caitlin, Chad, and Sean, Kev mounted up and reined up alongside Badger-Man.

"Do you need help with the body?"

Badger-Man went on chanting.

"Was it McTavish, or other Indians?" Kev asked, then stated, "Looks like white men to me. He's still got his hair, and those are shod tracks."

Badger-Man's chanting rose an octave.

"I have to go back to the herd, but I can stay here and help for a while if need be?"

Still, all he got in reply was the bone-chilling dirge. Finally, he reined away and made his way east on the ridge. When he got where he could see the herd, or thought he was as far down as they might be, he would work his way down the canyon to the flat surrounding the meandering Yellowstone. Once he found a ridge that would take him down, he whipped up the buckskin and it was hell-for-leather, slipping and sliding, until he reached the bottom.

He hadn't cut the trail of McTavish and his men, nor had the herd come that far yet, he realized as he made his way back at a gallop until he reined up alongside Sean, riding point.

Thank God, everything seemed fine with the cattle, and more thankfully, he could see both Caitlin and Chad, each riding flank. But where were McTavish and his cohorts? Surely they hadn't been satisfied just taking the life of Sleeps-in-Day. No, they were still out there. Caitlin was their real target.

But for the moment, they had to be second on Kev's mind.

He had to start looking for a crossing as he knew that Big Horn City and, farther downriver, the Army cantonment were both on the south side of the Yellowstone. And the farther downriver they went, the deeper or at least wider the water. He needed Badger-Man, and hoped he would ride into camp tonight, but didn't blame him if he packed up—and he already carried everything he owned behind his saddle—and headed back to the Rocky Butte country and his people.

Crossing the Yellowstone would be pure hell, if a plunging horseback swim in a freezing, rapidly moving body of water slaked with ice could be compared to the fires of perdition.

He'd hoped the river would be frozen hard over, but that would have been too much to ask. It looked like it would be a cold swim for all of them, and a hell of a good way to lose even more of the herd . . . if not worse. He couldn't imagine Caitlin, even as hardy as she'd proven to be, crossing that river on horseback.

But it had to be done eventually, and the sooner the better . . . unless they had time to wait for ice, and they didn't.

* * *

McTavish, Brennen, and Andre Toulouse moved quickly downriver. Where they could, they loped their horses. The weather was on them, and they knew where the herd was headed. Their only worry was that the Steels wouldn't stay with the herd, but them leaving was unlikely. With weather closing in, the Yellowstone Canyon—even as shallow as it was this far downriver—offered protection from the wind, and Big Horn City was the only hint of civilization until they reached the cantonment.

Caitlin Tolofsen and Chad Steel would head for Big Horn City.

The only thing that slowed the three of them was coming upon the track of many unshod horses, dragging travois, traveling south, pushing a few head of cattle. They estimated there to be several hundred Indians, more than three hundred. The three trackers veered north, wanting to fight shy of any contact with the savages. After a few miles, they moved back toward the river, but always keeping a sharp eye out for any signs of an Indian encampment.

It was the end of the day, with the wind finally stilled, when they saw a wisp of smoke in the distance. They very carefully approached the rim of the shallow canyon where the Yellowstone was now wide and wandering.

To their relief it was Big Horn City in the distance, a group of only a half-dozen buildings; and the Yellowstone River above the confluence with the Big Horn River had a fairly wide, and hopefully shallow, riffle. Still, it roiled along littered with ice.

They made the hundred-pace-wide crossing, only having to swim the horses for less than fifty feet, and kept moving rapidly until they reined up in front of the largest of the half-dozen log buildings—Hauptmann's General Store and Saloon.

Leaving their wet horses tied at the rail, they hurried inside a plank door marked KAISER'S SALOON—one of two in the building, with the other marked HAUPTMANN'S DRY GOODS—to dry off in front of Hauptmann's generous roaring fireplace. Hauptmann's was a log building, made from large ponderosa pines that must have been floated downriver, with a fine plank floor. The saloon portion had only a pair of four-place tables and a bar six stools long, but it might as well have been a palace after ten days on the trail. Still, as small as the place was, a three-by-four foot painting of a reclining scantily clad, amply endowed, blond woman with rosy cheeks graced the centerpiece of the back-bar, and almost a hundred bottles were lined up under her seductive glance.

Gustav Hauptmann, tall, gray, serious, and gangly with muttonchop sideburns, pushed through a pair of batwing doors between the store and saloon carrying three mugs of coffee to the shivering men. "You fellas lef' your horses at the rail?" he said in the way of a greeting.

"Yep," McTavish said between sips of the hot brew.

"They vet as you?"

McTavish eyed the tall lanky man skeptically, not liking being quizzed by some long lanky storekeep with a German accent. "Yeah, so what?"

Hauptmann's Adam's apple danced as he spoke. "I got da livery next door. I can haf' my man take 'em over and rub 'em down and grain 'em."

"And what's that cost?"

"Four bits a day."

"Hell, friend, it's a quarter a day in Bozeman."

"Dis ain't Bozeman . . . friend."

McTavish eyed him even harder. "You got me half afraid to drink this coffee now. I suppose it's two bits?"

"Coffee is on da house. You are gonna provision up?"

"We are."

Hauptmann smiled and refilled his coffee cup. "The horses?"

"Two bits, and *we'll* rub them down."

"Ain't the rubbin' costs, it's the hay and shelter."

"Jesus Christ," Brennen snapped, tired of the exchange. "Take the damned horses and quit yer jabberin'. You got anything hot to eat?"

Hauptmann was a bit taken aback by the big man with the crossed bandoliers on his chest, a pistol on each hip, and the rough tone. "My Siglinda, she da best cook on the Yellowstone."

"Then tell her to get on with the cookin'," Brennen snapped. "We need a room, and I want your man to bring my rifle inside before he takes my mount."

"Yes, sir," Hauptmann said, and hurried out of the saloon and back into the store.

"Too damn much money," McTavish groused.

"Damn sure will be, we get stuck here for the winter. I think we oughta ride back and shoot the hell out of those drovers, take the woman, skin her old man, and head upriver to get our money."

"When we can lay in wait here?" McTavish snapped. "By this hot fire, with some fat German

woman cooking for us, while they come mean-
derin' on in to us. To hell with that . . . "

"I agree," Andre said, the first time he'd entered
a conversation since he and Brennen had traded
words the day before.

"Nobody gives a damn what you agree to,
Frenchy."

"You two shut it up," McTavish snapped. "Your
mouths'll be full of hot food soon."

"You know, McTavish," Brennen said, his eyes
narrowing and his hand resting on the butt of one
of his revolvers, "you're starting to wear on me too."

"Let's see if they got a room," McTavish said, cutting his eyes away from the gunfighter, ignoring
both his companions.

"Fine," Brennen snapped. "I want to grub down,
suck up some whiskey, then sleep. Tomorrow may
be a big day in Big Horn, when I get to pay back
some back-shooting cowmen for this hole between
my wings."

"Humph," McTavish managed, "I thought we did
that yesterday in fine fettle. That was an arrow in
your back, not a bullet. If you hadn't already been
sucking the bottle, you probably woulda stayed
out'n the way of that arrow."

"The hell with you, McTavish," Brennen said with
a snarl, but McTavish was already out of the saloon,
his coffee cup empty . . . and this time wanted it
laced with rye, since he was sure they'd have no fine
Scottish dew of the heather in this hole. He'd
pushed through the batwings looking for the German before Brennen finished his insult.

"Tomorrow, we're going to finish this thing,"
Brennen called out behind him.

Chapter 16

It was the end of a hard day with a forever-lost friend, a half day of cutting wind, and a whole day of nervous cattle, when Kev spotted smoke in the distance. He'd ridden on ahead, scouting, not wanting to ride into a Hunkpapa encampment as he'd nervously passed the track of several hundred not a mile back, and was pleased to see the few buildings of Big Horn City not three miles from where the herd was moving steadily along. He spun his horse and galloped for a while, then eased off and loped back to rein up beside Caitlin.

"You're about to get your wish," he said, giving her the first semblance of a smile he'd managed since finding Sleeps-in-Day.

"Really?"

"Sure enough. Big Horn City, and that hot bath you've been grousing about, is just a couple of miles ahead."

"I'll have you know, Kev McQuade, I don't grouse. Tonight?"

"Nope, tomorrow. I don't want to start the herd across this close to dark. Should some be swept downstream, I'd never find them in the pitch black.

We should all rest, us and the horses and cattle, before we try the crossing."

Sean had overheard him. "Can I get a bath and a shave?"

"Sure enough you can get a bath. You're getting a bit whiffy."

Sean laughed. "And you'll have to take a chisel to your hide to get the crust off, Uncle Kev."

That night, after supper was done, camped in a grazing meadow only a mile from where Kev figured to cross, Badger-Man rode quietly into camp.

Caitlin hurried to make him some supper. He walked to the fire as she cooked.

"Sleeps-in-Day make this for you." He handed her a bearskin coat, rough-fashioned from the hide of the bear that they'd encountered.

She had already shed plenty of tears for Sleeps-in-Day, but when handed the coat, she broke down again, and had to walk away from the fire to find the nearby darkness.

Sleeps-in-Day turned to Kev. "She not like?"

"She likes. She likes you and she liked Sleeps-in-Day, and she weeps for him."

"Then that is good thing."

Kev rested a hand on Badger-Man's shoulder. "We all weep for him, in our own way."

Badger-Man cut his eyes away. Then he returned his glance to the fire, where a chunk of beef was turning black and smoking in the skillet. "Meat burn," he said, and snaked it out with his fingers. He walked away to make his own lonely camp, his shoulders uncharacteristically slumped, juggling the meat back and forth from hand to hand to keep from burning himself.

Caitlin returned to the fire, her eyes red and swollen, wearing the coat, rough-tanned and stitched with rawhide, but far warmer than the duster she'd been wearing.

"That suits you," Kev said quietly. "I'll keep you warm in the worst of it."

"When I get to St. Louis, I'll have a furrier refine this a little, and line it with silk . . . and I'll always treasure it. What would possess Sleeps-in-Day to give me something this grand and valuable to him?"

"You did for him, and Indians aren't much used to the white-eye doing for them. Indians are not like most think, Caitlin. I've lived around them most of my life, and they are a proud and giving people."

"So, what's different, other than how they look and dress?"

"Well, for one thing, in his culture an Indian is not judged by what he has, but by what he's given away. That's sure as the devil different from most of the white men I've known."

Again tears filled her eyes, and she turned from the fire.

Gustav Hauptmann smiled as two more men entered his establishment. This was going to be a good day.

"We'd like to board our horses for the night, get some hot food, and sleep in your hayloft?" Corporal Brian McGloughlan asked, stomping his feet and slapping his cold hands together. Barton Grigsby followed him, but walked promptly to the batwing doors and entered the saloon.

"It's four bits for the horses, with rolled oats and

all the meadow hay they can eat, and another two bits to sleep in the hayloft. Or we got one room in the back. You can share with those fellows in the saloon. Five of you and it's cheaper than the hayloft."

"That's a mite proud for a hayloft, friend," McGloughlan said, ignoring the opportunity to share one room and be with four others.

"Oh, we're proud of our hayloft. You can have an elk steak and all the trimmings, and my Siglinda's fine apple strudel, for another half-dollar."

"Well, it's not like we got a choice. Where do I take the horses?"

"My man vill take care of da horses. Go pour yerself a vhiskey and I'll be along to collect soon as I fetch my man over here."

Brian shook his head, but went next door, pushing through the batwings to join Grigsby at the bar. Three rough-looking men sat at a table near the fireplace. McGloughlan returned their nod, and joined the scout.

"A roof will be welcome," he said to Barton.

"It will"—he lowered his voice—"if we don't have to share it with the likes of those no-accounts over there."

"I already turned down that opportunity. You know them?"

"I know of them. A bad sort. Don't know the one with the Hudson Bay coat, but the other two . . ."

"Then we'll keep our own counsel." He picked up the shot glass Barton had already poured for him, and toasted him. "Here's to findin' a few hundred hostiles."

"I guess I'll drink to that," Barton said, and downed the rough whiskey. "But we should at least broach that subject." He moved the half-dozen paces to the table.

"Gentlemen. I'm Barton Grigsby, scout for General Miles."

"Howdy," McTavish said without extending his hand, merely eying Grigsby up and down.

"We're moving west, looking for sign of hostiles. You come from that way?"

"We did, and we passed plenty of track since leaving Bozeman."

"Can you be specific?"

"What's it worth to the Army?" McTavish asked.

Grigsby was silent for a moment. "Well, sir, it might be real valuable to any white men out there where a Hunkpapa might take his hair . . . you included."

"Still got mine, and plan to keep it."

"We all plan to, friend."

"I ain't the Army's friend, friend, but we crossed the track of several hundred moving south, pushing a few cattle, only five miles back."

"Thanks," Barton said. "Friend of the Army or not . . . I'll stand you all to a drink for that information."

"No, thanks," McTavish said. "But you can put it on the tab and I'll take it tomorrow. I've got a job of work to do real soon—"

"I'm Brennen, and I'll sure as hell take one," the big gunfighter cut in.

"And me, Andre Toulouse," the Frenchman added.

Grigsby brought a bottle off the bar and refilled their two glasses. He got no thanks, but merely shrugged and returned to McGloughlan.

* * *

Sitting Bull and almost four hundred Hunkpapa, warriors and old men, young women, children, and grandmothers, had crossed the Elk River, the river the white-eye called the Yellowstone, six miles west of Big Horn City. They now prepared to make camp for the second time since crossing, almost fifteen miles up the creek they followed, and only a few miles from the Big Horn River. Where they'd crossed was as close as Sitting Bull wanted to come to the white man's encampment, even though he sorely needed supplies from the trading post there. He'd traded with Hauptmann many times, and found him to be a hard trader, but always fair in the end.

But the walks-a-heap might be there. He knew they were looking for him and his people, and hoped they were looking north in the Fort Peck area—a region he normally frequented this time of year. This was much too close to a white encampment for comfort, and it was only this early snow that made him feel he could get away with this crossing.

Ever since he'd last met the walks-a-heap at Ash Creek, and had lost most of his people—now on a long walk to the reservation—he'd been much more careful.

One of his spies had told him that Bearcoat thought the Hunkpapa would head north, to the land of the Grandmother, the land they called Canada, and it was for that reason that he and the meager remnants of his band headed south.

He prayed to the Great Father that he would find Crazy Horse and his Lakota cousins, and that they would have found the *tatanka*, and their lodges would be full of meat for the winter—meat they would share with their Hunkpapa cousins.

And he prayed for snow, as he was sure Bearcoat and his soldiers would hole up for the winter when the real snows flew. Even though it would be hard on his people as well, this early winter was a blessing.

That night Kev bedded the herd down in a meadow very near the riffle, with Big Horn City less than a mile away. It was a quiet night, and they awoke to a flat gray sky, but no snow and no wind. It was as good a time to cross as any.

As they packed up after breakfast, Kev walked over to where Chad was saddling his horse. Chad had continued to get better. The wounds hadn't festered as Kev feared they would, and seemed to be healing nicely.

"Do you think we should build a raft to cross Caitlin?" Kev asked in a worried tone.

"No, I don't. It's a thoughtful idea, Kev, but I think she'd be better off horseback. With all the float ice out there, even though most of it looks slushy, there might be some chunks that would take the raft away."

"Good point. I'm just worried."

"She's a fine horsewoman—"

"Can she ride astraddle? That sidesaddle looks tough enough to ride normally."

Chad laughed. "She can, but she won't. I'm always amazed about how a woman can sit one of those damned things."

Kev shook his head in wonderment, then

changed the subject and his tone hardened. "We've seen no sign of McTavish and his boys, but they might be waiting for us in Big Horn City."

"Probably are, and I plan to ride ahead and find out as soon as we're safe on the other side."

"Bad idea, Chad. There's still three of them."

"And I don't want you and Caitlin facing the three of them. I plan to narrow the odds down a mite."

"Even if you could normally, Chad, you're still bad hurt. You and I can ride in and check things out, leaving Caitlin with Sean and Badger-Man."

"Nope. It's my problem. Besides, if something happened to you, Caitlin would never forgive me."

Kev studied on that a while, until Chad swung up into the saddle. "I'm real fond of her," Kev finally said.

Looking down at him, with a wry smile on his face, Chad answered, "And she's fond of you, and she'll be a single woman shortly after we reach St. Louis, that's why you're not going into Big Horn City with me."

"Got to."

Chad shook his head. "Let's settle it when we're across the river . . . the damn-cold and bloody-wet problems first."

Kev walked away to saddle his buckskin. "Hope you're well rested, old boy," he whispered to the big animal, then swung into the saddle. "It's gonna be a tough morning." He nudged the horse over to where Sean and Badger-Man sat horseback, surveying the herd, and waved Chad over. When they were all together, Kev laid out the plan for driving the herd across. He put Sean and Caitlin at the point, crossing first with the horse string and the

pack mules, as he thought that the safest position
Chad and Badger-Man spaced themselves out on
the downstream flank, which would be the tough-
est spot other than drag, which he would take
himself. From that position, he figured he had the
best chance to go after any cattle that might be
washed downstream, and more importantly, should
Caitlin or Sean or even Chad, in his condition, have
trouble, he could gallop down the bank until he
got in front of them.

As it was, his nephew and Caitlin should be safely
across by the time he entered the water.

They gathered the cattle into as tight a bunch as
possible. Then the plan was for Chad and Badger-
Man to push them a few at a time into the river,
while Kev took up the rear, making sure none
bolted or strayed.

He moved to the rear of the bunch, checked the
weather, had second thoughts again about the
proper way to attack this problem, then realized
he'd already worried about it most of the night.

Kev posted in the saddle, and yelled, "Push them
out."

Caitlin and Sean hit the water, able to stay dry for
the first fifty feet. Then Caitlin reached the main
channel, and she dropped out of the saddle and
clung to the horn as the horse swam for its life.

Chapter 17

Kev's stomach felt as heavy as bullet lead as he watched Caitlin's horse swim for the far shore with her dragging in the water at its side, literally hanging on for dear life. Then the animal gained his footing, and began to lunge in water only shoulder-deep. Caitlin, unable to hang on, dropped away, gathered herself in the freezing water, and began to stroke. For a second Chad feared chunks of ice would take her downstream, and wished he'd had the sand to suggest she remove the heavy skirt she wore, but he hadn't, and didn't, and he moved from the rear of the herd to a place higher on the bank so he could see her clearly and know if he had to ride hell-for-leather downstream to try and intercept her.

His heavy stomach now churned as he sat helplessly watching her battle for the shore. Then she had her feet under her, and the water was only waist-deep and she was only a dozen paces from the shore; then she was slogging among the river willows on the far shore—but now she was out, and safe, if wet to the bone.

Sean was able to regain the saddle before his big gray reached shallower water, and he got to the far shore right behind the mules and spare horses. They had put some of the morning's glowing coals in the coffeepot, and wrapped it in a tarp to keep it dry, so they could easily build a fire when they reached the far side, and he could see Sean already stripping a packsaddle, where the coffeepot was stored, off one of the mules as Caitlin, afoot, joined him.

God willing, they'd have a fire roaring by the time the rest of them reached safety.

Badger-Man and Chad began pushing the first of the cattle into the water, and soon the cattle too were clambering out on the far shore. As agreed, when half the herd was in the water or on the far shore, the two men hit the water. Without serious incident they made it to safety. Kev continued to push the herd, but the cattle had the idea and were following with little encouragement.

The big buckskin charged into the water, never hesitating, swimming powerfully when he reached the mainstream, and pounding up the far slope to shake like a dog and throw water everywhere.

By the time Kev had joined the others, Sean had a conflagration roaring. They circled the blaze, alternately putting their backsides, then their front sides to the drying warmth. They were there a half hour before speaking, now warm, if not totally dry.

"I believe," Caitlin said with a shudder, "that was the coldest I've ever been. If it's only a mile through this thicket to Big Horn City, when do we start? That warm bath sounds like heaven."

"I'm going in first," Chad said.

"*We're* going in first," Kev added.

"Not a chance," Chad said with finality.

"Caitlin," Kev asked, "you want your father to risk facing McTavish and his men alone?"

She looked from Kev to Chad and back to Kev. Chad was giving her a stern look, but it didn't faze her. "No, to be truthful, I don't." She studied them all for a moment, then her face lit up. "So far as we know, they never saw Sean. How about if he goes in to see if they're there?"

Kev pondered that a moment. "What do you think?" he asked Chad.

"I guess that would be all right. But it's up to Sean."

"You want me to find out if those men are there?"

Kev eyed his nephew. It seemed he'd aged ten years in the three weeks they'd been pushing cattle, a change for the better. "If you want to go. It could be dangerous. We don't really know if they were watching the drive from some hideout place, and they may have seen you . . . not that it's you they're after."

"That's true, they may have seen you," Caitlin said, now worried. "I don't think you should go either."

"No, I want to go. Can I take my shotgun?"

"No," Kev snapped. "You can wear your side arm, 'cause it would look fishy if you weren't armed, but don't you dare reach for it, no matter what they do . . . if they're even there."

"They saw that shotgun before, Sean," Chad offered. "In fact, I stuck its muzzle between McTavish's eyes in Bozeman. He might recognize it, as it's a rare weapon."

Sean nodded, satisfied, then went to fetch his horse.

* * *

McGloughlan and Grigsby had tarried far too long in Big Horn City, but had been promised a huge, and free, farmer's breakfast of pork chops, sausage, flapjacks, hen's eggs, biscuits, and gravy, all followed by apple strudel, if they'd help Gustav Hauptmann and his man lift the beams on a new smokehouse and slaughterhouse he was building out behind the dry-goods store and trading post.

As they did so, a job that had already taken more than two hours. Grigsby noticed that the bearded man, McTavish, had taken up a position in the hayloft, the highest spot in tiny Big Horn City, where he could watch the track that passed for a road coming into town from the west.

"What's he on the lookout for?" Barton Grigsby asked the shopkeeper.

"Don't rightly know," he said, but his hired man, a black man called Tobias, who'd jumped ship from a riverboat before the war, and long lived with the Crow until he decided to return to civilization after the war when he found he was now a free man, spoke up.

"I heard 'em talkin' when I was swamping out the saloon last night. They's a-waitin' for some woman run off from her husband in Bozeman. One of them is some kinda lawman."

Barton Grigsby and Brian McGloughlan stopped work.

Brian scratched his head. "I didn't know leavin' your husband was against the law. That some kind of territory thing?"

"Going against the law," Grigsby said, "and going

against the grain of some man is a different thing. But I don't know why some lawman would be involved. Seems like a personal thing to me."

Gustav Hauptmann merely shrugged his shoulders. "Not my business," he said and went back to the end of another beam.

"Sounds strange to me," Brian said to Grigsby, but joined him at the other end of the beam from Hauptmann and the black.

When they finished a dozen beams and were headed for the saloon, where the tables were used for meals, they were surprised to see another rider approaching, a lone rider leading a mule.

They reached the dry-goods store the same time as the new man on the scene, and were more surprised to see he was a youngster.

Brennen stood on the wide board porch watching the young man tie his horse and mule to the hitching rail.

McTavish was still in the hayloft, his rifle in hand. Andre Toulouse was across what passed for a road in an abandoned clapboard building, one of the five in the little town, by a glassless window, his knit cap pulled low on his forehead, watching carefully.

Sean McQuade, with the skill of a thespian, tied his horses and tipped his hat at the big gunfighter Brennen as he moved to the door. Brennen snatched him by the collar as he neared, just as Barton Grigsby reached them.

"Where you from, boy?" he snarled, looking down into the face of the youngster.

"Up in the Judith country. What's it to you, mister?"

Brennen tightened his grip on the collar, almost choking Sean.

"And what's your name, shoat?"

"He asked you a question, Brennen," Grigsby said, his hand resting on the revolver on his hip. "The shoat said, and I'm wondering myself, what's it to you?"

Brennen shoved the boy away, and took a step closer to Grigsby. "That's none a' yer damn business, breed," Brennen snarled.

But Grigsby was unfazed. "If you don't know this boy, you've got no call to put your hands on him."

Brennen too rested a hand on one of the two guns on his hip. "You best walk away and mind your own business, breed. We got official business—"

"The hell you do, that's no badge McTavish wears. He's a guard, no lawman, in the employ of some businessman in Bozeman. I was in Bozeman last summer."

"Still," Brennen snarled, "it's none of your concern." But he moved his hand away from his revolver.

Grigsby stepped even closer, an arm's length from the bigger man. "You know, Brennen, you're right, I'm half Crow and half white. And you make me glad I'm only half white. You're a big butt-ugly som'bitch, even if you had both ears. Now, if'n you can hear out of that ugly hole in your head, *leave the boy be.*"

Brennen's hand again moved slowly toward the butt of his revolver, and Grigsby matched him, inch for inch.

From behind Brennen, in the doorway of the saloon, McGloughlan's voice rang out. "Everything that happens in the territory is the Army's business,

Mr. Brennen, and Mr. Grigsby is in the Army's employ."

Brennen turned to find himself facing the large bore of a Springfield .45/.70 carbine, resting comfortably in the hands of a soldier who looked as if he was comfortable with it, and, Brennen noticed, the big hammer rested at full cock.

Brennen's voice lowered an octave, but seemed to quaver a little. "This is not the Army's affair neither, and if you'll look back over your shoulder, you'll see my friend McTavish has a Winchester leveled on your skinny back."

McGloughlan managed a wide smile. "I know where he is, but that won't keep me from blowing a hole in your chest that you could ride that mule through, should you draw a gun on my friend there . . . or me for that matter."

Brennen studied him. The man looked a little daft, red-haired and freckle-faced, smiling at him that way. Brennen dropped his hand away from the butt of the revolver. "There's no reason to get everybody worked up here." He turned back to the boy. "Now, young friend, I asked you a civil question—"

"Not so damned civil," Sean said, feeling a little smug now that he had considerable help.

"Well, maybe not." Brennen smiled. "But now, where are you from and what's your name?"

"Go ahead and answer him, son," Grigsby suggested.

Sean glanced up at a lone crow circling the chicken pen out back of the dry-goods store. "I'm George Crow, from the Judith country. I'm headin' downriver to pick up a riverboat to join my kin on the Mississippi."

Brennen shook his head. "Wrong time of year for that kind of journey. Try again?"

"Downriver to catch a boat," Sean said. "Can I get inside and warm up now?"

"No. You pass a cattle herd back a ways?"

"They're three or more miles back. They'll be two . . . three, maybe four hours before they wander in. I rode well around them, as I didn't recognize the outfit and it don't pay to ride up on strangers. My pa tol' me to mind my own affair out here."

Brennen continued to eye the boy, but seemed satisfied.

"You get on inside and varm up, son," Hauptmann said, who'd walked up for the last of the exchange. After Sean disappeared into the dry-goods store, Hauptmann turned his attention to Brennen. "We don't vant no trouble here, mister. Now you gather up yer friends if'n your vantin' some breakfast."

"Damn near mid-morning," Brennen snapped.

"You can save yer two bits, you don't want no pork chops and eggs, none of my elk sausage, or no more of Siglinda's strudel," Hauptmann said.

Brennen spun on his heel. "I'll fetch the others." Then he paused and turned back to Grigsby, who was carefully watching him. "It ain't over 'twixt you and me, breed."

Grigsby merely gave him a tight smile. After he walked away, Grigsby sheathed the knife he'd been holding out of sight behind his leg. He had no intention of letting Brennen draw on him, even though Brennen thought Barton Grigsby was ready to go for his revolver. Then he walked to the saloon door, where McGloughlan stood watching the big man stomp off. "I hear he's a real hand with them hog-legs he wears," Grisgby offered.

"Have to be to beat a cocked gun four feet from his belly," McGloughlan said, a wry smile on his face. "When he called you 'breed,' I thought you was gonna go for your own gun."

"Why? I'm proud of my blood: I got the best of both of 'um. You ready to eat?" Grigsby asked, returning the smile.

"Born ready," McGloughlan said, and pushed his way back inside where Mrs. Hauptmann had loaded both tables with an abundance of food. Sean was already in place, loading his plate.

Kev waited patiently, if a little nervously, for Sean to return. It was well after noon when he saw the boy working his way out of the thicket to the south. He rode up with a smile on his face, but without the mule.

"Why're you coming in from the south?" Kev asked.

"I told them fellers I was going downriver to try and catch a riverboat to the Mississippi, and hung myself on my own petard. That big one with the bandoliers crossing his chest was acting ugly enough, and I sure didn't want him following me when I backtracked."

"He give you some trouble?"

"Nothing I couldn't lie my way around. I never knew I was so good at it. I might just become a politician. Lucky there was an Army scout and a fella in uniform there, and they took up for me."

"So, they're there? McTavish and Brennen?"

"Sure enough. One with a big black beard and the real big one what gave me trouble and another Frenchman. I was as close as me and you for a couple hours."

"Anyone else in town?"

"Just Mr. and Mrs. Hauptmann, who own the store, and their man Tobias, and a couple of other families. . . . The other men are wolf hunters . . . and hide hunters. Didn't see hide nor hair of them folks. Boy howdy, that Mrs. Hauptmann can cook. I figured it would be real suspicious if'n I didn't join them at the table."

Kev smiled. "Real suspicious all right. Did you leave the mule?"

"Nope, rode out to the east toward the Big Horn, then soon as I got in the willow thicket, turned up-river and staked the mule out. I beat a trail getting back here and didn't want to drag him. Figured we could pick him up on our way out of town, or I could go fetch him."

"You did right."

Kev yelled to Chad and Badger-Man to join them from where they were tightening the herd up, and moved over to where Caitlin sat by the still-roaring fire. She had removed a pair of woolen petticoats and had them hanging by the fire to dry. She rose and moved over to where Kev and Sean sat their horses.

Kev eyed her carefully. How could a woman who'd just crossed a freezing river, and ridden two weeks on a hard trail surrounded by savages and bears and wolves, and slept on the ground, still move like she had a room full of violins playing for her own personal dance? He'd never seen anything like this lady, and wondered if he ever would again. It gave him a real sinking feeling, thinking that she might be leaving soon—*if* they could get by McTavish and Brennen and the remaining Frenchman.

Badger-Man and Chad reined up beside them.

"They're there," Kev said. "Now what?"

"Well," Chad said, his voice low and determined, "we can't go around with those bluffs and high country to the south, and we sure as hell don't need to cross the river again." He shrugged his shoulders. "So I guess I go into town and clear out the rats." He looked up at the gray dappled sky. "It's as good a day as any for those scum to die."

Chapter 18

"Then we all go. Agreed?" Kev looked to Badger-Man, who nodded in agreement. Then as an afterthought, he added, "Sean, you've done enough . . . no, you're going to stay and watch out for Caitlin as that's the most important job." Then he added before the boy had a chance to complain, "Now tell us all you can about the layout of things."

Colin McQuade was pleased with himself. So far he was making out just fine. He had a pile of hides in the barn to work with, he had his draw-down table, and his saddle was coming along fine. He had Pa's old scattergun that they'd kept in the barn, and plenty of buckshot and powder. Dugan had managed to salvage some potatoes, turnips, and carrots out of the root cellar, some of them half cooked, but that didn't matter as they froze up just fine, and he had a fat whitetail hanging in the barn alongside four cords of split wood.

He'd managed to hobble outside to check the remnants of the herd, and was pleased to see them fat and sassy, working on the huge pile of meadow hay that Dugan had opened up to them by tearing down the fence. A huge sheet of ice was beginning to form up the side hill where the hot spring on up the mountain flowed and cooled, and the snow was well beaten down where the cattle had been working their way up the mountain to water, and the river down below was accessible, still not frozen over. All in all, if things stayed status quo, they could make it through the winter with no problem.

When he ran out of meat, which he would before Christmas, if his brother and son didn't make it back, he could kill an old cow with the scattergun, let it freeze where it fell, go out every once in a while and hack a chunk off if the wolves or coyotes or a cougar didn't find it, and that would last him until spring. And almost as important to him right now, he had work to do. Getting the cow hides they had stored away ready for saddles and bridles was work enough.

He studied the skirts and fenders on the saddle on the draw-down table, pleased with himself. Now to form the leather around cantle and forks, the hardest part of the process.

If only Brigid was here to see what he had accomplished.

Sergeant Orin Starkey stood at attention across the makeshift table from Colonel Nelson Miles.

"The kitchen is replenished, sir."

"So, Sergeant, what sign of hostiles?"

"Only scattered small groups, sir. No more than a half dozen at any one time."

"And they didn't harass you?"

"No sir, fact is, all we saw was track."

"Any other incidents of note?"

Starkey cut his eyes away as he answered. "Nothing, sir. We passed the McQuade cattle herd ten or so days ago. They seemed to be making fine time and I'd estimate them here in under a week."

"We need those cattle, Sergeant. You check with Lieutenant Baldwin and make sure he agrees, but your orders are to get a good night's sleep, then march out with a small squad of men, say a half dozen, to intercept the McQuade herd and make sure they make this last few days in safely. The hostiles want those cattle as surely as do we. Escort them in, you understand?"

"Yes, sir. If I may, sir?"

"Go ahead, Sergeant."

"I burned my hand real bad . . . er . . . falling into the campfire, sir. It seems to be festering."

Miles rose and walked around the table. "Bare the hand, Sergeant."

Starkey pulled off his gauntlet and held the hand out for Miles's inspection. His other hand was in his trouser pocket, fumbling with the little red-and-purple-colored shell he'd taken from the McQuade house. He now considered it his lucky piece. But this time it didn't work so well.

"Seems to be healing fine, Sergeant. If you prefer, I can put you on wood detail."

"No, sir, escort is just fine. You do want us to go mounted?"

"No, Sergeant. I said *march* out. We're infantry, and we travel afoot. Wagons for supplies are one thing, but this is another. Get an early start. Draw two weeks rations and a hundred rounds per man."

"Yes, sir," Starkey said respectfully, but the disgusted look on his face said it all.

"You're excused," Miles snapped. Then his tone changed. "Good job getting the supplies here. Do the same good work as escort. We need those beeves."

"Yes, sir." Starkey saluted and spun on his heel.

Then Miles stopped him again. "Sergeant, take a pair of scissors to those dundrearies. Two-inch length will do just fine."

"Yes, sir," Starkey said, closing the office door with a little too much enthusiasm as he left.

Miles shook his head as Starkey left. The man had been a shirker ever since he'd been under Miles's command, and Miles had little respect for him . . . except when he was trying to save his own hide. Miles had noticed that adversity brought out both the best and worst in Starkey. The best was he was a capable fighting man when his back was to the wall, but the worst was he wasn't a company man. He seemed to operate only for the good of Sergeant Orin Starkey. And Miles had learned long ago, that was a condition that couldn't be trained or marched out of a man. Every man for himself was not the infantry way.

But it sure as hell seemed to be Orin Starkey's way.

McTavish was back in his position at the hay door in the loft of the stable, Frenchy in the window of the abandoned building across the way from the dry-goods store and saloon, and Brennen was inside the store itself, at a west-facing window, all of them carefully watching for the first signs of the herd. They had yet to see Chad Steel among the drovers, but knew the woman, at least a woman, had been with them, and knew another Indian rode with them.

It was mid-afternoon before the bell cow and a few

head of cattle began to filter out of the willows down-stream from the little town.

The Hauptmanns had watched the activity of Mc-Tavish and his men with interest and concern, and finally Siglinda Hauptmann walked over to look out the window next to Brennen, while Gustav Hauptmann continued to work behind the counter.

"You vatching for someones?" Siglinda asked.

"Nope, just watching the crows sail around," Brennen said sarcastically.

Siglinda eyed him with a little contempt. "Ve don't vant no trouble here, Mr. Brennen. That glass vas hauled a long vay upriver, and I von't have it shot out. You take yer guns and go on down the road, if you be vaiting for trouble."

Brennen brought his face closer to hers. "I'll open this window when and if the time comes. You're a fine cook, Mrs. Hauptmann. I'd suggest you get on back to your kitchen and leave man's work to us."

"Not if it concerns Mr. Hauptmann and me, Mr. Brennen. Now, you take yer guns and go."

Brennen ignored her and turned his attention to the storekeeper, who was wiping down his inventory of canned goods, but carefully watching Brennen's every move. "Hauptmann, if'n you don't want me to help this cacklin' hen of yours back to her kitchen, I'd suggest you do it."

Gustav Hauptmann hurried around the counter, took his wife by the arm, and escorted her back to her kitchen. Brennen could hear muffled talk, then Hauptmann returned.

"Yer not velcome here, Brennen," Hauptmann said, but his voice was not nearly so convincing as his wife's; in fact, it seemed a little tremulous.

"You'll just keep your pants on, Hauptmann," Brennen snarled at him, "if'n you know what's good for you. We got a little business, then we're off for Bozeman."

"Soon, I hope," Hauptmann managed.

"Couldn't be to soon for me," Brennen said, continuing to watch out the window, now carefully studying the herd that was beginning to work its way out of the willow thicket over four hundred yards from where he gazed intently.

In the loft, McTavish had been dozing. The three fat pork chops, sausage, biscuits, gravy, hen's eggs, and generous double portion of apple strudel he'd consumed were crying out to him to take a nap, but the pounding going on in the stable below conspired to keep him awake. The Army corporal and his smart-mouth friend, the scout, had discovered one of their horses shy a shoe, and were busily pumping Hauptmann's bellows and, with the black's help, shaping a new shoe.

McTavish yawned broadly, leaving his Winchester in his lap and spreading his arms wide. His yawn was cut short when the blade of Sleeps-in-Day's knife slid across his throat, and opened a smiling, gushing gap from ear to ear.

He saw the blood splash across his lap and the Winchester, but could do nothing but gargle. He tried to rise, but firm hands held him in place.

Very close to his ear, someone whispered, "That was the blade of man you kill, my friend, Sleeps-in-Day. He smiles as you die."

Badger-Man had managed to slip into the rear of the livery without being seen by the three men working intently at the forge and bellows, climbing into the loft without them seeing. He had no idea who they were, or if they were friends of the three who'd taken Sleeps-in-Day's spirit from him. But McQuade had cautioned him, harm no one other than the man with the black hair on his face, the man with one ear, or the man with the knit hat and Hudson Bay coat. Badger-Man, now in McTavish's position at the hayloft door, saw McQuade slip from the brush behind the abandoned log house, and move to a rear window. McQuade rose to where he could see inside, then vaulted through.

Kev lit inside, only a half-dozen paces from where the Frenchman, Andre Toulouse, was watching out the far window, his lever-action weapon leaning on the windowsill. Toulouse tried to spin, but his rifle struck the window mullion, and he found himself with his weapon still pointing outside and his body facing a man with a cocked and ready rifle leveled on his chest.

"*Sacre bleu,*" he managed.

"I'm not sure what that means," Kev said, "but I'm at least sure it means you're laying that weapon down."

Toulouse started to move so the weapon would clear the mullion, but stopped when Kev shook his head. "Grab it with one hand, by the barrel, and lay it aside."

He did so, carefully and slowly. "Now what?" the Frenchman asked.

"Now two-finger the revolver out and lay it beside the rifle."

He did so, looking as if he'd like to make a move. "I'd love to decorate the wall with your guts,

Frenchman, for the sake of the man you left tied to that tree."

Toulouse extended both hands, palm out, in supplication, and carefully rose to a standing position.

Kev motioned him away from the weapons. "You and your friends been laying in wait for me and mine. The next time I see you, I'll shoot you down for the coyote you are. You leave those weapons lay, walk out that back door, and go to running. Don't stop so long as you're in sight of this town, and then keep moving. We'll be gone tomorrow, only then can you come back and get your horse and weapons. I just watched the friend of the man you left tied to that pine open *your* friend McTavish up like a can of tomatoes. McTavish won't be going with you. Unless you want me to turn the Indian loose on you, you'll stay away until we're long gone, and never be seen by me again. Understand."

"*Oui.* I'll never get back to zee Bozeman without my horse and guns."

"Come back tomorrow, after we're long gone."

Toulouse headed for the back door.

"By the way," Kev said, "tell your boss, Tolofsen, that Kev and Colin McQuade will be there in three weeks with his money, and to fight shy of the Rocky Butte Ranch in the meantime."

"*Oui.*" He again started out.

"Hey, you might as well tell him that his wife is on her way to St. Louis, and he won't be a married man shortly after she gets there. An annulment, I believe they call it."

Toulouse nodded, then slipped through the back door.

"Don't slow down," Kev called after him.

Kev moved to the front door of the abandoned house. From where he was he could not see the side window of the dry-goods store, but he could see Chad Steel move around the building and slip into the saloon door.

Quickly, he moved to the front door, checked to see that Badger-Man had a clear view of him and the street, waved at him and got a nod in return, then bolted across to the boardwalk, up to the door, and inside.

He left his long gun on the saloon floor, palmed his Colt, and met the still-swinging batwing door and pushed his way into the dry-goods store.

"You too," a voice rang out. Kev was surprised at the scene that met him. Two older folks, looking as if they were the shopkeepers as both wore aprons, stood behind the store counter, both holding double-barrel shotguns. Kev presumed they were the Hauptmanns Sean had mentioned. The man's scattergun was leveled on the man Kev presumed to be the gunfighter, Brennen, and the woman's on Chad Steel, and now Kev as he was only four feet behind.

"You too," the woman's voice repeated. "Put that pistol back in your holster, and take yer trouble out of my store."

"You Steel?" Brennen asked, his voice low and cold.

"I am," Chad answered, "and you're the low-life scum that's been dogging our trail."

"No, I'm the man what's taking you and your daughter back to Bozeman."

Chapter 19

"Outside" the woman said to the ominous sound of her cocking both barrels of the scattergun.

"Sounds like we take this outside," Kev said quietly.

"You two," the man in the apron said, obviously speaking to Kev and Chad, "you back through the saloon doors and go out the front vay."

As Chad and Kev complied, they overheard the man instruct Brennen. "You go through Siglinda's kitchen, out the back vay. And don't be coming back."

Chad and Kev moved through the front door of the saloon, Kev recovering his rifle on the way. Chad whispered, "Go around that way, I'll take the other."

They were to circle the building, and hopefully, catch the gunfighter between them.

As Kev made his way between the saloon and the livery, he was out of sight of Badger-Man in the loft, and to his surprise another man stepped out of the back door of the livery. His eyes widened as he saw Kev, and he snaked his side arm smoothly out of his holster.

"What are you up to, neighbor?" he asked, his gun half raised.

Kev too held his rifle only half pointing at the man.

"The name's Kevin McQuade, and I'm pushing that cattle herd back there, heading this way. A couple of lowlifes have been giving us trouble, and we're about to make sure this is the end of it. And who might you be?"

"The name's Grigsby, Barton Grigsby. Army scout. And I got no love lost for those three, if it's Brennen and McTavish and that Frenchman you're stalkin'?"

"Well, that herd's going to the Army, so let me be so I can get this over and get on with the deliverin'."

"My pleasure," Grigsby said, reholstering his revolver as another man, in Army uniform, stepped out beside him.

As Kev moved forward, he could hear Grigsby explaining what he knew to the uniformed man.

Chad Steel had gotten ahead of Kev in rounding the building, and when Kev got to the rear, Chad was standing facing him with a puzzled look on his face. He shrugged, just as the privy door, twenty feet beyond where he stood, swung aside and the flash of a muzzle and roar and bellow of black powder smoke roiled out of the doorway.

Chad stumbled forward, shot in the back, but didn't go down.

Brennen charged out the door, a pistol in each hand. He fired again at Chad Steel, who'd spun but was backing away and firing his revolver.

Kev shot at the big man, at no more than thirty feet, and could not believe that he didn't go down.

Brennen swung his guns on Kev, as Kev levered

in to fire again. He dropped to one knee as he did so, and felt something burn his shoulder and spin him halfway around. Again he fired the Winchester, this time knowing he hit the big man as he stumbled backward. Kev glanced at Chad, who was also on his knees, one hand clutching his chest, one hand still firing the revolver.

Kev fired again, and Brennen went to his back, but he rolled and tried to regain his footing. Chad moved forward on his knees, firing time and again as Kev levered in and this time aimed carefully, the big bullet striking the big gunfighter in the side of his head, knocking him decisively into the mud, and stilling him.

The smell of gunpowder hung in the air, and the crack of gunshots echoed off the distant bluffs; then silence reigned supreme.

Kev regained his feet and ran to kneel beside Chad Steel, who was now on his back.

His amber eyes centered on Kev as red spread across his white shirt and soaked his waistcoat.

Chad's voice was little more than a whisper. "Kev, take care of Caitlin."

"Let's get you inside," Kev said, his throat thick.

"No. I've seen . . . my last . . . and it makes no difference. The only thing that matters . . . is that you . . . take care of Caitlin." His face went ashen, even as he smiled slightly, thinking of his daughter.

"I will," Kev said, reaching down to take Chad's hand.

"Swear it," Chad managed, nodding almost imperceptibly, a trickle of blood now running from the corner of his mouth.

"It's the easiest thing I've ever sworn to," Kev said with all the sincerity he could muster.

"See her . . . safely to . . . St. Louis. The lawyer . . . Mortensen . . . has papers for her."

"I promise, Lawyer Mortensen. She'll get there safe and sound."

Chad's eyes closed, and his breathing became heavy and labored. Kev rose and ran to the back door of the dry-goods store, and met the Hauptmanns there.

"I need a blanket for this man," Kev said.

"You be needin' a coffin for that man . . . for both of them, looks like," Mr. Hauptmann said. "And you'll be needin' some work on that shoulder."

Kev for the first time realized he'd been shot through the meaty part of his left shoulder and was bleeding freely. He turned back to see Chad Steel's arm relax from across his chest, and fall to the mud and snow beside him with finality.

He moved back across the few feet, and again knelt beside the man who'd become his friend over the last three weeks, again taking his hand, only this time it was limp. Carefully, reverently, Kev crossed Chad's hands on his chest, removed his hat, and placed it over his face, as it was clear Chad Steel had gone to meet his maker.

Kev rose and walked over to where the big gun-fighter lay, shot four times in the chest and once in the head. Even though he knew the man was clearly dead, Kev couldn't help but rear back and kick him squarely in the side. "You son of a bitch," Kev said.

"No need for that," Mr. Hauptmann said.

Kev moved back to the Hauptmanns. "This man's

daughter is back there with my cattle. You get this man inside and get him cleaned up and laid out proper before I get back here with her, you understand, and have that other son of a bitch out of sight . . . in the livery, or your dump, or somewheres where Caitlin doesn't have to lay eyes on him."

"That vill be a dollar," the woman said.

"You'll get your dollar, and you'll get a hell of a lot more if it's not done right, understand?"

"No need for threats, young man, or for that kind of language in front of my wife," Hauptmann said. "I'm Gustav Hauptmann, and ve own dis place."

"It's not a threat, Mr. Hauptmann, it's a by-God promise. Have him presentable for his daughter, who loves him very much, by the time we get back." Kev started away, then hesitated and turned back. "I apologize for my language, but this is a black day. You get him cleaned up and presentable. He's a gentleman . . . a gentleman who liked a clean white shirt."

"I vill take care," Hauptmann said, hurrying to Chad's side, while Mrs. Hauptmann moved to Kev and demanded he remove his shirt. He did so, and she did an expert job of packing, patching, and wrapping the wound, and the bleeding was quickly quelled.

Kev, a little unsteady on his feet, made his way back to the livery to make sure Badger-Man was all right, then saw that he wasn't. He was up against the livery wall, his arms raised, with both Grigsby and the soldier holding rifles on him.

"Here now, he's with me," Kev yelled out, and ran to stand beside them.

"He took a knife to McTavish up in the loft,"

Grigsby said, giving Kev a doubting look. "He did a mighty fine job of it too."

"He's my drover, and if you want your cattle to the Tongue River, you'll leave him be. He was acting on my orders."

"If you say so, but we'll take this up with Miles when we get back."

"Take it up with the Heavenly Father Himself if you want, but no harm's going to come to Badger-Man so long as I'm breathing."

Both of them lowered their weapons. "What was all the shooting?" Grigsby asked, the semblance of a smile on his face. "Looks like you took a bullet. Soon as the scared wears off, that's gonna go to hurtin'."

"The Hauptmanns can tell you what went on. I've got to get back to the herd and tell a daughter that she no longer has a father."

"Brennen?" Grigsby asked.

"Brennen's the son of a bitch that back-shot him, but he's ready to be fed to the hogs."

"Good," Grigsby said as Kev hurried to his horse.

When Kev and Badger-Man rode up, Caitlin and Sean were both at the back of the herd, moving them quietly along as agreed.

"You're hurt," she said, a worried and apprehensive look on her face.

"It's just a flesh wound, and it'll heal. . . ." Then his tone softened. "But Caitlin, it's worse than that." Kev dismounted, and walked to the side of her horse.

"My father?" she asked, but the haunted look in her eyes said she knew the answer.

"Yes," he said with a tentative nod. Then she slipped off the sidesaddle and into his one good arm.

He held her for a long time, with no one saying anything as she buried her face in his chest and silently sobbed. Then she looked up. "I heard the shooting, and something inside told me. I prayed to God it wasn't both of you."

"Brennen and McTavish are deservedly dead. I ran the Frenchman off, and we've seen the last of him."

"Did he go hard? Father, I mean?"

"No, his last words were of you . . . that he loved you and that I was to take care of you."

Again, she buried her face in Kev's chest. After a long while, she raised her tearstained face. "Can I go see him now?"

"Yes, he's being well taken care of by some nice folks who own the dry-goods store. Let's go in."

Barton Grigsby and Corporal Brian McGloughlan rode south out of Big Horn City, away from the Yellowstone, along the Big Horn River, after Kev had reported to them his seeing several hundred Indian tracks heading south, and only a few miles back.

They moved upriver as quickly as their mounts could carry them without killing the animals. By nightfall they'd traveled a dozen miles, and they made another hard slogging dozen before the next midday, after making a cold camp and leaving well before dawn. It was there they cut the track Barton had been looking for.

"I knew they'd be crossing to the Big Horn, and heading farther east. And I'll bet a month's pay, it's Sitting Bull and his bunch."

"How do you figure?" McGloughlan asked.

"'Cause Miles thought he was heading to the Grandmother country, Canada. The young fox let him believe that, and probably planted the thought in the minds of whoever was giving Miles information. He'll head south, but southeast like this here track shows. Due south would take him up into the Yellowstone country, too damn high and too damn cold for a bunch of women and little ones. Nope, it's probably somewhere high up on the Buffalo Tongue, which don't rise nearly so high in elevation as the Yellowstone. And there's plenty of game seems to winter there."

"So, now what?" McGloughlan asked.

"We're going to follow them another dozen miles or so, and if we don't cut their camp, we'll swing south and follow the Yellowstone back to the cantonment and report to Miles. To my way of thinkin', it's up the Buffalo Tongue he'll want to go, if'n he wants to catch this bunch."

"He wants 'em all," McGloughlan said. "Ever' last one of them."

"Let's move. By midnight, day after tomorrow, we can be in the cantonment kitchen sippin' that hot mud the cook calls coffee."

With that, Grigsby spurred his horse into the Big Horn River, following the track of unshod horses and travois southeast. Up and out of the Big Horn drainage.

In a clean white shirt provided by Gustav Hauptmann, Chad Steel was buried on a knoll overlooking the confluence of the Big Horn and the Yellowstone Rivers.

They had all had their hot baths the night before, but it was without the joy that might have been. Caitlin took hers in a leather tub in the privacy of Mrs. Hauptmann's bedroom, while Kev and Sean used the same tub later in the kitchen behind the dry-goods store.

Badger-Man was happy with a pot of hot water, retiring to the livery, where he shared a room off the stalls with Tobias.

By noon, after the words were said over Chad Steel, and a simple cross was erected on his grave, they were again on the trail, pushing northeast, less than fifty miles from where the beeves were to be delivered to the 5th Infantry.

Kev had tried to hire Tobias to accompany them, as they were now down to the four of them, Kev, Sean, Badger-Man, and Caitlin, but the Hauptmanns had insisted they couldn't spare him. Kev even checked with the other two occupied cabins in Big Horn City, hoping their menfolk had returned, but they were still out poisoning wolves and there was no sign of them, nor did they have any adult children who could be hired out.

It was up to the four of them.

Chapter 20

Kev rode drag with Caitlin as they let the bell cow pick her own way, and as Badger-Man took one flank and Sean the other. The crossing of the Big Horn had been easy, with the river only belly-deep on the horses. Caitlin was able to lift her skirts and ankles and avoid getting wet at all, and it was a good thing, as it was even colder than it had been when they crossed the Yellowstone.

For almost two hours Caitlin talked about her upbringing; her mother who she'd never known and who'd died in childbirth; her mammy, the black woman who'd raised her; and her father. It was obvious, even more so than Kev had already surmised, that Caitlin Steel had worshiped her father, but not so much as to not go against his wishes from time to time. Kev got the impression that she did so to get her father's attention, as she continually said how hard he worked and how so often he'd been away from their home in St. Louis.

Kev let her talk, knowing it was probably better than weeping, not that she didn't fall to that from time to time.

Finally, after a long silence, Kev asked her? "You know a lawyer named Mortensen?"

"Yes, Edgar Mortensen, in St. Louis."

"Your father said he would have papers for you. Right before he passed."

"Mr. Mortensen was a good friend of Father's. I'm sure he has Father's will, among other things."

Again there was a long silence. Then Kev added, "How about his business there? You going to sell it, or . . . ?"

She seemed to carefully consider her answer. "Father would never let me spend any time there, and would not like the thought of me running the place. So, I don't know what I'm going to do."

Again there was a long pause, before Kev cleared his throat and turned to her. She met his gaze with those deep amber eyes. He was hesitant, and cut his eyes away from hers as he asked, "Would you ever consider . . . ?" He seemed to choke on his words, then cleared his throat and began again. "Have you thought of . . . ?" About that time, a steer bawled, and Kev saw a half dozen break away from the flank of the herd, unseen by Sean, and move into the brush.

"Damn knot-heads," he said, and spurred his horse, leaving Caitlin wondering what he was trying to ask.

The next morning, and for three days following, the sun shined, but the cold was penetrating; then the day before Kev figured they would reach the cantonment, the wind picked up and the snow came in earnest.

It had been an uneventful four days, until now. Kev had never returned to his conversation with Caitlin, always changing the subject when she brought up what he'd been trying to ask. He was attentive to her every want and need, but also he had to attend to the cattle. They slept, each in their own bedroll, but under a common pack tarp, with Caitlin tucked between Kev and Sean. Kev awoke one morning with Caitlin's arm thrown over him. He lay in bed for an hour past when he normally would have arisen, enjoying the nearness of her and the familiarity of her arm across his chest.

Midday on the third day out of Big Horn City, Sergeant Orin Starkey and a troop of six men marched up alongside the herd.

Without fanfare, Starkey advised Kev that three of his men would take the point, afoot, and two, including himself, would march on the flanks. The soldiers camped apart from Kev and the others, keeping their own counsel, acting only as escort, except for the first night they were there. Starkey had appeared in camp, just after supper, his hair and whiskers slicked down, and clumsily invited Caitlin to take a stroll down by the river. She politely refused, and he left in a bit of a huff, his fists clenched at his sides. That same afternoon, Barton Grigsby and Corporal Brian McGloughlan rode up alongside the drive. But they didn't tarry, wanting to get news of the large band of hostiles back to Miles.

The last morning the drovers awoke under eight inches of fresh snow.

"This should be the last day's drive," Kev assured Caitlin as she worked to make a breakfast fire.

That morning, Starkey walked over to the drovers' camp. "We should make the cantonment just after midday," he announced tersely.

"Won't be any too soon for me," Kev said. It was all that Starkey had to say, and he quickly returned to his position on the flank, waiting for them to begin moving the herd out.

Later, riding drag with Caitlin, both of them wrapped as if they were beginning an Artic expedition, with coats flapping in the hard wind and hats pulled low over their faces, Caitlin got a faraway look in her eye, then turned to Kev, having to almost shout to be heard. "So Kev McQuade, will this be the last day I have the pleasure of your company?"

"I have to get the money I collect from this herd back to Bozeman, Caitlin." A slight smile crossed his face. "We owe some no-account banker there a few hundred dollars."

"Mark . . . Mark Tolofsen of Bozeman Merchants and Miners?"

"One and the same."

"You can't just go riding into Bozeman, Kev. The Frenchman will have gone back there, and Mark will know all about what's happened."

"So?"

"So, Mark Tolofsen knows the law and the judges in Bozeman. Two of Mark's men have died. It won't be safe for you there."

"He's got to be paid, Caitlin, or he'll own the Rocky Butte."

"I'm afraid for you."

"Don't be. I'm in the right; everything your father and I did was in the right."

There was a long quiet time before she said in a low tone, just loud enough to be heard over the howling wind, "Oftentimes a man's been right, all the way to the grave."

"Still and all, I have to go."

"And your promise to my father?" she said, her tone a little accusatory.

"I plan to keep it, but you'll have to wait here at the cantonment for me to go back to Rocky Butte, and to Bozeman. It could be spring before I can get back here."

"That's a lot to ask, Kev."

"I know it is," was all he said. Then he added, "Of course, you could go back with me."

"I can't do that, Kev. I've gotten away from Mark, at great cost. I can't go back now. Besides, I have business to take care of in St. Louis."

"Well, then, I guess that corks it," he said as he spurred the buckskin and rode up to the point.

Miles assigned Caitlin one of the officer's rooms and had two of his majors room together. Kev and Sean were assigned quarters in the soldiers' barracks, and Badger-Man camped with Barton Grigsby away from the other Indian scouts as they were Crow, and his people had no love lost for the Crow. Even though Grigsby was half Crow, his white half had come to like Badger-Man, who was rapidly taking on white man's ways.

That first night, Caitlin, Kev, and Sean were invited to dine with Colonel Nelson Miles and the majors who'd been inconvenienced to make room for Caitlin.

In honor of Caitlin's attendance, the table had a clean white cloth, crockery rather than tin plates, and there was even an arrangement of dried flowers adorning the center of the setting.

After they'd enjoyed the first course of soup, a

bullion, while one of the handsome majors was re-
galing Caitlin with tales of Indian wars in Texas, Kev
broached a new subject to his host. "I'd appreciate
being paid in the morning, Colonel. This weather
is worsening, and we have a long hard ride back upriver."

"What's your hurry, Mr. McQuade?" Miles asked.
"Is my hospitality so bad?"

"No, sir, it sure isn't," he said as a well-browned
steaming roast, roiling a mouthwatering odor, was
placed on the table—centered among a large platter of potatoes, onions, and carrots. Another bowl
held bubbling brown gravy, and yet another dried
apples that had been boiled and reconstituted to
plump perfection. Fresh fat golden-brown dinner
rolls adorned the bread plate at the side of each of
their crockery plates.

Miles eyed Kev with interest. "Then why don't
you let me make a proposal to you?"

"What's that, Colonel?"

"Barton Grigsby, whom I believe you know, has
reported a large movement of hostiles, just what
I've been waiting to hear. We'll be moving out very
soon, up the Tongue River in pursuit of that body
of Indians, and I'd like to have fresh meat along for
my men. I'll pay you and your nephew here, and
your other man, handsomely to drive and care for
three-or four-dozen head of beef. I'll provide you
with two wagons, six ups, and drivers to haul fod-
der, to ease your job."

"You mean go along on your campaign?" Kev
shook his head. "Can't do that, Colonel. I have to
get this money back to Bozeman . . . to a bank
there. Our very ranch may depend upon it."

Miles was silent for a long while. "Can you trust young Sean here to get it back?"

"I wouldn't ask young Sean to do that. It's too tough and too dangerous a trip for a youngster . . . in fact, for anyone alone."

"But you would trust him to deliver the money?"

Kev smiled at his young nephew, who was following the conversation with interest. "I'd trust him with just about anything after they way he handled himself on this trip."

"Then sending him on alone is your only concern."

"I guess that's true."

"Good, then it's settled. I have a troop of two-dozen men marching out to Bozeman in the morning, accompanied by a wagon and four-up. Sergeant Starkey, who I believe you've met as he was in charge of acquiring the cattle, and of the troop who escorted you in, returned from Bozeman with the report that three of our men, deserters, were being held in the Bozeman jail for some petty theft, and I want them back here for Army punishment. Young Sean can accompany the soldiers, your money will be well protected and assured of getting to Bozeman, and you and your Indian drover can work for me for a few weeks."

"I don't know—"

"I'll pay you packer's wages, Mr. McQuade. That's six dollars a day since you have your own animals, and I'll pay your man as a scout."

"That's a lot of money, Colonel, but I still have to get back."

Miles tone hardened. "You know there's the matter of a hearing regarding your man, Badger-Face or whatever he's called, for killing a white man."

Kev's tone grew even harder than that of Miles. "Badger-*Man* did that at my orders, and for good reason. In fact, he was acting in my stead, and if he's to have a hearing, then I should also. He's no less or no more guilty of that man's death than I am . . . not that it wasn't well justified."

There was a long silence; then Miles smiled and changed the subject. "Sergeant Starkey was authorized to pay up to nine dollars a head for good fat beef on the hoof. What did the McQuades settle for?"

Kev cleared his throat, then rather sheepishly admitted, "Seven dollars."

"How about I make it *nine* for every head delivered. That's another three hundred and eighty dollars or so, plus six dollars a day for every day you spend on the campaign with us. I understand you lost some cattle to hostiles, and that will help make up . . . in fact will more than make up for that loss. I want fresh beef for my men on this very tough assignment. . . . Can you afford to turn that down?"

Kev thought for a moment. He knew what his sister-in-law, Brigid, would say, that this was when two fools met, the one who upped the price, and one who didn't take it, if he should turn it down. Another four or five hundred dollars would go a long way on the Rocky Butte.

He smiled at the colonel. "And you'll pay in the morning, in gold coin, so Sean and your troop can be on their way?"

"I'll pay the original seven agreed upon. You'll

have to wait for the other two until we return and you've fulfilled your side of the bargain."

"And you'll concede the fact that Badger-Man was acting on my orders, and to protect the Army herd?"

"We'll still have a short hearing, for the sake of the record, but my recommendation will be in his favor." Miles smiled. "And my recommendation seems to carry a little weight around here."

"And Mrs. Tolofsen can wait here in comfort until we get back?" Kev glanced at Caitlin, who gave him a broad smile.

"She could do that under any circumstance. Under the full protection of the 5th Infantry."

"In that case, Colonel, I don't know how I can refuse." Kev extended his hand and shook with Miles.

When the supper was over, and the men had finished their brandy and cigars, and they'd said their good-byes and expressed their gratitude to the colonel, one of the handsome majors offered to escort Caitlin back to her quarters. Laughing for the first time since getting news of her father's death, she turned those beautiful amber eyes on Kev. "Thank you, Major, but Mr. McQuade has already promised to see me home, in fact all the way home to St. Louis."

"I'll walk you to your quarters," Sean interrupted, with boyish enthusiasm.

"Thank you," Caitlin said, pulling the boy to her and kissing him on the cheek, which immediately reddened as he flushed with embarrassment. All the men in the room chuckled, and he reddened even more. "But you need your rest, Sean Mc-Quade. Kev will walk me to my quarters."

Kev gave the major a stern yet triumphant nod, then smiled at Caitlin and offered his arm.

When they reached her door, with the wind howling and movement in the camp stilled and dark, but with clear skies overhead peppered with a million pricks of light, she turned to face Kev. "Thank you, Kev McQuade, for all you've done on this very difficult trip, for soothing my father's last moments, and for helping me through a terrible time."

She moved closer to him, her chest pressed against his. He looked down at her, his eyes only inches from hers, uncertain what she expected, until she coiled a slender hand around the back of his neck and pulled his lips down to meet hers. The kiss was long and thorough, and when they parted, he couldn't resist wrapping her up with his arms and lifting her off the ground, kissing her again until his own knees were weak, the frustration of spending weeks intimately close to her surfacing in the passion of that one moment.

When he returned her to the ground, she pushed away from him with a gasp, concern crossing her moonlit face. "Did I hurt . . . your shoulder?" she asked, a catch in her throat.

"No," he said, smiling slightly. "If I'd had an arm blown clean off, I'd wouldn't have noticed while I was kissing you."

"I'd better go in," she said, looking at him with liquid golden eyes each a pool of warmth, her breath quickening.

"I hope I didn't do anything . . . anything improper . . . " Kev stammered a little.

"I'm the one who's acting improperly, Kev Mc-Quade, and I don't care. But I'm going in now, while I can still save some semblance of propriety." She started to close the door, then hesitated and turned back long enough to say, "But I will tell you, McQuade is a much finer last name than Tolofsen, and I envy you that."

Her door closed quietly, and Kev stood for a long time outside considering what she'd said, until he regained his composure and his breathing quieted. Then he walked slowly back to the barracks.

Colin McQuade had trouble falling asleep, even through he'd had a long hard day. For the first time, he'd gone back to their house and poked through the ashes, now covered with a blanket of six inches of snow.

Flashes of disturbing memories kept niggling at him as he used his crutch to turn over scorched and burned items. Tears had come to his eyes more than once as familiar yet destroyed mementos were revealed to him. He gathered some of the shells Brigid had collected to take back to his cabin in the barn. Each one he picked up, most of them scorched and cracked, caused a catch and burning in his throat. He'd been so feverish and ill the day of the fire that he could barely remember the fire itself, or what had happened and who was there.

A strange but oddly familiar face kept coming to mind, a face he just couldn't tie to a name, a face that troubled him so much it made him physically ill to recollect.

It was a man, that was about all he could remember for sure; a big man, one not normally in the household. He put his face in his hands, and more came back to him. A man who was well dressed, but who lacked manners to match his clothes. For some strange reason, Colin had flashes of yelling, of trying to struggle out of his sickbed. Trying with all his might and concentration to get to the bedroom door, because something had been wrong, Brigid had been screaming.

Had it been the fire, or had it been something else?

What was it she had screamed?

All night long he intermittently awakened in a cold sweat, the blurred features of that big man, a man with whiskers, haunting him.

When he awoke again in the morning light, he feared he would not sleep well ever again, not until he tied that face to a name and recollected what it had to do with the day of the fire.

Chapter 21

Colonel Nelson Miles was furious. The scout Tom LaForge stood before him, a rather sheepish look on his face.

Only an hour before, a party of Sioux had ridden down the face of an embankment a mile or so from the cantonment, each carrying a lance topped with a white flag, each unarmed, carrying a peace pipe across his forearm.

LaForge was in charge of the Crow scouts, with over a hundred Crow camped away from the cantonment, between it and the embankment from which the Sioux approached.

Over two-dozen Crow met the oncoming Sioux, the Crow on foot, also appearing to be unarmed. The Crow approached the peace party with hands outstretched as if in greeting, then when hands were clasped, jerked the Sioux from their horses and fell upon them with formerly hidden knifes, killing each of the five, while another dozen sat atop the embankment, forced to watch the massacre, unable to do anything but ride down and become victims themselves.

Miles stammered, spittle flying in anger, "Finally, we get an . . . a damned opportunity for peace . . .

and your bloody treacherous Crow kill not only the Sioux, but probably all opportunity for any peaceful settlement with Crazy Horse and Sitting Bull."

"I never would have guessed they'd do such a thing, Colonel," LaForge said with a shrug.

"I want them stripped of all Army mounts and arms, do you understand?"

"Yes, sir. I've already taken their arms."

"Take their mounts, and any you know who participated in this travesty I want driven out of camp, on foot, with an escort to return them to their reservation—unless they have their own ponies they go afoot, understand?"

"Yes, sir. They may not make it out there in this damned cold, particularly without mounts." Laforge hesitated a moment, then added, "Of course, all the Crow knowed was that you wanted the Sioux caught or killed. They was doing what they thought you wanted done all along."

Miles shook his head, refusing LaForge's attempt to explain away the actions of the Crow. "The Sioux came in under a white flag. Run the damned Crow out. They'll have a better chance, even afoot, than they gave the Sioux. Damn the flies, the Sioux coming in on their own accord to parlay, and now it'll be hell to pay. They'll never trust my word again, and you have no idea how angry that makes me."

LaForge stood his ground. "We need them scouts, General."

"All right, damn it, keep the four best, so long as they don't have blood on their knives. But the others go."

LaForge spun on his heel and left the colonel's office as Miles yelled at his orderly, "Get my majors and lieutenants in here. We're marching out within a fortnight."

Kev had a sick feeling in his stomach as he watched Sean, his saddlebags full of gold coin, ride out following a marching troop of a dozen soldiers. Even though it meant a lot of money to the Rocky Butte, he couldn't help but wonder if he'd made the right decision.

He was somewhat reassured by the fact that Badger-Man had decided to go back with Sean. After the Crow had killed the Sioux peace party, Badger-Man couldn't abide being anywhere near the Crow. And Kev was just as happy that he couldn't as he trusted the man's skills, and knew that on the trip back to Rocky Butte he'd watch after Sean.

The good news was it gave Kev a week or more of leisure time to spend with Caitlin. And as that week wore on, they were able to take a few long walks, when the weather would permit, and spend many long hours in front of a potbelly stove, talking about what each of them wanted out of life, what they'd like in the way of a family, and even what they expected from a mate, even though there was no talk of marriage. They agreed on most everything, except as to where each of them wanted to live. Caitlin wanted the city life, at least wanted to be close enough that she could visit the city weekly, but Kev craved the ranch life, and the city meant little to him. Still, three more nightly kisses at her door brought him more and more to believe he couldn't live the rest of his life without her.

Things got a little busier for him the end of that

week, as a Sioux raiding party of a half-dozen men had swept down on the herd the night before they were scheduled to ride out, and driven off more than half the herd, along with two-dozen mules and a half-dozen horses. The two lone sentries were found with throats slit. The Indians had more than seven hours headstart.

Again, Colonel Miles was sputtering in anger.

He called Kev and Barton Grigsby to his office.

"I want you two to ride out and track that damned raiding party. I'm sending a squad of a dozen men with you, with instructions to capture or shoot down the raiders, and even if they can't, to make sure they don't get back up the Tongue with those cattle. Shoot the damned cattle and mules if you have to, rather than let the Sioux have them. Winter and hunger are our best allies, and it's *imperative* we don't let the Sioux have those cattle."

"Yes, sir," Grigsby said. "Can we have McGloughlan to command the troop?"

"You can. I've promoted him to sergeant, at Lieutenant Baldwin's recommendation. Be back on the Tongue within the week, wherever you think is the closest spot on the river that you can reach, and pick up our trail if we've passed, or wait if we haven't until we arrive, even if you don't catch up with those thieves. If you do, and you've got cattle and mules, have McGloughlan direct half his troop to move them back to the cantonment. Just in case, take tack along for a half dozen riders, who can mount the mules or horses. I'm moving out before dawn, with over four hundred men, two field pieces, and a half dozen wagons. I've got to use oxen on two of the wagons, as the damn Sioux drove off some of our good mules. That's going to slow us down. But we're going. It's time we ended this."

Grigsby scratched his chin. "That snow's getting deeper, Colonel. And it'll be deeper yet the farther you go up the Tongue."

"Good. I want it deep. Now go and do your duty . . . make sure those cattle don't get upriver. McQuade, I'll have a couple of my men drive the cattle we're taking along, until you can catch up."

As Kev left with Grigsby, he couldn't help but thank the Lord that he'd collected his money for the cattle before the Sioux had struck. At least now it was Army cattle he was chasing.

Early the next morning, Kev knocked on Caitlin's door, wanting to say good-bye as they were leaving as soon as the men got their early breakfast down.

She was already dressed, and invited him inside for the first time. He carefully left the door slightly ajar, but not so much as to allow the wind to whistle inside.

"I'm about to leave," he said.

"I have two things for you," she said, a mischievous smile on her face. She moved close to him and pulled his lips down to hers for a long kiss, then pushed away. "It's Christmas Eve and you'll be gone tomorrow." She fetched a small package.

Kev was surprised, as the time had flown. "I'm embarrassed," he said. "I had no idea it was upon us."

"No reason to be," she said, again flashing that smile. "It's just that it's my favorite day of the year, and I wanted you to have something."

"Should I open it now?"

"No, it's a Christmas gift. Open it tomorrow, if you have time."

"Oh, I'll have time." He stuffed the small package in one of the wolf-skin coat's big pockets, then gathered her up again and gave her another kiss.

He smiled down at her. "I promise, I'll have something for you when I return."

"You've done so much for me, that's my Christmas. Just come back safe, that's the best present I could receive."

Then, reluctantly, he pushed his way out the door into the quickening wind.

It had taken Kev over five weeks to drive the herd downriver, but it took Sean and the party, marching and riding hard in an effort to stay warm, only twelve hard days to return, even through it was upriver and the weather was not kind.

Sean could hardly contain himself as they topped the last rise that looked down on the Rocky Butte; then he and the gray stood as if the gray was nailed to the rock ledge; shocked, his gut wrenching, Sean could see the house was gone. A house he was born in, suckled in, raised in for all his young years. A house, a home, that was all he'd ever known. He whipped up his horse, followed closely by Badger-Man, and galloped away from the troop down through the deep snow the last half mile to the barn and the twisted remnants of the house.

Colin McQuade cast the shotgun he carried aside into the snow as he recognized the riders and as Sean dismounted and ran to him. They embraced, almost knocking Colin from his one good foot.

"My God, Pa, your leg," Sean said as his father held

him at arm's length, balancing with the help of his hands on Sean's shoulders.

Colin's face fell, and he took a deep breath before he gave Sean the horrible news. "It's worse than that, Sean. Your mother, Pattiann, and your grandpa . . . all of them, in the fire."

Tears welled in Sean's eyes and he moved past his father, slogging through the snow and up the hill past the tangled, fallen, badly scorched beams of the house to the little fenced area that served as the Mc-Quade graveyard.

It was a long time before he returned.

In the meantime, Colin stood and visited as best he could with Badger-Man, getting filled in on where Kevin was, why he hadn't returned, and how the drive had gone.

Then he saw the approaching column of soldiers, and suddenly his blood ran cold. A uniform, that's what the man in the house had been wearing. A uniform; a man with side-whiskers, dundrearies, in uniform. It came to him with the shock and chill of an avalanche; Orin Starkey had been that man. Orin Starkey had been the reason he couldn't sleep at night. Sergeant Orin Starkey had been the man who . . . who had done what?

It still wasn't clear to Colin. Then it came to him in a rush of emotion.

Brigid had been yelling, "No, Starkey, take your hands off me. Damn you, damn you." That's what had compelled Colin, as weak as he was, to roll out of the bed and fight his way to the door. Brigid never cursed, never. It had to be something terrible that Starkey was doing to make her scream at him, curse at him.

There was no reason his family couldn't have gotten out of the house if there was a fire. Even the old man could have gotten out, unless he was held there, or beaten unconscious. Starkey had gotten out; Starkey had been nowhere to be found. And he'd been there when the fire started. Colin knew he had, for he'd heard Starkey yell out, curse, about the same time Colin had seen the smoke and flame overhead.

Colin's stomach was knotted as tightly as his jaw when Sean returned, streaks of tears frozen on his young face. Colin put his arm around his son's shoulders, and allowed the youth to help him into the barn, and into the small cabin, while Badger-Man cared for the horses.

When they were seated in front of the small stone fireplace, Colin eyed his exhausted son, and mouthed one of the hardest things he'd ever said. "You've got to go back to the Tongue, Sean."

Sean McQuade stared a little incredulously at his father.

His scouts, who he called his wolves, had ridden in earlier in the day, reporting to him that the walks-a-heap were on the move, and moving upriver.

Crazy Horse stood in front of the council fire, even angrier than Colonel Nelson Miles, and he had been so for days, since the death of his peace emissaries had been reported to him.

He fumed, walking around and around the fire between it and the circle of chiefs.

"Bearcoat lies. The *Waseca* all lie. They will come now, there will be no peace, but we will pick the time and place to fight."

Sitting Bull rose, and waited until Crazy Horse stopped fuming before he spoke. "Bearcoat is strong and has more men than each day from winter to winter. He has the long guns that destroy our villages from ten times the length of an arrow shot . . . no, twenty times. We should ride east, then north, stopping only at Fort Peck, then on to the country of the Grandmother, beyond the line Bearcoat will not cross."

Sitting Bull returned to his sitting position as Crazy Horse reddened, his fists clenched. Finally, he regained enough composure to speak. "It was you, Sitting Bull, who wanted to send the offer of peace to Bearcoat. It was you who sent five of our chiefs to their deaths. I do not want to hear of peace from you. I have forced even the summer roamers to stay with us. The ones who wanted to crawl back to the reservation to hide in the winter moon. We are strong. We have eight hundred lodges, and we have guns and ammunition."

Again Sitting Bull arose. "Yes, we again have many men, many who are sick. Many who have sick women and children to care for. Your own wife, Black Shawl, coughs with the rattle of death. We should leave now, before the snow flies again, and we can be across the Elk River even as Bearcoat and the walks-a-heap reach this place."

"No," snapped Crazy Horse. "Now is the time to make a stand. We will move upriver, slowly, keeping ahead of the walks-a-heap, drawing him ever closer, eventually to the Creek of the Prairie Dog, where the hot water flows from mother earth and never freezes. There is firewood there to last the winter. We will send our wolves downriver to skulk in the cover of the hillsides and watch the walks-a-heap. As he nears, we will move upriver, always drawing him onward, until we are where his wagons and big guns cannot reach. Each day he will tire more, each day he will become weaker, until we pick our place on the bluffs of Wolf Mountain to fight. We will have the high ground, and we will kill all the walks-a-heap and take their strong horses and winter lodges and buffalo coats. We will win."

Sitting Bull's voice softened. "Yes, like we took the coats and horses at Greasy Grass from the horse soldiers of the Golden Hair, which we should never have done. They fought bravely there, and they should have been left in the field as the brave men they were. Instead, we stripped away all they had, our women gouged out their eyes, and cut away their manhood. They were shamed. Now, their brothers fight like maddened wolves, or the great bear defending her cubs. We have had no rest since that day, and I fear we will never rest again."

"We will kill them all," Crazy Horse said with finality. He ignored Sitting Bull and turned to the others. "I want warriors to move downriver, to harass Bearcoat, but to stay in front of him, luring him on, luring him into our trap like the foolish sage hen. They will hit and run, shoot into his camp, make him angry, and thus foolish. Each of you select as many as you have fingers. One of you lead them. Send them with the morning sun."

Sitting Bull sat and remained quiet. Yes, they would fight, but he knew that unless the walks-a-heap lost many men and many horses on the march up the river, they would not win. They too were tired and weak, and worse, sick. Almost all of them had broken lips and bleeding noses from the cold, and too many of them had the cough that caused their hands to be speckled with spots of their lifeblood. And he had seen the walks-a-heap take their wagons and cannons places that no man should have been able to take such loads. And they came, and came, and came, as sure as the big Muddy Water River flows.

The walks-a-heap were determined, more determined than Sitting Bull had ever seen them. It was a bad omen, one that he believed came from the shame that had been bestowed on the Golden-Haired One and his horse soldiers at Greasy Grass.

Sitting Bull decided then and there that he would bide his time, and when ready, he would take his people and head across the Elk River, across the largest of all, the Muddy Water River, and on into the cold winds until he was in the country of the Grandmother, where Bearcoat and the walks-a-heap would not follow. Where they would not cross some imaginary line in the snow drawn by their grandfathers in the place they called Washington.

He was saddened by this decision, but knew in his heart that it was the only place his people would be safe.

The next morning, over one hundred warriors, called the decoys by Crazy Horse, in full paint and feathers, rode out of camp.

Kev had ridden out with a troop of a dozen marching men. Miles had decided that marching was the only way they could press into the dark of night, a forced march of eighteen hours a day that would allow them to catch up with the cattle thieves. One wagon followed, carrying corn for its own six mules and the horses, foodstuff and spare arms and ammunition for the soldiers, and tents for the men, leaving the men without heavy packs and able to move quickly. The wagon would follow as long as possible, until the rugged country precluded its passing.

The hell of it was that some lazy quartermaster had shipped summer-weight tents to Miles and the 5th, and they offered little protection against this kind of cold. The men slept in pairs, each man in a heavyweight buffalo coat, wrapped in his own pair of blankets, back-to-back with his tent-mate. Many of the men did not bother to erect the lightweight canvas, preferring to wrap it about themselves and their tent-mates like katydids in cocoons.

It turned out that the Sioux had driven off over a hundred head, leaving fewer than they took, and in the process gathered up two-dozen mules and some horses. That was the bad of it; the good of it was the cattle, mules, and the Sioux mounts beat flat a fine-compacted trail that was not only easy to follow, but smooth as a highway—as over four hundred hoofs broke trail and packed the snow in front of the marchers. So long as there was no new snowfall, they could follow at a brisk pace.

But the Sioux were pushing hard also, and even marching eighteen hours a day, it took three hard days until, late in the afternoon of the third day, the pursuers came upon cattle dung still steaming in the winter cold. They had not been bothered by snowfall, but the cold was bitter, well below zero. As cold as it was, for the cattle and mule droppings to still be steaming meant the herd, and the Indians, were just over the next rise.

Chapter 22

McGloughlan quickstepped up alongside Kev and Grigsby. "Gentlemen," he said, "if you'd ride ahead and scout the situation. I'm going to leave the wagon here with the freighter and two soldiers as guard, and the rest of us will move up close to the top of the rise. Come back here and report to me before you take any action."

There was a tree line up-slope above a small rim-rock from where they sat, only a half mile from the rise over which they figured the cattle were moving along, so Grigsby, with Kev close behind, whipped up his mount and headed uphill.

After finding a small cleft in the rimrock, they reached the tree line, mostly thick cedars where the snow was even deeper in the shade, and rode well inside its cover before turning south, until they figured they were well past the ridge below, then carefully moved out to the edge of the copse. As expected, they could clearly see the cattle, no more than a half mile below them, moving ahead of a half-dozen Sioux riders at a leisurely pace.

"They seem damned confident," Grigsby said quietly.

"Or damned tired," Kev offered in an equally low

tone. "As deep as this snow is, those cattle have little feed, the mules won't stand for it for long, and they've had to work hard to keep pushing them along this far."

"You satisfied?" Grigsby asked.

"I wish I could say I was. I'm still wondering why there's only a half dozen of them."

"Damn sight better than half a hundred. Let's get back to McGloughlan."

They had to retrace their trail in order to stay out of sight of the Indians, but did so, and in a matter of minutes were reporting to the sergeant with the new chevrons on his sleeve.

"How far ahead of us?" McGloughlan asked.

"Not more than three quarters of a mile," Kev offered.

"Then we can double-time and catch the herd?"

Grigsby scratched the five-day beard on his chin. "There's rough country south, ahead of the way they're going, rimrock to the east they can't cross, but a clear way downhill to the west, I'd guess all the way to the Tongue, which I recollect is not more than five or six miles. You can't close on them without they see you coming, as there's damn little cover. What say McQuade and I circle around to the west, and get 'twixt the herd and any way they might be drove on the run. Y'all come in on them from behind, and with luck get close enough to bring a few of them down. If possible, we'll keep the herd from getting drove off to the west."

"What do you think, Kev?" McGloughlan asked.

"I think Grigsby's idea is fine. I doubt if the devil himself could get those cattle to running, as wore out as they look to me. The mules might break and run, but not the cattle."

"Good, then go." McGloughlan pulled a pocket watch from a pocket deep under his buffalo coat, and checked the time. "I'll give you twenty minutes, and try to keep as close as possible behind the herd without being seen, then we'll double-time it. You'll hear the shooting soon as we're close enough to set up five to a skirmish line; then you can close in from the west."

It took Kev and Grigsby more than twenty minutes to get into position, a half mile west of the herd. Just as it had been between the soldiers and the herd, there was little cover between them and the cattle.

They barely had time to wind their horses when the shooting began.

"Let's move," Kev said, and he and Grigsby whipped up their tired mounts.

Before they'd ridden more than three hundred yards, they were faced with a wide oncoming herd of charging cattle.

"I thought they wouldn't run," Grigsby chided, shouting at Kev.

"Can't be right all the time . . . over here," Kev yelled, and they reined to a group of a half-dozen pines, the only trees for hundreds of yards in any direction.

By the time they got dismounted, tied the horses, and raised their rifles, the cattle were coming hard, only a few dozen yards away. Both of them fired just over the heads of the charging cattle, and caused a breach between them as they parted, partly because of the trees, partly because of the roar of the weapons.

In moments they had pounded past, and Grigsby was able to turn his attention, and his Sharps, on the Indians flanking the herd. The closest rider was well over two hundred yards away and riding hard in the deep snow when Grigsby fired the first round. It didn't seem to hit the rider, but his mount folded under him and he somersaulted, throwing up a shower of snow. Another Indian spun his horse and came back, hooking arms with the first and loading him on behind. Before they could whip up the horse, Grigsby had fired again, and the man who'd come to help his comrade was blown partially out of the saddle. The first Indian was able to reseat his friend, and whip up the horse. In moments, all that was left was tracks.

It took McGloughlan and his men several minutes to catch up with them.

"Well, that was . . . a damn . . . fine thing," he said, panting hard as he tried to catch his breath.

"Did you knock down any of the bloody bastards?" Grigsby asked.

"We got one brave down, and no one of us was hit. You?"

"Knocked one halfway out of the saddle, but his friend carried him off."

"What now?" McGloughlan asked.

"Hell, boy, you're the sergeant," Grigsby said with a half smile.

"Let's take to their tactics," Kev said.

"How's that," Grigsby asked.

"As you know, I'm surprised they got them to run at all, but they won't run far before those cattle are winded." He looked up, checking the sun with a gloved hand shading his eyes. "It'll be sundown in an hour or so, and they might push on for another hour or so, but those cattle are going to be damn hard to move after that run, and as cold as it will get soon as the sun falls. I don't know if you saw, but the mules split off, and they'll be heading back down to where the snow is lighter and they can graze, and probably work their own way back to the haystacks at the cantonment. Let's wait till the hostiles bed down for the night, and hit them in the dead of night like they hit the herd in the first place. Grigsby and I can drive them off, right into a skirmish line of soldiers. If they give chase, they'll run into a wall of infantry lead."

"Grigsby?" McGloughlan asked.

"Sounds right to me."

McGloughlan sent a runner back to inform the wagon and bring it and the two guards accompanying it forward, while Kev and Grigsby moved on, tracking the herd and trying to find out exactly where they'd bedded down.

The soldiers took a well-earned rest, building a small fire and making coffee.

Now it was wait, for the wagon to catch up, and until they knew where they were to set their trap.

As the sun was about to fall behind the low foothills to the west, Sergeant Orin Starkey rose from his sickbed in the hospital, and called out to the cantonment doctor. "Major Wilkins, I'm sure as heck feeling a lot better. Maybe I could go back to my quarters now."

The tall graying Wilkins crossed the room, moving around a couple of bunks containing men he thought actually were sick, to Starkey's bunk. "You mean now that your comrades have moved out. . . . You know, Sergeant, I don't think you ever had a damned cramped gut. I think you came in here and doubled up because you're a shirker, and had no intention of going upriver with your men."

"Oh, oh, damn, there it goes again," Sharkey said, doubling over, holding his stomach. He moaned convincingly, falling back on his bunk and crunching into a fetal position, then said in a rasping voice, "Oh, sweet Jesus, I never had nothing hurt me so. Can't you give me nothing?" He moaned again.

Wilkins walked across the room to a wall-mounted cabinet. He removed a small square bottle and a tablespoon, then recrossed to the bunk. "Sit up, Starkey."

The sergeant complied as Wilkins unstoppered the bottle and poured a tablespoon of dark liquid, then held it out for Wilkins to swallow.

He did so, then winced and shook his head rapidly, like a wet dog. He coughed, then spat on the floor. "Damn, man, that's a terrible bitter brew."

"It's damn, *sir*, to you. And don't you ever spit on my floor. And it should be a bitter brew as it's Cockleby's Fine Old Foreign Bitters. You'll get three doses a day from now on, and liquids only to eat. The rest of us are having stew and biscuits for supper."

It was only fifteen minutes later when Starkey again called out to the major. "Major, sir . . . I really do think that Cockleby's brew did the trick . . . sir."

"So, that wood detail I'm assigning you to doesn't

look so bad now?" Wilkins had a wry smile on his face.

"I sure wish I could have gone south with my fellas, but the wood detail will have to do, sir, as I'll never catch up to them now . . . and it'd be no trip for a man alone. Sioux would scalp me, sure as hell."

"Then get up and get out of here. If you cramp up again, come on back for another dose. Tomorrow, it's the wood detail, or back here for bitters and nothing but liquids."

"Yes, sir," Starkey said, quickly rising, stripping off his nightgown, then fetching his long underwear, trousers, blouse, and coat off a hook by the bunk.

"If there're any details going to catch up with the main body and Miles, count on going with them, Starkey." But Starkey's back disappeared out the door without his acknowledgment. Wilkins shook his head while watching Starkey stomp quickly past the hospital window, reminding himself to write a short report regarding his belief that Starkey had faked an illness to get out of the very cold and very long march that Miles and the Fifth had set upon. A report that he sincerely hoped would get Starkey busted back to corporal.

Starkey was suddenly cold to the bone, but not so cold that he didn't walk out of his way to pass the door of Caitlin Steel's quarters. He moved slowly by, carefully inspecting the window as he did so, but the crude curtains were drawn tightly.

When he'd discovered that Caitlin Steel was to stay in camp, at least until Miles and the troop returned from this expedition, he decided that he too would figure a way to stay, and he would get his chance at her. She'd shamed him, refusing even to walk with him. If things kept going badly for him in Miles's command, and he had no reason to suspect they wouldn't, he'd slap her snotty nose out of the air, then he'd haul her back to Bozeman. He didn't need the Army any longer, and she was worth a pile of gold if the scuttlebutt he heard around the camp was true.

And he planned to collect it. It would give him a good start on his way to Oregon.

And he planned to give her one more chance to be nice to him, one more chance to trust him, as it would make his plan easier if he could get her alone, away from the cantonment.

They managed to keep a big fire roaring, but even that, as frigid as it was, would only keep one side of them warm at a time. Each man had two blankets, and they'd pulled the wagon up to up-wind of the fire, to serve as windbreak, but still the side away from the fire was always cold as a banker's heart.

After it had been dark for a few hours, it was so cold that ice was beginning to form in the men's beards and mustaches from their breath. Among the supplies in the wagon had been a number of burlap bags. The men on the march had wrapped their feet so the burlap would fit inside what was now very snug boots, but Kev and Grigsby had wrapped theirs on the outside as they were to be mounted.

Kev looked up at the moon, now at its highest in the clear night sky, then across the fire at Grigsby.

"Shall we ride out and find those boys, and see if we're to have a shot at them this night?"

"Sounds right," Grigsby managed, and they headed to saddle the horses, walking on feet wrapped in burlap.

It could have been Kev's imagination, but he thought the buckskin, his muzzle covered with ice, almost welcomed his coming, and the opportunity to be on the move.

The meadow down which the cattle and their Indian drovers had gone narrowed and became a ravine, then in a couple of miles, widened and became a flat-bottomed, steep-banked barranca. After a couple of miles moving along the bottom, Grigsby reined over alongside Kev. "Let's split up and ride the rims of this wash."

"Well be in tougher snow than following in their trail," Kev said.

"I'm afraid we're going to come on them soon, and they'll be looking for us to be in the track."

"Sounds right to me," Kev said, and broke away to the north side, leaving the south to Grigsby.

"When we find them, drop back a couple of hundred yards and we'll join up in the track again," said Grigsby.

Kev merely nodded, wrapping the hood of his wolf-skin coat tighter around his neck and face.

It was another two miles before the moonlight revealed the humps of cattle bedded down in the ravine bottom. In the silence of the frigid night, the crunch of horse's hoofs in the hard-crusted snow seemed as loud as the crack, crack, crack of hammer on anvil, their heavy breathing and blowing as loud as a steam train letting off pressure—not an auspicious way to approach a camp of hostiles. Kev quickly reined up and sat studying the scene below him, surreal with steam rising off the bodies of over a hundred animals in the midst of a white field, sparkling like acres of broken glass in the moonlight.

Kev immediately reined up away from the herd as he could not identify any of the lumps as being or not being men among the animals, and had no intention of riding dumbly into trouble and being chased and shot at by a half-dozen angry Sioux.

He circled back, and found Grigsby awaiting him.

"Did you see the Sioux?" Kev asked.

"Did not, but I saw the glow of a fire on your side. Worried you might ride up on them. Their fire is very low, and banked against the north wall."

"Let's fetch the others and get this over with."

Chapter 23

They moved back toward the camp at a quick walk, getting no reluctance from the horses as they were more than willing to keep moving.

After a quick parlay with McGloughlan, they all set out to their appointed positions. Kev and Grigsby north of the herd, the soldiers well south in a skirmish line.

After an agreed half hour, Kev and Grigsby whipped up their mounts and charged down the slope, firing their weapons and yelling like banshees. The herd was less than eager to stampede, and Kev was positive the Indians would fall upon them while they were moving back and forth, driving the cattle forward. But nothing happened, other than getting the cattle into something less than a stampede, and only getting them at that pace until just after they'd passed the low copse of trees agreed upon as the skirmish line.

Kev and Grigsby circled back after the cattle settled down.

"No Sioux?" Kev asked McGloughlan, but the answer was obvious as there had been no shooting. The sergeant merely shrugged.

"They pulled out in the night," Grigsby offered.

"I'd guess they knew they would not get away with the whole herd, and picked the animals they thought was up to the move. I saw some track going on west, maybe three-dozen cattle and the Sioux mounts."

"Should we keep moving after them?" Kev asked, dreading the answer as he wanted to get back to the job at hand, and that job was to join up with Miles and find and kill, or hopefully capture, the main band of Indians, so he could get back to the cantonment and Caitlin.

"Miles wants you with the main force," McGloughlan said in response. "Grigsby can track them a while if he thinks necessary, but I'm having half the troop drive this main bunch back to the cantonment, and I think you and I and half the detail should press on north along the Tongue."

"In the morning," Kev said, dismounting and untying his blankets from behind the saddle, then dropping the saddle from the buckskin. Eying the fire the soldiers were building, he added, "I can still get three or four hours before sunrise."

Grigsby offered, "The Tongue's only a mile or so down the ravine. With luck, Miles is well past by now."

Kev and Grigsby curled up as close as they could get to the fire, already circled by soldiers. Kev's last thoughts before falling into a hard sleep were of Caitlin. He would return to the cantonment as quickly as possible.

Then Kev had a major decision to make. Go back to the Rocky Butte Ranch and confirm that things were all right there, or immediately begin to fulfill his obligation to Chad Steel and set out with Caitlin downriver all the way to St. Louis.

Kev knew that was what Caitlin wanted, but it was so bloody unreasonably cold, and going to Rocky Butte meant she could continue to lay up in warmth and comfort at the cantonment, and the fact was Kev knew she would be safer there, even safer than moving on downriver with him.

It was going to be a tough decision.

The next day, mid-morning, they reached the Tongue, following the trail of the Sioux and the small herd they still possessed. After counting the cattle, they decided the Sioux had managed to get away with just over forty head. Miles would not be pleased. He had not yet reached the spot where they came upon the river, so Grigsby rode to a high spot; returning, he reported that the column was not but a mile or two downriver. Grigsby and Mc-Gloughlan decided that since Miles was so close, they'd wait to pursue the remaining captured cattle until receiving new orders.

Kev and Grigsby helped move the cattle south until meeting up with Second Lieutenant Oscar F. Long and his engineering detachment, who were well ahead of the main detachment of seven battalions. The construction crew was corduroying the banks, placing timbers in a stair-step so the wagons could negotiate the steep slippery sides of the river where it had to be crossed. In addition to the men, two cannon and six supply wagons followed.

Kev and Grigsby stopped and helped with the work until Miles and his soldiers caught up, with Long and his construction crew hurrying on ahead to prepare the next bank necessary to cross. It was

New Year's Eve, and that day they'd already made a half-dozen crossings of the twisting Tongue, and it seemed many more were to come.

Miles had a short discussion with McGloughlan before sending him on his way back to the cantonment with the main herd, then sent for Kev and Grigsby.

"Well, it seems the Sioux still have a good many of our cattle?" Miles tone was accusatory.

"They do," Kev answered, "but they'll never get them to the Indian encampment if it's any distance, if it's more than two or three days upriver. Those cattle are about done in, and unless they have some meadow hay along the way, which looks damn unlikely, as cold as it is and as deep as this snow is, they'll lay down and die."

"I hope you're right, Mr. McQuade. I hope you're right. Please go back and relieve the men I have acting as drovers . . . and do the job you've been paid to do."

Kev felt the heat rise to the back of his neck. "That's what we've been doing, General. And what I'll continue to do."

Miles stared at him a moment. The whiskers on his face seemed to bristle. Then he relaxed. "Just relieve my men, and see that we keep what cattle we have."

"My pleasure, General," Kev said, and turned and mounted the buckskin, spurring him into a canter around the column.

Miles turned to Grigsby, who stayed behind. "Seems Mr. McQuade takes offense?"

"McQuade does his job, and as you know, it's not Corporal McQuade or Sergeant McQuade. He's not used to the Army way. He'll carry his weight and plenty more, if the past is any professor."

"Good. Go give him a hand, Grigsby. I'll send a runner if I need you for anything more."

Grigsby, even though he was neither corporal nor sergeant, gave Miles a perfunctory salute, and went to his own mount.

When they finally circled the wagons, they'd made forty-six miles from the cantonment, crossing the ice-slaked Tongue almost a hundred times, seven times that day alone.

It was New Year's Eve. Nonetheless, by far the majority of the men were asleep the instant they were relieved from duty.

The next morning, not but two hours after the four-thirty reveille, with light just casting its first lemon glow, only a mile upstream they came upon the first dead cow with a half-dozen crows happily perched upon its frozen, bloodied, carcass, hurriedly stripped of its back-straps. As Kev had predicted, and if this single cow was any indication, it seemed the cattle would not make it far upriver.

After they found the third steer, only another two miles upstream, Kev, who was following well behind the wagons and cannon, saw a man trotting back his way.

"The general would like to see you," the runner reported, and Kev spurred the buckskin up past the cannon, wagons, and seven companies of infantry, 460 men, only one company of which was mounted.

Without preamble, Miles gave Kev a nod. "It looks as if you were right, Mr. McQuade. We've now found three head of dead cattle, and I'd judge there're more to come. I'd appreciate it if you and

Grigsby would stop and butcher these two, and add the meat to the supply wagons."

"Again, my pleasure, General. By the way, Happy New Year."

Miles merely nodded, but he did give Kev the hint of a smile. Kev whipped his horse up, and returned at a trot. It was interesting for Kev to note that Miles was not a man to dismiss the fact he'd been wrong. He had no problem admitting that Kev was right, nor pointing out that fact. Not only that, but when he asked Kev to do something he hadn't been hired to do, he prefaced it with, "I'd appreciate it. . . ." More and more, Kev was gaining a grudging admiration for the man.

On Christmas Day, a week ago, Caitlin had been surprised to find a tiny package propped up against her door. She took it inside, and with a smile lighting her face, opened it. The smile faded as she read the note inside. "Merry Christmas. This is almost as pretty as you. Orin Starkey." It wasn't from Kev, but from Sergeant Starkey. It was a small red and purple shell, a beautiful thing, but something she certainly wouldn't keep. She had one of the major's aides return it to Starkey, with a note of her own. "Thank you, but this is much too precious and it would be improper for me to accept the kind gift. Wishing you a happy holiday season. Mrs. Tolofsen."

She heard nothing more from Starkey.

A week later, to Caitlin's great surprise, Sean McQuade struggled into the cantonment, riding his father's big gray and leading a strong sorrel, with

Badger-Man following closely also leading a spare mount.

She met him as he dismounted, giving him a hardy hug, then holding him at arm's length. "Why in the world are you back?"

"We rode hard, changing mounts every hour, leaving before sunup and not quitting until after sundown."

"But why?"

Sean cut his eyes away. "Got to get to Kev. My ma, grandpa, and sister, all dead." He turned back to her, and she could see the hurt in his eyes and hear that his voice was about to break. "The home place was burnt to the ground, with them in it."

"My God, Sean. Tell me that's not true."

"It is, and my pa thinks that big ugly sergeant, Starkey was his name. . . . He thinks there was foul play and wants him held until we can get to the bottom of things."

Caitlin hesitated only a moment, before she spun on her heel. "Let's go see Major Jenkins."

As the day wore on, the wind turned and began coming from the southwest, continuing to warm. Snow began to melt, and though the warmer weather was a blessing, the melting snow and the mud it created were not. Where the men had been having to break trail in ankle-deep and ofttimes deeper snow, now they sloshed, and the banks became even more difficult to negotiate.

The country was relatively smooth in the river bottom, but the river itself oxbowed back and forth from high bank to high bank, and the bottom lay thick with barren cottonwood, blowdown, and undergrowth.

Later, on that New Year's Day, as the column neared Otter Creek with the Wolf Mountains rising in the background, shots rang out from high on the embankments across the Tongue from the column.

Kev and Grigsby tightened the herd and moved them closer to the cannon and wagons, as far in front of their position Miles gave the order to take cover and the men did so, as best they could in the relatively open meadow on the alluvial deposit they were crossing.

In the thick cottonwood stand ahead, Kev could see riders, then realized they were feathered and shouting, shaking lances, bows, and rifles as they galloped through the thick stand of trees.

It was a quick hit-and-run tactic the Sioux were pursuing, and before Miles was finished shouting orders and the men had set up their skirmish lines, the Sioux disappeared around the next bend in the river.

The mounted battalion pursued the Indians only until they might have lost sight of the main body of infantry, then turned back, not allowing the Sioux to draw them into ambush.

Kev continued to check the slopes on either side of his herd, expecting Sioux to sweep down on them, and Grigsby even spurred his mount to the top of a nearby slope to gain a better view, but the Sioux did not appear to be after the cattle, as there was no flanking action on their part. In a half hour, things returned to normal.

With the warming weather, snow turned to rain, then after they'd made camp across Otter Creek, night brought colder weather, sleet and slushy rain.

It seemed as if the Good Lord would continue to deal them a tough hand to play.

It was a cold miserable camp that awoke to continue to pursue the elusive Sioux.

In some ways, the travel had become easier, as the river this far upstream was frozen solid. No more sloshing through freezing water merely slaked with ice floes. Of course, now they had to worry about breaking through the ice, unless it soon got colder. At each river crossing after corduroying the banks, Lieutenant Long and his engineering detachment built huge fires so when and if wagons broke through and men were soaked, they could quickly get warm and dry.

They trudged on.

It was the following day, after Sean and Caitlin had met with Major Jenkins, that the major called Sergeant Orin Starkey before him. Starkey stood at attention in front of the wagon tailgate that Miles had used as a desk. Across the room, Jenkins's aide sat in a straight-back chair, a lap desk in position on his thighs, a quill in hand, waiting.

Jenkins had wanted to interrogate the men that had accompanied Starkey on the vegetable mission to Bozeman, but to a man they were south with Miles. He was left no alternative other than confronting Starkey with only hearsay evidence without corroboration.

"It has been reported to me that you were involved in some . . . some misdeeds at the McQuade ranch upriver."

"Misdeeds, sir?" Starkey asked, the picture of innocence.

Jenkins hesitated. He really had very little to say unless he got cooperation from his sergeant. "Yes, misdeeds. A Mr. Colin McQuade"—Starkey seemed to blanch at the mention of Colin McQuade's name—"has reported that you were present when his wife, daughter, and father, I believe it was, were killed and his ranch house burned to the ground."

It was all Starkey could do to acknowledge that Colin McQuade might be alive to talk, and it shook him to the bone, but he managed a straight and very concerned coutenance. "I don't know what he's talking about, sir. We stopped at the McQuade ranch to check on the delivery of the cattle that I'd purchased from them . . . at General Miles's orders, the cattle that arrived here three weeks or so ago. When we left the McQuade ranch, all seemed right as rain. . . ." Jenkins said nothing, continuing to listen carefully. He turned to his aide, noting that the man was writing furiously. Nervously, Starkey continued. "At her request, I did assist Mrs. McQuade in amputating her husband's leg, which had gone green after receiving a gunshot wound from some savage. You know I've been Army long enough to have seen several such surgeries. . . ." Jenkins continued to listen, his face set like stone. "Mr. McQuade was delirious, and was still unconscious when we drove out." Starkey seemed to grow more confident as he talked. "In fact, Mrs. McQuade was very appreciative of my help, and even fed me and sent some stew out to the men who were bivouacked in the McQuade barn during our short visit, only a few yards from the house. We left there soon after offering our assistance when assured there was nothing more we could do."

Jenkins walked to the window and stared out for a short while, his hands folded behind his back. Finally, he turned back to face Starkey. "Don't leave the cantonment, even for wood detail or any other duty. You're confined to close camp until I say otherwise. We'll take this up again when the men who were on that trek with you return. Understand?"

"Yes, sir," Starkey said, giving the major a sharp salute.

Starkey spun on his heel, then turned back. "Sir, right after we left the McQuade place, only a couple of miles out, we passed the track of two dozen or more hostiles, Hunkpapa I'd guess. If something happened at the McQuade place, I'd guess it was at the hand of the bloody savage." Starkey shrugged, then left with a wry smile on his face unseen by Jenkins.

But Starkey left knowing his days in the Army were numbered. All he needed was a little more of a break in the weather, and he'd be on his way.

As Starkey crossed the compound, Sean and Caitlin were on their way to the laundry, Sean with an armload of Caitlin's bedding. She pulled up short, not wanting to get anywhere near the big sergeant.

"I thought Major Jenkins would arrest him," Sean said, crestfallen.

"Major Jenkins is a good man. He'll do what's right."

"I don't know," Sean said, obviously both worried and agitated.

After Starkey had passed, Caitlin offhandedly mentioned to Sean, "He tried to give me a Christmas present, but I returned it."

"What was it?" Sean asked.

Chapter 24

"A shell. A beautiful little red and purple shell," Caitlin said.

Sean's face fell. "About this long?" He held his thumb and finger indicating about an inch and a half.

"Yes. Some kind of sea snail, I'd guess."

"It was my mother's, given to her by my father years ago when they were married."

"Maybe she gave it to Starkey."

"Never. Never, never. It was one of her most prized possessions. I'm going to go get it, and find out what that low-life scum did—"

Caitlin grabbed Sean by the sleeve as he turned to leave. "No, Sean. You're not. Just wait until Kev returns. The last thing we need is you hurt. Kev would never forgive me. Kev has to take care of this."

Sean hesitated.

Caitlin tried to soothe him. "I'll go see the major again. Maybe he'll put Starkey in chains when he knows about the shell."

"He's Army. They all stick together."

"Let me see what I can do." She dug in the small reticule she carried and handed him a dime. "Go to the cookhouse and have a cup of coffee. Give the cook this, and maybe he'll put a dollop of chocolate in it. I'll meet you back at my room."

He looked confused, then shrugged. "I'll help you, then go."

Caitlin and Sean delivered her laundry to the camp followers who had set up business in a steaming tent just a few steps from the last camp building. Then she turned to Sean. "Do you want to come along?"

"Don't think so," Sean said, staring away. "I'll go to the cookhouse."

"Then meet me at my room?"

"Sure."

Caitlin was forced to wait most of an hour in the anteroom until Jenkins was finished with a meeting with the mail contractor, whose wagon had been attacked by the Sioux, with the mail stolen, one of his men killed, and most of his stock driven off. Caitlin overheard the gist of the meeting and heard Jenkins arguing to no avail, the result being that there would be no more mail delivered to the camp until the Indian problem was resolved.

She had a very short and again unsatisfactory meeting with the major, disappointed to learn that Jenkins had met with Starkey already and had simply merely confined him to camp, unwilling to do more until the men who'd been in Starkey's detachment the day he'd visited the McQuade place returned from the excursion up the Tongue.

She was far more disappointed to return to her quarters, where she expected to meet Sean, finding a note slipped under her door. It was short and succinct. "I've gone upriver to find Uncle Kev."

Caitlin ran to the corrals where the riding stock

was kept, but the boy was nowhere to be found. She then hurried to try and find Badger-Man, and discovered that he'd ridden out of camp the day before, planning to return to his people.

Heartsick, her lungs aching, cheeks bright red, and hair askew from running in the cold, she again went to see Major Jenkins, but he merely shrugged his shoulders, pointing out that Sean was a civilian and free to come and go as he pleased. He certainly couldn't spare soldiers to fetch some errant civilian youth.

She returned to her quarters, threw herself on her bed, and cried until her throat ached and tears refused to come. If she'd been able to convince Jenkins to put Starkey in the guardhouse, Sean wouldn't have gone. If she hadn't told Sean that only Kev could take care of this, Sean wouldn't have gone. Now he was out in the freezing weather, alone, in country full of Sioux and Cheyenne.

And it was all her fault.

The march dragged on, with Miles keeping up a relentless pace. Finally, on their ninth day out, after a grueling two-and-a-half-mile morning march, and finding a perfect horseshoe bend in the river in which to camp, with an abundance of firewood, Miles decided to let the men rest and repair their things.

He'd concluded, by the number of dead cattle and still-warm camps they'd found, and from the fact that the cattle had not been butchered, that the fleeing cattle thieves were not far in front of them. If they wouldn't take the time to butcher the cattle that fell, then they must have been worried that the infantry would overtake them.

Miles took the opportunity to send Luther "Yellowstone" Kelly and his scouts on ahead. Late in the afternoon, they returned with several prisoners. Nine Northern Cheyenne women and children. Kelly and Miles came to the conclusion that the women were also searching for the camp of Crazy Horse and Sitting Bull.

Miles decided that the main hostile camp could not be far, maybe as close as two days in front of them. He wanted to become more maneuverable, and decided that this would be a good place to leave the supply wagons and most of the stock. They would go on ahead for a quick two-day reconnaissance with only pack mules, leaving only one company behind to guard the wagons and stock.

He again summoned Grigsby and Kev. "I'm leaving a small body of men behind to guard the wagons and stock. I can use you both as scouts, so leave the cattle to my soldiers, my rear guard, who'll have little else to do."

Grigsby was eager to move ahead, but Kev seemed to hesitate. Miles continued. "McQuade, I know this isn't what you hired on for."

"General, I want to get back to the cantonment as quickly as possible. If you tell me the fastest way to do that is for me to ride into the Indian camp and bring you back Sitting Bull's hair, I'll give it a go."

Miles smiled. "Good. We're moving out well before light day after tomorrow, double time. Get rested, but get your animals and equipment ready to go. You both have plenty of ammunition for your Sharps and Winchester?"

"All we can carry," Grigsby said.

"Good, you may need it very soon."

His words proved prophetic, as almost as soon as they left his mouth, another group of scouts rode up and Liver-eating Johnston leaped from the saddle. "Indians, sir, up where those women was caught. Twenty, maybe thirty of them. Looks like they're trying to figure out what happened with their womenfolk."

"Wait here," Miles instructed Grigsby and Kev. Then he turned to his scouts. "Get Kelly and the others over here."

In moments Yellowstone Kelly, Tom LaForge, George Johnson, James Parker, and John "Liver-eating" Johnson were in front of him, and moments later, all of them, accompanied by Grigsby and Kev McQuade, were at a gallop to rout the Sioux and Cheyenne warriors.

Before they'd traveled two miles, alternating between a fast walk and a cantor, they saw the warriors, still milling about, a few hundred yards up a ravine.

Believing theeir party to be unseen, Kelly led them to the side, where a small rise continued to keep them unseen until they were less than two hundred yards from their quarry.

In a wide line, they burst over the rise, firing at random at any target they could find, quickly closing on the Indians.

The hostiles spun their horses and galloped up the ravine, with the scouts not fifty yards behind.

As soon as they reached the spot where the Indians had originally been spotted, forty or fifty more rose up out of the brush along the hillside, and all hell broke loose.

It was a carefully planned Sioux ambush.

Kev dropped low in the saddle, lead whistling overhead. Grigsby, riding only two lengths in front of Kev, went over his horse's head as the animal went down, dead before it hit the ground. Kev offered him an arm, and he swung quickly on behind. The buckskin gave it his all, snow flying behind his powerful hindquarters in a plume. They were now only five or six lengths behind the rest of the scouts, who headed for a copse of trees in a small side ravine.

Without being hit again, they reached the tree line and quickly set up barricades from windfall.

Two scouts had had horses shot out from under them, but no serious injuries had befallen the scouts. Liver-eating Johnston had a crease on his skull, and was missing a few locks of hair.

It had been a close call, but now, even though they were severely outnumbered, the scouts set up behind a sturdy breastwork of logs and rocks. They might fall, but they'd take a lot of warriors with them if they did.

Back in camp, hearing the gunshots, Miles quickly set up defenses, forming skirmish lines around the bivouac.

Miles dispatched Captain James Casey and his company to take one of the field artillery pieces to a nearby plateau, then sent Lieutenant Charles Hargous and his mounted infantry to the relief of the scouts. By the time they were in position, the number of hostiles surrounding the scouts' position had increased to over a hundred.

Small-arms fire continued until sundown, then the artillery piece had begun to find its range around the perimeter of the scouts' position.

The Indians fell back and the scouts took the first opportunity to make a run for the main camp, only attracting a few shots that went wild in the darkness.

By nightfall, silence reigned over the valley. But Miles was anything but silent. He presumed the Indians were regrouping and preparing for an attack on his main force. He dispatched two companies a quarter mile forward to stand guard against a direct attack.

Luckily, the valley was surrounded by rugged broken country, and the horseshoe bend that hosted his main body was encircled by especially hard country. Across the river, due north of the camp, cliffs precluded any mounted attack. Open floodplains offered a good field of fire both east and west. And to the south steep foothills would slow any attack.

It was a good place for a defense.

The Northern Cheyenne brave, Big Horse, pushed his mount hard. As he moved north along the Tongue, he cursed the women: Sweet Taste Woman, Crooked Nose, Twin Woman and her children, Finger's Woman, and the others; all of them were fools. He'd instructed them not to venture out of their hiding place while he scouted the smoke they'd seen in the distance.

On their journey north they had crossed the track of many walks-a-heap, and he knew the soldiers were somewhere on the Buffalo Tongue, but

he also knew that Crazy Horse was camped somewhere on the river. He'd returned, without being
seen, from discovering that the smoke was from the
walks-a-heap camp, to see the women being captured by the *wasicu,* so many of them there was
nothing Big Horse could do.

But what he could do was find Crazy Horse, and
tell him where and how many were the walks-a-
heap.

With new vigor, he pushed his tired animal onward.

It had continued to warm, and was only just
below freezing at night.

Caitlin picked at her dinner in her room, as
she'd been invited to do by Major Jenkins when
and if she preferred that to eating with the officers.
Then mustering her courage, not wanting to
bother Jenkins's aide, she returned her dishes to
the cookhouse, then took a brisk stroll around the
interior courtyard of the small L-shaped fort, trying
to walk off the meal, but more so the jitters she'd
suffered since Sean had ridden away. As much as
she could under the circumstances, she was enjoying the clear crisp night with men sitting about
smoking pipes and cigars and playing mouth harps
and fiddles, when suddenly the stars were occluded
by a dense, bone-chilling fog that rolled in as if a
blanket had been thrown over them. She moved
quickly back to her quarters, dropped the bar
across the interior side of her door, stoked up her
small potbellied stove with a few sticks, and made
ready for bed. In her nightgown, she forked out a

few red-hot coals, dropped them into the long-handled bedwarmer, and passed it around between the flannel sheets, secretly wishing she was warming the bed for Kev and herself.

She eyed the *Leslies* on the bedside table, thought about reading a little, but decided against it, turning down the coal-oil lamp until it extinguished.

Every day since Sean had left had been a nervous one for her. She couldn't seem to relax. She'd read everything in camp, and the *Leslies Magazines* and St. Louis papers, most of them months old, at least three times.

Sleep finally became her ally, and she quickly fell deeply and totally into sleep's black oblivion.

In the fog, not a dozen steps from her window, sheltered by a large cottonwood, Sergeant Orin Starkey waited. He smiled as the light in the room was extinguished.

This fog was the blessing he'd been awaiting. As soon as it had gotten dark, and he'd noticed the bank of fog coming, he'd managed to slip four horses out of the corral without being seen. Earlier in the week, he'd managed to sneak two riding saddles and bridles and two packsaddles, with pack covers and lead ropes, out of the tack room—among the dozens there he knew they wouldn't be missed—and had them all hidden in the copse of cottonwoods between the encampment and the river. For days he'd been hoarding dried meat and fruit, and had managed to slip away with a half-dozen blankets and almost twenty pounds of corn for the animals, hiding it all in the cottonwoods. When that was gone, the animals could make do on cottonwood bark, and there was no shortage of that between the Tongue and Bozeman.

Now, all he had to do was wait for the camp to go dark.

And that wouldn't be long.

Chapter 25

The brave, Big Horse, rode into the Camp of Sitting Bull and Crazy Horse, howling like a wolf. It was a sign that he carried big news. As he reached Sitting Bull's lodge, the whole camp was beginning to gather around him.

He began relating the news of the large encampment of walks-a-heap as Crazy Horse approached. Hearing his tale, and his report of the capturing of the women, Crazy Horse wasted no time.

"We will ride to fight Bearcoat, catching him in his camp, taking him by surprise. I know this place, Otter Creek, and it's a good place where we will have the high ground. We will kill them all."

In a matter of hours, over four hundred braves were painted, armed, and mounted. They rode out, fired by Crazy Horse's continuing rhetoric, knowing that thirty miles or so down the Tongue would be as good a place to die as any.

Every night Sean had thanked God for the buffalo coat. He'd left camp riding the gray, and leading the tall sorrel he'd brought back from the Rocky Butte.

It had been ride two or three hours, then change mounts, having to unsaddle both animals as the off-animal had to carry the packsaddle full of corn and the few supplies he'd managed to finagle out of the camp cook. But the packsaddle gave the off-animal some rest, as it weighed even less than Sean. And the time it took to change the saddles gave the animals a chance to blow.

It hadn't been hard, following the trail of seven battalions of men and several dozen animals, but he hoped he would soon find them. The ride itself had been grueling. Rather than try and follow the soldiers' track directly, he'd oftentimes moved up-slope so he wouldn't have to cross the river, but consequently he had to break snow. But it was far better than breaking ice, being dunked in the water, and freezing to death. Even though the weather had warmed, it was still dangerously cold. He'd constantly worried about Indians, keeping his fires small and refusing to try to bring down what few animals he'd seen, but the fact was he'd seen almost no life of any kind. It was as if the country had hibernated in the cold. Even the normally raucous crows remained quiet.

But yesterday, he'd seen life. He'd come upon the soldiers returning the main body of cattle to the cantonment, and they'd shared the fact that the Miles and his brother were not far ahead. It spurred him onward.

He'd found an embankment high on the hill to camp this night, but had arisen from his early bed more than once, as he sensed gunfire in the distance. He couldn't be sure, as it seemed little more than a feeling.

He was getting ready to bed down again, after his small fire had burned to coals, when he noticed he'd just put the last of his dried meat in his mouth. He made the final bite last a long time, finally swallowing. He had to find his Uncle Kev soon, or he'd be hunting crows for soup, and even the crows were scarce.

As it darkened, he was surprised to see light glowing over a low rise just upriver. He arose again as the wind turned, positive this time that it *was* gunfire. Then again, only stillness. After his fire was well out, he imagined he smelled smoke.

Could it be that he was so close he could see the glow of their fires?

It was too dangerous to travel at night, so he decided that he would move out quickly, but carefully, at first light and see if he'd finally caught up with them.

Then he and Kev could return to camp, and they would take care of that big ugly sergeant.

And then they could all go back to the Rocky Butte, and take care of his father, and begin rebuilding the ranch.

But first, he had to find his Uncle Kev.

Caitlin awoke struggling for breath, with a rough hand over her mouth and nose and a huge weight on her chest.

Then she recognized the gravely voice. "If you yell, I'll knock you plumb into next week . . . understand."

Starkey. Starkey was in her room. Oh, God. Her chest filled with knots and fear flooded her, but she was still unable to move, and was afraid she was going to pass out from loss of breath. When he finally released the hand, all she could do was gasp for breath; then a rag was forced around her mouth and tied tightly behind her head.

His voice was a harsh whisper. "I'm gonna get off you now. You can get up and get dressed. But you try and yell, or make noise, and I'll knock you cold as it is outside . . . understand?"

She managed a barely perceptible nod.

Again she gasped for breath, having trouble as the rag inhibited her breathing. Her chest heaved as the big man lifted his weight off her. He stood beside the bed, his eyes sweeping over her, but still controlling her with his rough hands as she arose.

He carefully stayed between her and the door. She dressed, leaving her nightgown on, pulling her woolen petticoats and skirt on over them, then her blouse and finally her bearskin coat on over all.

He spun her around and bound her hands in front her, then said, "Let's go."

She bolted for the door, but he roughly stopped her and spun her around. "The window, damn you."

Only then did she realize that the window was open, and the wind coming in was dreadfully damp and cold. She again struggled, trying to break for the door, but he struck her in the stomach and she folded to her knees, unable to get her wind. She sunk onto the floor, whimpering between gasping breaths.

"Yer old man probably wouldn't pay so much for you if'n you was froze stiff, but I can arrange that, you try and run again. Understand?"

She managed another nod, this time letting him pick her up to her feet and guide her to the open window. Her mind racing, she thought about how she could run if he put her through the window ahead of him, but the last thing he did before lifting her up was to bind her ankles.

He shoved her through the small window headfirst, and she crashed to the ground outside. Had it not been for the six inches of snow, she probably would have been seriously injured. As it was, even with hands bound, she was able to break her fall.

She lay there stunned as he forced his big body through the window behind her. Thankfully, she managed to roll aside as he crashed beside her.

He placed a big arm across her, holding her to the ground for a long while in silence, making sure no one heard as the snowfall increased, then arose, brushing new snow away, jerking Caitlin to her feet. Across his shoulder, as if she were a sack of grain, he carried her into the deep shadows of the cottonwoods.

In moments she was tied facedown across the saddle, her soft belly crushed against the hard McClellan, the harsh hemp rope cutting into her back and legs. She died a thousand deaths as he pushed the horses hard, away from the cantonment, away from safety. Into God only knows what.

For the first mile she prayed that she would fall from the horse and that he'd ride on without knowing, then as they went farther, she prayed that the horse would fall on her and she would die.

Then she hurt so badly, she couldn't pray at all.

All she could do was silently cry as her ribs raked back and forth across the saddle, her legs were ripped and gouged by underbrush, and her circulation was quelled by tight rasping ropes.

Sean was up with the sun, surprised to find his rough camp covered by over a foot of new snow, saddling and mounting without bothering to make the last of the coffee he had. He moved out toward where he'd seen the glow of light the night before.

Having only traveled a half mile, he slogged to the crest of the rise, and smiled as he looked up the Tongue River Valley to see a large encampment of men ahead and across the river from him; then his smile turned to a frown as he heard the pounding of hoofbeats, then bloodcurdling screams from the hillside above him.

He snapped his head around to see a half-dozen braves no more than a hundred yards up the hill from him, coming hard and fast, their horses plunging through a deep snowbank.

He gave his heels to the gray, and the big horse bolted downhill. Sean was almost dragged from the saddle, trying to hold onto the sorrel's lead rope, so he cast it aside. Again he looked back. The sorrel was following, but with little enthusiasm. By the time the big gray was up to stride, the Indians had closed to fifty yards. A shot whizzed past Sean's ear, holing the wide brim of his hat, and he dropped low in the saddle.

Kev and Grigsby, spreading corn on a couple of tarpaulins for the cattle, looked up. All they could see in the distance was a lone rider, hunkered low in the saddle, whipping his horse with the tail of his reins, a riderless horse following—and a half-dozen Indians close behind it.

"Get that Sharps," Kev yelled to Grigsby. Luckily, both men had saddled their own mounts first thing on rising, but the saddles weren't cinched tightly.

It took a moment to do so; then they were mounted and moving toward the galloping man, but having trouble in the deep snow.

A sergeant yelled at Grigsby and Kev, commanding them to hold their position, but they ignored him. A troop of infantry, lead by the sergeant, moved forward behind Kev and Grigsby to form a skirmish line protecting the cattle.

Sean looked over his shoulder and realized that two of the Indians, obviously on faster mounts than the others, were closing ground on him and if he didn't do something quickly, they would be upon him.

He was nearing the river, and could have gotten much closer to the infantry encampment before he had to take the river, but it would mean riding in the open for several hundred yards.

Instead, in a bold move, he jerked the reins to the right and drove the gray into a wall of underbrush, tearing their way through, then down a steep embankment to the ice-covered river below.

If he went through the ice, all would be lost, and it would literally be like shooting fish in a barrel for the Indian warriors firing down on his position while he floundered in the freezing water.

The gray set his back legs, sliding down the embankment, underbrush ripping and grasping at horse and rider. Sean gasped involuntarily as the horse hit the ice, sliding a half-dozen yards out onto the slick surface. Then the animal got his feet under him, and made headway.

The Indians reached the edge of the slope above, and would have had a clear field of fire at the rider below, had the brush not been so thick. Instead they too had to crash through the underbrush to reach the surface of the river.

Sean was halfway across when the ice began to fail. He could feel the horse begin to sink under him, but the animal flailed its forefeet and managed to regain it's footing. Again Sean looked over his shoulder to see the Indians dismounting and dropping to one knee, their rifles coming to their shoulders. Luckily, they were heaving for breath with the effort of the chase through the deep snow, and it would take a moment before they could zero in on their target.

Sean hugged the horse, praying that the Indians were poor shots, as the horse reached a lower embankment on the far side of the river and charged up—but slipped and went to its side, pinning Sean's leg underneath against the muddy and snow-covered riverside. Sean cried out, then realized he wasn't really hurt. The gray came back upright and Sean clung to the saddle; then the animal had its legs under him again. Lead slugs peppered the bank beside horse and rider, throwing up plumes of mud and snow; then the horse lunged over the edge.

Just as it seemed the Indians would zero in on their rapidly disappearing target, two riders approached, leaping from their saddles. Dropping behind a deadfall of cottonwood, they returned fire.

Sean pounded toward them, the gray running flat out for all he was worth. They reached the deadfall and the horse and rider sailed over, causing Grigsby to dive to the side.

Kev McQuade stared in utter surprise as he recognized his young nephew. Sean spun the horse, stopping, and flew from the saddle.

He scrambled up beside his uncle, as Grigsby found the range and knocked an Indian from the saddle. The Indians retreated, clambering up over the embankment, now on the far side of the river from Sean and his rescuers, dragging their fallen comrade with them.

The next they were seen, they were leading the sorrel over a distant rise, still shaking their rifles, some of them firing back ineffectively at their enemies, now over four hundred yards behind.

"What the hell?" Kev managed.

In a rush of words and emotion, Sean related the events of the past three weeks to his uncle.

When he'd finally run out of words, Kev stood for a long moment, turned away, his face contorted with emotion, then collected himself and said, "Let's go talk to Miles." But when they arrived, Miles was firing orders left and right, and he dismissed them offhandedly with a wave. Kev wouldn't have it under the circumstances, and insisted.

"General, this can't wait."

Miles snapped at him. "It damn well better wait, McQuade. In case you haven't noticed, we're being surrounded by hostiles. It looks like we'll end this thing in the shadow of the Wolf Mountains. Tend to your cattle unless you hear from me otherwise." Then the general noticed that Sean was present.

"Your nephew. Good, he's on the payroll. He's to relieve Grigsby. Tell Grigsby to report to me."

The presence of the hostiles in a formidable force was a circumstance for which Kev had no argument, and he dragged Sean aside as the general barked orders to his subordinates while at the same time lifting his field glasses to his eyes and checking the disbursement of the growing number of Indians in the rugged hills at several hundred yards distance.

Kev yelled to Sean as he mounted up. "We got to make damn sure we keep those cattle. When this is over, I promise you, we'll see the Army deals with Starkey, and if they don't, we damn sure will. Right now, we have a more immediate problem." He whipped up the buckskin, and galloped back to the small herd where Grigsby waited, with Sean following close behind.

In moments, Grigsby was mounted and riding to report to General Miles.

Chapter 26

The infantry camp was south of the river in the crotch of a horseshoe bend, with the open side to the south and reaches of the river on both east and west. Southwest of the river on the same side as the encampment lay a kidney-shaped plateau with a knoll swelling from its center; a dry creek bed circled the rear of the knoll and came to the river from the south. A narrow floodplain lay between the knoll and the river. Across the river to the north rose imposing bluffs. But to the west across the river from the camp lay a broad plain, and that was the way from which Miles presumed the attack would come.

Miles directed E Company to the knoll, which would give them a wide view of the valley floor. The knoll's western face was nothing more than a tall cliff, at least eighty feet high, so any attack on the knoll would have to come across a wide flat to the east.

Miles sent K Company under Lieutenant Mason Carter to take a position in a stand of cottonwoods on the river's far bank.

They waited impatiently for the Indian attack to come. When nightfall came, they were still waiting;

then sporadic fire began to come from the hills across the river, but no attack. Only the harassment of blind fire into the camp, keeping the men ill at east but doing no real damage.

They settled in to wait. It would be a long night.

As Kev and Sean unrolled their bedrolls in the last of day's glow, Kev pulled Sean's hat from his head and stuck his finger through the bullet hole in the wide brim. He managed a tight smile at his nephew. "Close," was all he said, and Sean shrugged as he climbed between his blankets, covering them with his buffalo-pelt coat.

"Close don't count," he said, burying his head beneath the covers.

Kev sighed deeply as he did the same, and before he fell into a fitful sleep, he thought, *if nothing else good has come of this, it's sure as the devil made a man out of Sean McQuade . . . and I've met Caitlin Tolofsen, soon to again be Caitlin Steel, and sometime in the future, who knows.*

Caitlin lay quietly across the fire from Orin Starkey. He had been silent for most of the afternoon, only speaking to her as he untied her and allowed her to sit up in the saddle, then binding her legs to the cinch and her hands to the saddle horn. Now her back and belly felt some better, but her legs and wrists were badly chapped and gouged from the rough hemp rope.

But nothing hurt as badly as the anticipation of what he might do with her.

She pulled the blankets up to her nose, not wanting to take her eyes off him as he'd been slowly sipping a jug of whiskey since they'd camped, and she was frightened as to what he'd do if he got drunk, but she was also hopeful he'd get drunk enough to pass out. But he'd bound her hands and feet, and tied a six-foot rope from her wrists to a turn around one of his wrists. She figured they were no more than fifteen miles from the cantonment, and she was game enough to try that, even if on foot, should she have the chance and should she be able to get loose.

But he set the whiskey aside, rolled out his own bedroll, rewrapped the rope around his wrist, and was soon breathing deeply.

When she was convinced he was asleep, she began to work on the ropes on her wrists with her teeth.

He spoke without opening his eyes. "If'n you worry those ropes, I'll bind you sitting up to that there tree trunk, and you'll get no sleep this night. I'd be sleepin', as you'll need it come morning."

She took a deep breath, which caught in her throat, but she had resolved not to cry. If she was to take advantage of any opportunity tomorrow, she would need some rest tonight. She took his advice, let the bindings be, closed her eyes, and tried to sleep.

Miles might have been more aggressive had he known that Crazy Horse and four hundred more braves were riding through the night to join the original one hundred.

The snow continued to fall, but not enough to impede the progress of the Indians. They arrived before dawn. Big Crow and half the warriors crossed the Tongue and began to find cover in the hills to the south of the infantry camp. Crazy Horse, Medicine Bear, and the others continued down the northern bank, making no attempt to conceal their coming.

Reveille sounded at four A.M., but it was unnecessary as no one had slept with the continued blind fire into the camp. And each man had been contemplating his mission for that morning, missions that Miles had planned the night before. As all men do when facing battle, they prayed, praying mostly that they would not shame themselves, that they would do their duty, and that none of the bullets that must find some of them would find them personally.

With the first rays of light, Miles sent his scouts into the field, now covered with two to three feet of fresh snow.

It took little time for them to return at the gallop, shouting warnings of an approaching band of warriors.

Miles mounted up and rode to the plateau, where he could get a clear view of the field and the hills beyond. With field glasses glued to his eyes, he watched Crazy Horse's men disburse through the hills to the west.

The sight of the Indians did not excite or dismay Miles as this was just what he'd been waiting for, but it did surprise him. They were dismounting, and forming firing lines a few hundred yards from the camp. They slipped from horseback, with the horses being led out of sight, then moved down every ravine and lined every crest. It was a completely new tactic for the hostiles. No more wild firing from horseback. They'd taken a page out of the infantry book.

"Damned if they don't look like a field of Prussians," Miles muttered under his voice.

"Sir?" Lieutenant Mason Carter asked.

"Nothing, Lieutenant. Watch for the savages to slip up on your lines. They're dismounting and fighting on foot."

"The hell you say," Carter said, his look as astounded as Miles's had been.

Miles turned to his aides, who'd followed him to the plateau, pointing out exactly where his units were to be deployed. Captain Casey with A Company and Lieutenant Hargous's mounted infantrymen would join Ewers and Miles on the plateau, supporting Lieutenant James W. Pope's two artillery pieces. Miles sent his big guns to the northwestern bank of the plateau.

Two more companies were deployed to join Carter's K Company across the river in the cottonwoods. D Company, one of the few groups from the 22nd Infantry, would remain on this side of the river. Remaining in the bend of the river at the original camp, Lieutenant Cornelius Cusick and F Company, also of the 22nd, would guard the supply wagons and cattle. He kept two companies, C and D, in reserve at the base of the plateau, facing the east. These companies were commanded by Lieutenant Robert McDonald and Captain Edmund Butler.

Miles considered his forces well deployed, and it was a good thing he'd done so quickly as, at seven A.M., all hell broke loose. Cheyenne warriors charged K Company and its two supporting companies in the cottonwoods across the river. The fighting in the distance was heavy and furious, until Pope's artillery rounds began to find the range and the hillsides just to the north of the cottonwoods began to explode with plumes of earth and deadly shot cut the air. The Indians fell back, regrouping in the hills out of sight of the artillerymen.

Again they struck, this time at the far east of the cottonwoods, probing, looking for a weakness. Rifle fire and arrows peppered the cottonwoods. But heavy rifle from the good cover of the cottonwood windfall and undergrowth, and artillery fire from the butte, again repulsed them.

Deciding that the cottonwoods couldn't be broached, Crazy Horse took another tack, this time deploying his forces to the high bluffs overlooking camp. Rocks protected Indian braves, and they fired at will, offering covering fire to others who charged over the river to the hills southeast of Miles's position.

Heavy fighting in the western valley encouraged Medicine Bear, and he and his mounted braves galloped along the northern bank and crossed the river to the hills across the plain from the plateau. Miles quickly responded, shifting his forces to form a line extending from the edge of the plateau to the bank rising up from its southwestern extremity. Natural cover of rocks and cuts allowed the infantry to form skirmish lines and direct deadly fire at the riders.

Medicine Bear, a man of great religious belief, rode into the open, waving a talisman, challenging the infantry to try and defeat his good medicine, to try and bring bullets to sear his flesh. His intent was to bring all the walks-a-heap bullets his way, thus away from his men. It worked for a good long time, frustrating the infantry riflemen and fortifying his braves' courage, until Pope's artillerymen swung their weapons Medicine Bear's way. A direct hit to the horse's flank careened him around, but failed to explode. Still, Medicine Bear wisely and hastily beat a retreat into the hills.

But Medicine Bear's tactics were wise, as he knew that if he and his men could broach the lines and get to Bearcoat and the big guns, the battle would be won.

Miles knew that as well as Medicine Bear, and he deployed E Company to the southern base of the knoll, protecting the cannon.

Indians now were well entrenched in the hills to the north, and the bluffs to the south of the plateau and horseshoe bend. Miles and his infantry were surrounded.

Kev and Sean were out of the thick of things, with only the occasional stray slug buzzing overhead. They worked the cattle on foot, not wanting to get above the cover of the animals and nearby wagons.

The cattle milled about nervously, and Kev thought they would bolt every time a cannon was fired, particularly the Rodman gun, a three-inch ordnance rifle, which made a resounding crack across the valley, much louder than the larger-bored twelve-pound Napoleon cannon.

It must have sounded a little strange, and even more maudlin, when Kev began singing "Rock of

Ages," one of the few songs he knew from front to back . . . at least the first verse.

Sean moved to his side. "You want to spook 'em for sure."

"Very funny," Kev said. "Join in, it seems to quiet them."

So Sean did, and finally, the infantry company encircling them fell in as well.

For an instant, the firing in the whole valley stopped, as a chorus of voices rang out, "cleft for me, and let—" But the silence was short-lived, as soldiers on both sides again took up volleys at the enemy.

The battle roared on, with the Indians attacking, and Miles and the infantry defending, then counterattacking, but never getting out so far their backs were exposed to anyone other than their fellows. Finally, following Miles's orders, Captain Casey and his A Company formed a skirmish line and charged, at a slow walk as the deep snow and the heavy winter gear they wore precluded any other pace. They took volley after volley from Medicine Bear's forces, but not a man was hit. At long last, they commanded the first low hill, but there the attack stalled.

Three higher ridges faced them, and the warriors regrouped behind the first of them. When Miles raised his field glasses, he moaned as his attackers took cover on the crest of the low hill. Their forward movement stalled. Quickly he dispatched D Company to join Casey's forces. D Company, under the command of Lieutenant Robert McDonald, followed in the track of A Company, then veered to the left of A's stalled forces, driving to the base of one of the higher hills and falling under raining rifle fire and arrows.

But it was not to be as easy an objective as the first low hill. Fierce rifle fire splattered into the snow from above as the men clambered to gain footing, slipping back two steps for every three gained.

An astonishing sight greeted them, as on the hilltop a Northern Cheyenne medicine man, Big Crow, was dancing, waving, and occasionally firing his rifle, his long headdress nearly dragging the ground, unless he spun and it cut the air behind him.

Nearby, even Crazy Horse seemed astounded, particularly when Big Crow paused in his dance to come back behind the rocks to borrow a few more rounds from his comrades, then returned to his dance.

This time the display was not long-lived, as soldiers from D Company zeroed in on the big warrior from two hundred yards below the crest of the second hill. The long Infantry-model Springfield .45/.70's were too accurate for Big Crow's medicine, and he collapsed spread-eagled in snow.

It was not only a killing blow for Big Crow, but for all the warriors gaining strength from his display, as Big Crow was renowned among his people for his bravery and invincibility. Many of his comrades ran to his aid and dragged him from the field, but many more ran from the battle, escaping over the next rise. The Lakotas filled the ranks of the departing Cheyenne, and the battle resumed.

They were led in a screaming assault against the walks-a-heap by Crazy Horse himself. They charged across a connecting ridge between hills two and three to within fifty yards of McDonald's position.

The shrill cry of eagle-bone whistles pierced the air as they came, the banshee cry of warriors willing to risk all to save what had been theirs, and their ancestors', for centuries.

Almost three hundred of them came, braving volleys of fire from the soldiers, slogging through snow above the knee to charge on, into almost certain death.

From his vantage point on the plateau, Miles watched in morbid fascination as the brave warriors advanced. Crazy Horse's mere presence, and his willingness to lead into the wall of lead, brought them into a frenzy of strength and determination.

Miles, somewhat shaken, ordered another company, C Company, to the left face where the Indians would be in their direct field of fire; they ran at double time, at the risk of exhausting themselves in the deep snow.

Then Miles saw something that dismayed him even more. More and more Indians were occupying the third and largest hill. He ordered Lieutenant Frank Baldwin to carry a message to Butler, who was still driving forward to reinforce D Company.

Chapter 27

"Don't fail me, Frank," Miles said.

Baldwin mounted his horse and galloped, his animal plunging through the deep snow until he reached Butler to redirect him around McDonald to the third hill for a charge up its infernal slope to rout the Indian reinforcements.

Indians seemed to be everywhere—behind every rock, in every ravine. It seemed no force could rout them, but D Company charged on.

Butler, seeing the opportunity to take the high ground, and the necessity to come to the aid of the badly outnumbered C Company, led his men in a bold charge across the ravine between hills three and four. His horse pitched forward, dead before it hit the ground, and he went flying headfirst into the snow, only to be dragged to his feet by his following infantry. As quickly as he went down he was up, waving his side arm and charging, his men at his heels.

Finally, Crazy Horse and his warriors fell before the onslaught of bluecoats, but only far enough back to take positions on the crest of the third and highest hill.

From seven hundred yards across the valley, Pope

brought his artillery to bear on the Indians' superior position, firing over the ranks of his own soldiers.

With infantry-like precision, under the bombardment of exploding shells, the Indians began to give way, but not in a rout as Miles anticipated, rather in an orderly military fashion. Falling back, regrouping, falling back, regrouping. Miles smiled as he watched through his field glasses. Crazy Horse was a quick learner, quicker than some of the West Point graduates he'd known.

The infantry pushed on behind the hostiles for nearly a mile, but then the snow began to fall in earnest, and it would mean coming to within thirty or forty yards of an enemy before a target was seen.

And worse, the artillery was offered no targets. To fire the big guns blindly would mean risking hitting one's own forces.

Exhausted and almost out of ammunition, Butler, now in the lead, ordered a retreat and regrouping.

All across the battlefield, where smaller skirmishes were under way, the snow compelled a secession of the fighting.

It had been five hours since the first of the firing had begun, and thousands of rounds had been fired. The soldiers regrouped and retook their original positions defending the encampment, while the Indians faded into the growing storm.

A hospital tent was set up on the butte and the wagons unpacked. To the amazement of Miles, only one man, August Rathman, had been killed, and only eight others wounded. Later, another man, Bernard McCann, would die of his wounds.

Kev and Sean remained unscathed throughout the battle, and were able to keep the cattle and wagon stock milling in a tight circle, but not bolting.

Kev had done his job, and he left the cattle in the quiet snowfall to Sean, and crossed the wide plain to the butte and on to the knoll where the officers had set up their tents.

Outside the perimeter of the tents, he paused by a large campfire when he saw Grigsby and Mc-Gloughlan among the men gathered there. He exchanged greetings with them, glad to see that both of them were unscathed if exhausted. Grigsby seemed reluctant to express it, but finally said, "Them damned Sioux and Cheyenne was tough as horseshoe nails. I never seen the like. I was out there with the scouts until a few minutes ago, and the hills are red with blood. They was hurt bad this day, but still, it was a proud day for the red man."

Kev was not a bit reluctant to agree.

Kev went on to Miles's command tent, and waited outside for the better part of an hour in the growing darkness and increasing snowfall until Miles finished a meeting with his officers. Then he was summoned inside.

"What is it now, McQuade?"

Kev took his time explaining to Miles his predicament; this time Miles listened. Then he offered, "First, let me tell you that Starkey was interrogated by Major Jenkins back at the cantonment. A courier rode in last night with a number of communiqués, including a copy of that interview. I fully intend to follow up. . . . I'll determine who they are, then summon the men who were on that mission with Starkey. Then you can, along with me, question them in the morning. God willing, I'll have time. If justified, I'll send you back with written orders to have Sergeant Starkey held in confinement until a proper inquiry can be made. If not . . . if there's no indication of misconduct, then you'll ride on out to your ranch tomorrow, leaving Starkey to the Army. Satisfied?"

"Yes, sir, for now."

Miles shook his head, smiling tightly, as Mc-Quade turned to leave, then called out behind him. "There're still plenty of hostiles out there in the hills . . . you sure you want to ride out?"

"Yes, sir, I'm sure."

"Stay with your cattle, McQuade. I'll send for you in the morning."

While the battle raged on, Orin Starkey and his prisoner rode farther and farther from the cantonment. At no time did Caitlin feel she had any opportunity to bolt and run. It was odd, riding astraddle the saddle, without her sidesaddle, but she was gaining confidence doing so. Finally, halfway through the day, he untied her wrists, now chaffed and seeping blood. But he left her ankles bound to the cinch. He let her rein her own horse.

It had been snowing all day, and didn't seem as if it was going to let up. In fact, it was getting worse. She wondered how he knew where he was going, but didn't ask. The less she talked to him, she figured, the better.

The only words he'd said all day was at a hot spring when he'd untied her wrists while they were eating. "This dun of mine will run that grulla down in a heartbeat, missy, should you try and bolt for it. So don't, 'cause if you do, I'll beat you like an orphan and tie you twice as tight next time."

She believed him.

They'd ridden from before daybreak until after sundown, with only jerky and hardtack to eat, and some water that tasted of sulfur from the hot spring.

She decided that Orin Starkey was certainly a worthless scum, but he was a very tough one, never faltering, never tiring. She continued to wonder as to when he was going to attack her, but she certainly was not going to broach the subject.

All day long, all she'd seen was his back, except for the fifteen minutes or so at midday when he'd stopped at the spring to eat.

But now she had another night to face, and she said a silent prayer as she dismounted.

"Make a fire," he snapped at her as he unsaddled the stock.

"I'm exhausted. All I want to do is wrap up in my coat and bedroll and go to sleep."

"Made a fire, damn you, and don't sass me. If it weren't for getting that money from your damned husband, you'd be finding out what a real man was. Now, do as I say."

She did, without further argument.

He made coffee, and they had it with the jerky and hardtack.

She slept under the boughs of a large pine, with the snow still coming.

* * *

It was shortly after breakfast when the runner came to fetch Kev.

Six men were lined up at parade rest outside Miles's tent when Kev got there.

When Kev was shown in, Miles was abrupt. "This can't take long, McQuade. I've got some Indians to run down."

"Doubt if anyone will be doing much running down in this snow, General."

Miles merely grunted.

One by one, Miles called the men before him, with Kev standing off to the side. Only one of the first five mentioned Starkey's burnt hand, but all of them remembered Starkey staying behind as the rest of them drove the wagons away from the McQuade place.

Finally, the number two in command of the detachment was called inside. Corporal Jason Donklin was a lanky man, with ice-blue penetrating eyes and prematurely gray hair. He came to attention in front of the wagon-tailgate desk that Miles had usurped from the freighters as soon as the column made a semipermanent camp.

"Stand at ease, Corporal," Miles said. "You know Mr. McQuade here?"

"We met on the trail when we passed the cattle drive, sir," Donklin said.

"It seems, as I'm sure the men who were interviewed before you have reported, that some terrible things happened at the McQuade place about the time the vegetable procurement was returning from Bozeman. What can you tell us about your stop at the McQuade Ranch?"

"In regards to what, sir?"

"In regards to the possibility of misdeeds on the part of Sergeant Starkey, or any of the other men."

"Starkey was the only one to go into the house, sir. It's my understanding that he assisted in a surgery on the man of the house, removing a leg, or so I understand."

"And you men . . . ?"

"We remained in the barn out of the weather, cooking our dinner and resting ourselves and the stock."

Miles eyed him. "Cooking your dinner? It was my understanding Mrs. McQuade brought out some stew."

"No, sir. We cooked our own meal. We never saw Mrs. McQuade, not once."

"So, did anything untoward happen?"

"Starkey came out to tell us to hitch up and move out, and that he would join us later. He was injured, which I thought odd, and he seemed out of sorts."

"Injured?"

"Bleeding from the mouth. Said he'd burned his tongue on hot stew, matter of fact. Then said he'd bitten his tongue as a result. Fact was, he could have done something as stupid as that, as he was drunk as a toad backstroking in a keg of brandy."

"Drunk?"

"Drunk as McKirdy's goat, sir. And I happen to know from firsthand knowledge that Orin Starkey is a mean drunk, mean as a scalded cat."

"That all of it?"

"No, sir, not really. When Starkey came along later on horseback, he had a hand wrapped up. Said he'd burned it falling in a campfire, but we put our fire out and doused it before we rode out of the McQuade place. Strange thing was, he had three or four excuses for burning that hand, depending upon who he was talking to and who was listening. Starkey couldn't have burnt it in our campfire."

"Anything more?"

"Yes, sir. As we were driving the wagons over a rise, some two or three miles from the McQuade home place, I was sure I saw smoke coming from back near where the house and barn lay. I questioned Orin . . . Sergeant Starkey . . . about it when he came riding up, but he put it off to the McQuade boy putting coal oil and torch to a pile of brush out in the pasture. I saw no pile of brush around the place . . . not that there couldn't have been."

For the first time, Kev spoke up. "Then it comes down to the fact you think Orin Starkey was up to some kind of no good, maybe even hurt some people and got hurt in the process, and maybe set a fire to cover up what he'd done?"

"None of that would surprise me, Mr. McQuade. Circumstance would lead one to believe that something was amiss at your place while Orin Starkey was there."

"Thank you," Miles said. "You're dismissed."

"Yes, sir." Donklin gave him a sharp salute and spun and started out.

Miles's eyes brightened for a moment, and he stopped Donklin with another question. "Did you see sign of hostiles just after leaving the McQuade place?"

"No, sir. It was twenty miles before we saw any sign."

"Dismissed."

"Sir."

Kev edged over in front of Miles's desk as Miles reached for a quill and ink. "That was an old man, a young woman in her prime, and a twelve-year-old girl who never hurt nobody in her few years that Starkey murdered, then burnt up to conceal his crime. General? Well?"

"I'm writing the order, McQuade. Starkey lied to Jenkins about several things, and I don't like my officers lied to."

The weather improved the next morning, even though Starkey and Caitlin had to dig their way out from under the pine boughs they'd used for shelter.

For the next three days the sky remained a mottled pewter, and they were not blessed with sunshine, but as they approached Big Horn City, the snow began again.

Starkey had continued to push hard, and the horses were all but done in by the time they reached the shore of the Big Horn River, but the Kaiser Saloon awaited Starkey across the ice. He hesitated long enough to dismount and walk back to stand beside her.

"Missy, you want to get out of this snow, we got to stop here. I'm going to untie your legs, but you make any move or try and talk to the Hauptmanns, then I'll have to do grave harm to you and them. Understand?"

"I want a bath. I don't have to talk, but I want a bath."

"You'll have your bath"—Starkey stroked his sidewhiskers and eyed her hungrily—"but it'll be in the room they got to rent out. You're to tell them that you and I was wed, and I mustered out of the Army, understand?"

She was physically repelled by his leer. "I can't bathe in any room that you're even close to, much less inside of."

"You can hang up a blanket, but I'm in the room, just like we was newlyweds. Understand?"

She sighed deeply. The snow was coming down so hard they couldn't see across the river. "I understand. But if you lay a hand on me, or even come near the blanket, I'll scream like you never heard. Do you understand?"

He chuckled for the first time since they'd left the Cantonment. "You mean for one little peek, you'd risk me doing harm to those good folks."

"Yes, that's what I mean. I give you my word, I'll go along with your dreadful lie, but you're to keep your distance. Remember, you want to turn me over to my husband, and if I tell him you laid a hand on me. . . ."

His look soured. "Just you act like the newlywed, and we'll get on just fine. We'll ride out tomorrow, rested and fed, and you scrubbed down, if'n there be any chance of moving through this storm."

They crossed the ice without incident. As they dismounted outside the saloon, he cautioned her again. "Don't make me do harm to these folks."

She nodded, and they moved up to the double doors of the Kaiser Saloon.

Chapter 28

Kev and Sean had ridden steadily to get back to the cantonment, seeing no sign of hostiles along the way. Miles had negotiated Kev down on the increased price for the cattle, since he did not stay to complete the campaign, but he still left with over two hundred dollars extra, and each of them had an Army horse in tow in addition to Kev's buckskin and Colin's gray that Sean rode.

It was afternoon when they reached the cantonment, and Kev went directly to Caitlin's room, knocked on the door, then went to the cookhouse, where the cook told him she hadn't been seen for days. He was not particularly alarmed as she'd mentioned that she would take most of her meals in her room. But he nervously anticipated the fact that she'd found some way to go downriver, return to St. Louis, and that he'd never see her again.

Major Jenkins had his aide bring Kev straight in when he arrived.

"She's gone missing," he said without preamble.

"What the hell do you mean, missing?"

"Three or four days ago, she just wasn't in her room come morning."

"So, what have you done?"

"I've had patrols out, but this snow's been hell. Tracks would have been covered in a matter of a couple of hours . . . and there's something else."

"What?"

"Sergeant Orin Starkey."

"What about Starkey?"

"He's absent also. Missing the same day as Mrs. Tolofsen."

Kev flew into a rage, stomping back and forth across the office, accusing Jenkins of being a complete incompetent. He threw Miles's communiqué down on Jenkins desk. "Then I guess it's a little late for you to obey your general's orders. If you'd locked him up, as I requested, none of this would have happened." Kev spun on his heels, cursing Jenkins as he stomped out.

He headed straight to the cookhouse, where he'd left Sean. He grabbed a cup of coffee and told the head cook he'd like to buy some food for the trail.

Sean gave him a worried look. "Where's Caitlin?"

"Damned if I know, Sean. But I'm going to find her. Starkey is gone, and so's she. I fear the worst, that he's taken her. The hell of it is, where?"

Sean looked both frightened and worried. "She wanted to go downriver . . . to St. Louis."

"I don't think they'll be going where Caitlin wants to go, Sean. He dragged her away in the dead of night. It's my guess he's taking her back to Bozeman, to cash in with her husband. At least I pray that's it. If not, we'll never find them." Both of them were silent a moment; then Kev laid a hand on Sean's shoulder. "I'm going to ride out of here as soon as I'm reprovisioned. I'm taking your extra horse, so I have two spare animals and can make double time. Maybe I can catch up with them by the time they reach Rocky Butte."

"I'm going," Sean said.

"No, you're staying here until the next Army detachment rides out to Bozeman. Then you come along with them in better weather."

"No, Uncle Kev. I'm coming with you."

"I forbid it."

"Fine. Then after you're gone, I'll follow. You know I will."

Kev turned away, staring out the cookhouse window. Then he turned back, shaking his head. "I won't make as good time, dragging you along."

"*I'll* be dragging *you*, Uncle Kev."

"You're damn sure becoming a typical hard-headed McQuade. Let's go, get ready."

In less than a half hour, they rode out into the snow, each dragging a spare animal, each with the determination of a cougar stalking a fat elk.

Mrs. Hauptmann was overjoyed to see Caitlin again, but in moments her joy turned to concern.

All of them were around a table in the Kaiser Saloon, enjoying a meal she'd quickly prepared. Leftover elk roast was sliced into a hot gravy, and boiled potatoes heated. Fresh bread and apple sauce also adorned the table. Even as it was only leftovers, both Orin and Caitlin ate with a relish.

Starkey ate in concentrated silence, only nodding when questioned by Gustav Hauptmann.

"You seem vorried," Siglinda finally said to Caitlin as she tucked a strand of hair back into the dust cap she wore.

"Worried?" Caitlin said, forcing a smile. Her tone implied otherwise, but her look was gaunt and fearful.

"Yes, vorried," Siglinda repeated, glaring a little at Starkey.

Starkey ignored Siglinda and eyed Caitlin, stroking his dundrearies with a hand, his look saying "caution" and his eyes burning into her.

"It's this storm, is all," Caitlin said, forcing another weak smile. "This weather will be the death of me. In fact, it almost was the death of us both." That she could say with complete honesty, as it was true. "It's terrible out there."

"And getting vorse," Gustav said, his tone cautionary.

Siglinda did not seem satisfied, but didn't press the issue. The rest of the meal was eaten in silence. When they'd finished and Siglinda rose to clear the table, Caitlin made no move to help.

Finally, the German woman said to Caitlin,, "Help me carry these in, and you an' I can chat whilst I vash tings up."

"No," Starkey snapped. "She's all tuckered out, and she's going to the room to take a rest. We're paying good money for the room and this here meal, and it don't call for no helpin'."

Gustav Hauptmann rose, disgustedly throwing his cloth napkin in his plate. "Der's no call to be snappish, Sergeant. Mrs. Hauptmann vas only vantin' some womanfolk company while she vorks."

"Mrs. Starkey is plumb tired out. We're going to the room. Heat some water. She'll be wanting her bath," Starkey said, rising and circling the table to take Caitlin by the arm and lead her away to the room at the rear of the dry-goods store.

Moments later, Gustav stood beside his wife at the kitchen cabinet, drying dishes as she washed.

"Somethin' mighty strange wit them two," he said.

"I tink so too. He sure don't treat her like no newlyved. She seemed so taken mit dat handsome young rancher, Kev McQuade. Something is very, very strange 'bout this."

"Well, they von't be going in this veather, it's blowing up a real norther out there, so ve'll be having some time to find out vat's up."

She eyed him, nodding her head, continuing her washing.

Kev pushed hard, only staying astride a horse for a couple of hours before changing off. They took a mid-afternoon break, but it was no real rest as the wind continued to pick up, and even sitting with their coats wrapped about them was miserable. Still, Sean managed to fall asleep where he sat on a snow-covered boulder, and Kev stayed an hour longer than he felt he should, letting his nephew rest—then he woke the boy and they pushed on until well after nightfall. Finally, it was blowing so hard that they had to stop and find shelter as the animals were barely making headway.

By morning it had let up somewhat, but was still miserable, with a thirty-mile-an-hour wind driving snow into their faces. The horses trudged on, hanging their heads, plodding. By the end of the second day, Kev began to worry about the skunk-striped dun he'd purchased from the Army. The horse was actually wobbly on its feet as he unsaddled and rubbed him down. He seemed better after a hatful of corn. They slept for six hours before rising and pressing on.

But by noon on the third day, the dun had gone lame. Kev unsaddled him and spread the load from his packsaddle to a pack behind his saddle on the buckskin and to Sean's spare horse.

"Should we butcher him?" Kev said tiredly.

"We got dried meat, Uncle Kev. Let him have a chance of finding his way back to the cantonment."

Kev nodded and remounted the buckskin. They would trade off leading the blue roan that was Sean's second horse.

They rose early the morning of the fourth day, no later than four A.M.

After they'd had some coffee and fed the horses, Kev turned to Sean. "We've made good time. We should find Big Horn City by midday. There's a chance Starkey has holed up there, so we'll be a little careful going in."

Sean merely nodded. As they set out, the wind intensity grew even more, cutting their faces with whipped snow. Both of them were wrapped so nothing but eyes showed, but the eyes burned and teared, and the tears froze on their cheeks.

By the time they reached the top of a rise, looking down on what Kev hoped was Big Horn City—since the snow was flying so thick he could only guess—the horses were laboring with every step. Kev waved Sean up alongside.

He had to shout to be heard over the howl of the wind. "If I got my bearings right, we'll hit the Big

Horn River down at the bottom of this long slope. As much as we'd like to get out of the cold, we'll head straight for the barn. You'll hole up there while I check things out. Understand?"

"Yes, sir."

Kev reached across and laid a hand on his nephew's shoulder. "Sean, I haven't said nothing but I want you to know I'm real proud of you. You've done a man's work and more this whole trip, and I'm proud to have you as kin."

Sean smiled at him, but as Kev could only see his eyes, all he got in return was the light in them.

As Kev had suspected, they found the river, nothing more than a flat spot covered with snow, and trudged across with no problem. When they finally got to the barn, Kev swung the door aside and they entered, welcoming the relative silence out of the howling wind.

Tobias, the Hauptmanns' hired man, stuck his head out of his room in the barn to find Sean and Kev stomping about, beating their sides with gloved hands, trying to get some circulation back in cold hands and feet.

"Lord, Lord, look at the two of you, out in this weather. Come on in here and have yersef a cup of Joe."

Kev immediately noticed four horses in the stalls, horses that hadn't been there the last time he passed through. "You got an Army sergeant and a lady staying here?" Kev asked, the anticipation about to drive him mad.

"We do."

Kev exhaled, realizing he'd been holding his breath.

Tobias continued. "Mr. and Mrs. Starkey . . . you remember her, Caitlin is her given name, and you was here when her pa was shot. That sergeant done mustered out o'da the Army, and they's on they way to Oregon." Tobias parroted the story Starkey had given the Hauptmanns.

"The hell you say," Kev said, momentarily shocked, then he had second thoughts. *Of course Starkey would give them a tale of some kind. He wouldn't want them to know Caitlin was his prisoner. They might not take well to a man having a woman as prisoner, no matter what the reason.*

"Tobias, could it be that Starkey is holding her against her will?"

Tobias seemed to study that a moment. "Well, sir, that sure could be as they been actin' mighty strange. The missus was mighty kind to me the last time y'all was here, even though she was grievin' her pa. Now she don't have a thing to say, and come to think on it, she's never out of that sergeant's eye. He won't let her have a moment alone with Mrs. Hauptmann, and you know how womenfolk normally is."

After they'd unsaddled, rubbed, and grained the horses, they joined Tobias in his room for the coffee he'd offered.

Kev wanted to rush in, his guns blazing, but that would endanger not only Caitlin, but the Hauptmanns. He thought about his predicament as he sipped the hot brew and warmed up. Then he turned to Tobias.

"Tobias, do they call you Toby?"

"My kinfolk back home did."

"Do you mind if I call you Toby?"

"That would be right fine, Mr. McQuade."

"Then you call me Kev, okay?"

"That would be right fine also . . . Kev."

"I want you to do me a big favor."

"Be pleased to do what I can."

"I want you to go in the store, or the Hauptmanns' quarters, or wherever Starkey can be found, and give him a little cock and bull and get him out here."

Toby's eyes seemed to light up. "Can't say as I have much to say good about Mr. Starkey. I suppose I can find a way to get him away from the lady."

"How about you tell him one of his horses is down, stove up, or foundered, or whatever."

"You gonna shoot a few holes in the ol' boy, like you did to that big ugly Brennen fella?"

Chapter 29

Kev eyed the Hauptmanns' hired man, wondering if he could refrain from shooting Orin Starkey down like a dog.

Then he said, "Not if I don't have to, but I am going to take him back to Bozeman to stand trial. You see, Toby, we're sure he killed my father, sister-in-law, and niece . . . Sean's sister."

"I believe I'd just shoot 'im down, could I get him in my sights."

"Me too," Sean said with enthusiasm.

"No. We're gonna do this right, and takin' him prisoner, and getting him in front of a territorial judge and out of the hands of the Army, is what's right."

"I'm going on in," Toby said, standing.

"Get him out here, and we'll be ready. I'd suggest then you find an excuse to go back inside the store, though, Toby."

Toby nodded, and headed for the door.

"Sean, I want you up in the loft with your shotgun, understand?"

"Yes, sir."

"But you stay hid out, and don't show your face unless you hear some shooting and then I call for you, but if I don't call, and the head that pokes up into the loft is wearing whiskers. . . . Understand?"

"Then what?"

"Then it's Starkey, and it means he's shot me down and you have my permission to blow his damn head off."

Sean smiled. "Good." He headed for the loft.

Kev moved over to the cover of an upright supporting the loft above, only a dozen paces from the barn door.

He waited for the better part of a half hour, then heard a voice over the whistling wind. "It's only old Toby, all alone, coming into the barn."

Kev relaxed somewhat.

Toby came in alone, and Kev stepped out from behind the upright. "He wouldn't come?"

"Sure 'nuf." Toby held out his palm. A four-bit piece was cradled in its center. "He done gave me four bits, said to care for the animal, and that he wasn't coming out into this cold for no lousy four-footed critter."

"Figures," Kev said.

"He was in the room with the missus."

"She's not his missus," Kev snapped. "That's a lie, and he's real good at lying. She's already married, and can't get unmarried until she goes back to St. Louis."

"Still an' all, he won't come out."

"Come on down, Sean," Kev yelled up to his nephew. "We've got to find another plan."

Caitlin had grown restless from being locked in the room for the last three days, only going out for meals. It was a surprise to her, but Starkey had been true to his word, and not bothered her while she used the Hauptmanns' leather tub to bathe. Nor had he laid a hand on her at other times, even though he continued to nurse a jug of whiskey he'd purchased in the dry-goods store. The threat of what her husband might do to him, should he molest her, and more so the fact that her husband might not pay the reward he'd offered, seemed enough to make Starkey keep his distance. He slept in the bed, and she'd made a pallet in a corner of the room, hanging a blanket up for privacy. He'd had to borrow a hammer and nails from Gustav to accomplish the task, explaining that his "wife" was modest, and wouldn't dress or bathe in front of him.

She'd fortified his fear by telling him more than once about the hard types Mark Tolofsen kept on his payroll. Of course he'd scoffed at that, but she thought it had had some effect.

"I'm going into the store," he said after making another trip to the window and pacing nervously.

"I've read everything the Hauptmanns' have. Please ask Mrs. Hauptmann if I can borrow her Bible, so I have something to read."

"Humph," he mumbled, but nodded his head as he opened the door. He paused in the doorway. "Don't you be stickin' your head out. Understand?"

She nodded, then demanded, "And please empty the chamber pots. Just because there's bad weather doesn't mean I have to live like an animal." He fetched them, then closed the door.

If Starkey had gone to the window once, he'd gone a hundred times, checking the weather, waiting for a break so they could ride out, but the weather had remained consistently bad.

As soon as he walked out, she went to the window, wondering if she could survive out in that cold, if she could slip out the window, saddle a horse, and be gone into the whiteout before he discovered.

She concluded that she probably could escape, but into what, sure death? Probably, as the wind was howling and the snow blowing horizontally.

She perched herself on the single ladder-back chair in the room, put her face in her hands, and sobbed.

Where was Kev? Had Sean made it to Miles and the detachment without being dragged down by the Sioux? She would not allow herself to cry in front of Starkey, but now that he was gone, she sobbed with self-indulgence and self-pity. *Damn, damn, damn, where was Kev?*

She dabbed at her eyes with a hanky, then glanced at the window as a shadow passed by, then looked in astonishment as a face appeared. For a second she thought she was hallucinating. It was Kev, Kev McQuade. Her prayer had been answered.

She ran to the window, and pried it up with Kev's help from the outside, then threw her arms around him and they hugged, but for only a second, as the hug was continued by his dragging her through the opening.

"We've got to get you to the barn," he said, dragging her across the open area to the barn's rear doors, then through.

She came face-to-face with Sean, and hugged him fiercely. "We don't have much time," Kev said, prying them apart. "Toby is inside, trying to keep Starkey busy at the bar."

Kev spun, ready to head out.

"Wait," Caitlin said, grabbing him by the shirt-sleeve.

"I can't wait," Kev said.

"Let's just stay here. He won't come out in the storm."

"Caitlin, he killed my family. I have to take him in."

"No, let's ride out, head back to the canton-ment."

Kev grabbed her by both arms and stared her directly in the eye. "That's not going to happen. I have to get back to the ranch and see that my brother's all right, and Starkey has to pay for what he's done. He'll soon know you're gone, and he'll come looking for you. I want to face him down in the saloon, without anyone in the way to be hurt."

"He'll kill you, Kevin. He's a madman, and strong as an ox."

Chapter 30

Kev's voice softened. "Caitlin, I have to take care of this."

She spun on her heel and put her face in her hands. "If you have any feeling for me, Kevin McQuade, you'll let this go and take me back to the cantonment where I can be safe."

But his answer was to head out the door, his Winchester in one hand, his Colt palmed in the other.

Sean walked over and laid a hand on her shoulder. "I'm to stay here and take care of you."

But that only made her sob even more.

Toby stood behind the bar, pouring another drink for Orin Starkey. And he was pouring them at the house's expense, unknown to the Hauptmanns', who were busy in the dry-goods store.

Both men snapped their heads toward the door as Kev busted through, the wind howling through the door he left open behind him.

Orin Starkey found himself standing with nothing but a drink in his hand, facing a man with a Winchester leveled at his belly.

"Thought you was upriver," Starkey said calmly.

"Toby, get into the dry-goods store and tell the Hauptmanns to keep their distance."

"Yes, sir," Toby said, walking to the end of the short bar, but having to step in front of Kev as he headed for the batwing doors into the store.

As soon as he stepped in front of Kev, Starkey went for the Army Remington, butt-forward on his left side.

Toby saw it happen, and dove to the floor to get out of the line of fire.

The Winchester and Remington roared at the same time, but both men were diving to the side as they fired, and both missed.

Toby scrambled on through the batwings as Kev dove behind the cover of the bar and Starkey backed away, knocking over a table and chair as he did so.

The Winchester was too long for the tight space, so Kev pulled the Colt. Two shots in rapid succession splintered the corner of the bar, then Kev heard rapid steps and the slamming of a door. He stood quickly, ready to snap off a shot, but Starkey was nowhere in sight. There was a door at the rear of the small saloon. Kev moved to the batwing doors and yelled through to Toby. "Where does that back door go?"

"Storeroom, but they's a window out to the back."

Kev remembered looking into a dark storeroom when he was searching for the window to Caitlin's room. He fired two quick shots through the door, but didn't charge it; rather, he ran out the front door into the storm and rounded the building, hoping to catch the big man climbing out the storeroom window. But Starkey was faster than Kev might have imagined, and another shot splintered the corner of the building as Kev rounded it, forcing Kev to dive into the snow.

Starkey was at a dead run, heading for the barn, firing blindly as he ran, trying to make sure Kev kept his head down so he could make the barn in safety.

But realizing Starkey was heading for where Caitlin and Sean were holed up, Kev jumped to his feet. Starkey was a good seventy-five feet away, at a dead run, when Kev snapped off a shot. Starkey spun a complete circle and went down, but almost as quickly was back on one knee, leveling the Remington at Kev. His shot cut through Kev's coat, and Kev again dove to the side as Starkey, holding his bloody side, scrambled to and through the barn door.

Kev heard the report of the shotgun as Starkey charged inside the barn.

He scrambled to his feet and ran for the barn, throwing aside the doors, damning the consequences. Starkey lay with his back to a stall, holding the wound in his side with one hand, his left thigh half blown away from Sean's shotgun work, but the big sergeant still held the Remington with the other hand and he had it raised and aimed at Sean, who must have fired both barrels as the shotgun was broken open and Sean was madly trying to fit shells into the chambers.

Kev fired quickly, slamming a shot into Starkey's chest, but the big man managed to fire the Remington one more time.

Kev fired again, then realized that Caitlin was

backing away, her amber eyes wide and pleading, holding her chest.

"No," Kev yelled. Then he emptied the revolver into Starkey, walking forward, firing the last two shots at point-blank range.

He ran to Caitlin's side. She was down on her back on the hay-covered floor of the barn, holding her chest with both hands, gasping.

"Oh, God. I'm so sorry," Kev said, his eyes filling with tears.

She gasped for a breath, and a fine trickle of blood found its way out of the corner of her mouth.

"I . . . I really did . . . care for you," she said.

"Oh, God, Caitlin," Kev said, lifting her into his arms.

"I don't want . . . to go back . . . to Bozeman, Kev."

"You won't have to."

"By my father, please."

"What?"

"Bury me . . . next to Papa."

Kev moved her away so he could look her in the eyes. "Hang on, Caitlin." His voice rang with desperation. "Sean, get Mrs. Hauptmann. She can do something."

But Sean didn't move. He stood with tears running down his cheeks. He'd dropped the shotgun to the barn floor.

"Caitlin," Kev said, but her eyes were shut, and in a heartbeat, her heart had stopped. Her slender hands slipped away from her chest. Kev stood, picking her up in his arms as he did so.

"Go on ahead, Sean. Tell Mrs. Hauptmann we're coming."

* * *

They waited a week until the weather cleared to bury Caitlin, then started home. This time, for the first time in a long while, they were able to take their time.

When they arrived at Rocky Butte, to their surprise, they were met by a mounted Colin McQuade, who rode through the foot-deep snow up the slope and intercepted them half a mile from the house.

He'd fashioned a sleeve of leather attached to the side of his saddle that his stub would exactly slip into, and a second stirrup on the left side of the horse so he could drop it down when mounting, a stair-step of stirrups, then tie it up alongside the other when riding.

To watch him ride with the stub firmly seated in the leather sleeve, you'd think he had two good legs and both feet firmly in the stirrup.

They spent only a few days at the ranch, then set out for Bozeman with the money to pay Mark Tolofsen and the bank.

Kev had very few words for Tolofsen, not bothering to sit when they made their appearance across his desk at the bank, but did advise him that his wife had been killed, shot by Sergeant Orin Starkey, who was shot dead by Kev himself, and that she was buried next to her father in Big Horn City.

When Tolofsen started to question him, Kev placed both hands on the man's desk and leaned forward, looking him hard in the eye.

"I've said all I'll say to you, Tolofsen, ever. Don't

ever speak to me or look me in the eye again, and if you see me coming down the street you'd better cross to the other side. Two good men are dead because of you, Chad Steel and a good man who went by the name of Sleeps-in-Day, and worse, a fine woman . . . an angel of a woman . . . is dead because you thought you owned her."

"But—"

Kev slammed his hand down on the oak desk. The whole bank silenced, and the customers and employees turned toward them. "That's the last word I want to hear you say, or it may just be the last you ever do say! Understand?"

Tolofsen merely nodded.

Kev stomped out of the bank.

Colin rose and fitted his crutch under his arm, then cleared his throat before he spoke. "I guess we'll be needin' a receipt, Mr. Tolofsen."

While Kev was in Bozeman, he also took the time to write the lawyer, Mortensen, in St. Louis and advise him of the death of Chad Steel and Caitlin.

It was late the next fall, while visiting Colin in Bozeman, where he'd opened a saddlery, with Sean as his helper, that Kev learned that Mark Tolofsen had inherited Chad Steel's saloon and was moving to St. Louis, as Caitlin was Chad's only heir, and Mark Tolofsen was hers.

"Damn the flies," he told Colin as they enjoyed a bourbon after Colin had closed for the day, "it just don't seem fair."

"Hell, Kev, this country ain't fair. Don't go around looking for fair or just, and sure as hell not for God's good grace . . . particularly if you're gonna stay in the cattle business. The good news is, Tolofsen has done left the territory."

"That's damn little consolation. But somethin' is better than nothin'."

Author's Note

The story of the McQuades is fictional, but there was a stock contractor who delivered cattle to the cantonment just before Miles set off up the Tongue for the last great battle with the Sioux and Cheyenne. And the Sioux did drive a good number of those cattle away from the infantry encampment.

The Battle of Wolf Mountain(s), also known as the Battle of the Butte, was portrayed here as it was reported in a number of historical sources. Miles's winter campaign, in one of the worst winters in Montana history, was a bold bit of strategy, and against the wishes of General Terry and Miles's immediate superiors—but coincided with the belief of General Sherman, who commanded all the Western forces.

It would be only a short time before Miles was again made a general.

Miles City, Montana, formerly the site of the Tongue River Cantonment, is well worth the visit. I hunt there at least once a year, and it's the home of some fine antelope herds and some of Montana's biggest and most spectacular mule deer.

Based on the amount of blood in the snow in the hostiles' position, Miles ordered the infantry to return to the cantonment after the battle, deciding that the expedition's objectives had been met.

The general conclusion by historians is that the Battle of Wolf Mountain, or Battle of the Butte if you prefer, was a draw, but in fact it was the last hurrah for the Sioux and Cheyenne. The non-agency bands of Indians began to separate in February and to find their own way to surrender to Bearcoat at the Tongue River Cantonment, or to make their way back at the Great Sioux Reservation.

Only Crazy Horse and his band remained at large, in the area, into the spring.

Finally, due to hunger, fatigue, and utter disillusionment, on May 6, 1877, about four months after the last great battle, Crazy Horse rode into Camp Robinson, Wyoming Territory, and shook the hand of Lieutenant Philo Clark, the commander of Indian scouts at the fort.

The Great Sioux War was over.

But Sitting Bull, the Hunkpapa fox, outsmarted them all and lived free in Canada until 1881, having led his people well around the Army position, finding his way to the Grandmother country—Canada.

He lived on the reservation until 1890, when he was murdered at the Standing Rock Agency just prior to the Wounded Knee massacre.

Miles's memoirs, *Personal Recollections and Observations of General Nelson A. Miles,* are available in two volumes, in trade paperback, from the University of Nebraska Press. *Yellowstone Command,* by Jerome A. Green, is another excellent source of information about the battle, also from the University of Nebraska Press. Luther "Yellowstone" Kelly's recollections are also published, and are a fascinating read.

My good friend Terry C. Johnston—hopefully now palavering somewhere above Montana's big sky with all those great historical characters he so accurately wrote about when alive—has a wonderfully informative novel on the subject of the battle, *Wolf Mountain Moon*.

Hope you enjoyed *Wolf Mountain*.

L. J. Martin
Rock Creek, Montana
E-Mail: wolfpack@gunrack.net
Webpage: www.ljmartin.com

THE LAST GUNFIGHTER SERIES BY
WILLIAM W. JOHNSTONE